DEATH CHARMED

ERICA REEDER

FERRY TALES, LLC

Cover by Bookfly Design

Editing by Book Nook Nuts

Get new release updates and exclusive content when you sign up for my
mailing list!
Oh, and you also get a FREE BOOK!

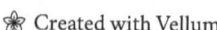 Created with Vellum

ACKNOWLEDGMENTS

Thank you to the man of my dreams, Steven Davis, for giving me the space to be my own person and loving me for the quirky, clumsy, got-my-shit-together person I am, not in spite of it. You've given me back parts of myself that I thought were lost forever. That's a gift more valuable than a truckload of diamonds. Thank you for proving even now why I should be writing this by coming over and kissing me, even though you have no idea I am writing about you.

Thank you for showing me that dreams really can come to life; spider bites are something to be be happy about; and that the most special place in this world is with you in our bed.

QUEENS & KINGS

To all of the Queens and Kings out there, thank you for coming on this journey with me.

CHAPTER 1

Fairies clung to the rafters like leaves after a storm, exhaustion hung from them like fresh dew. I got it. The last few hours had been packed with more action than they'd seen in a century. Despite that, and the fact that the dark of the night was long past and starting to break into the light of dawn, they couldn't sleep. Not when their fates were being decided. Anything could happen now. Would they be left to fend for themselves in a strange world they'd never seen before? Or would they go to live out the rest of their days in a mound they'd never even seen before? And wouldn't that be just like trading one prison for another? The glitter sifted down from them, where they perched on the Guildhall's rafters. They didn't have to ask. Their multicolored snow of glitter on our shoulders made their questions apparent without them having to say a word.

"Well, I'm not taking them back," I said, my tone final.

I had been hammered for the last hour about why I should be the one to bring the rag-tag group of faeries back. And while I did agree they should go to Knockaine, I didn't understand why it had to be me. Wasn't it enough that I'd risked my skin trying to save them last night?

The tips of my wings bent underneath me as I plopped down onto one of the crates. Dozens of them were piled behind us like a poor man's Christmas tree, so it wasn't hard to find a free one. My teeth gnashed. Charles Carmichael, with his arms, propped on his round belly, looked more like Santa Claus than the leader of a transmundane organization.

"I don't see who else can. Nobody else knows where Knockaine is." He said in his too-sensible, nasally voice.

Frankly, I didn't care who did it. I just didn't want it to be me. All of the other faeries might want to live there, but to me, it was the equivalent of prison. And I'd gotten out twice already. The last time I'd had to escape, and it almost killed me. I wasn't about to take that risk again.

But the problem with rescuing over a dozen faeries is that I was responsible for them. So here we were.

"Kittie knows where Knockaine is. What about her?" I asked.

Even as I said it, I felt lousy for volunteering the little pixie. I owed my life to her. I'd forever be in her debt, but I would sooner get the chickenpox than admit that to her.

"The Pixie King pulled her for an assignment." Sven said as he stepped away from where he leaned against the cracked wall.

His dark hair should have looked sinister the rebellious way it fell over his arched brow, but it just made me want to push it out of his face and kiss his pillow-soft lips. I tried to focus: kissing later, crisis prevention now.

"We can't keep them here." Mitzi put in, her pink trench coat billowing behind her with the force of her walk as she strode past.

"Mitzi's right," Charles confirmed as she strode out of view again. "We can't keep the presence of over a dozen faeries, mum. If word gets out that there are faeries here, the Court is bound to come calling. We can't afford to have the Court's eyes on our little organization. And to be perfectly frank, the faeries won't be safe anywhere else."

He didn't say why he didn't want the Court to investigate, but I knew why. His wife was a faerie. Wing-bearing faeries weren't allowed to live outside Knockaine. That, of course, was the reason I'd had to escape myself. That being said, at least I could take care of myself.

"Isn't it about time you and Mrs. Carmichael went to Knockaine anyway? Mrs. Carmichael has no way to defend herself out here with just her healing abilities to aide her. She's at risk with those wings, and you know it. You could apply for an exception, maybe the Court would let you in since you have a history of reliability. It really is safer there for her." I said the last as a gentle reminder.

"The same could be said for yourself." He said, pointedly looking at my new wings.

My frown deepened. It was much more complicated for me. I had a mother who was forever trying to rule my life and give me unfair responsibilities, or I just wasn't cut out for. Granted, being a faerie princess brought those things around, but Mother had a way of making them painful.

They didn't need to know any of that, though. "That just isn't happening."

"Well, just who do you propose brings the faeries back?" Asked Charles and then added. "Because they can't stay here."

I popped my lips in thought. Nobody but faeries and pixies knew where Knockaine was. And none of the faeries above me knew. They'd been taken before Knockaine had existed. If I could get another pixie, this issue would be a moot point. But I couldn't bring myself to go to them. Pixies had killed my father. To say I didn't trust them was an understatement. It had taken a lot for me to trust Kittie.

There was no avoiding it. I was going to have to bring the faeries to Knockaine myself. Exhaustion sank into my shoulders. I tried to push past it. Maybe it wouldn't be so bad. I would take them to the door and leave them there. If I was smart about it, I could do it and be back home before anyone in Knockaine was the wiser.

The crate screeched against the cement floor when I stood up. "Fine."

"Splendid," said Oren floating down from the rafters like an angel.

It was an apt comparison. He had to be more saint than sinner to have survived being locked up for the last 150 years as a human milk machine.

"Ok, grab anything you want to take with you. We'll leave at the top of the hour." I projected my voice so the rest of the fae could hear.

That only gave them 15 minutes, but I'm sure they didn't have much to gather. Making an escape didn't exactly give you an option to bring many things with you.

"We shall be ready." Oren said.

There was a gleam in his eyes. I could tell he was anxious to be reunited with the other faeries. I wasn't surprised. The rest of the survivors probably were too.

As if on cue, the other fae floated down from the rafters one by one. A tall, thin faerie padded up to me on delicate stems of legs as soon as she dropped down. Wendy.

Her wings fluttered ever so gently. Now that she was going home, I didn't know what she had to feel nervous about. I so didn't have the energy to hear it either. That probably made me a bad person. But how else was I supposed to feel after being almost killed and now being strong-armed into a mission? Mostly, all I wanted to do was sleep, a long, blissful sleep. About 100 years might do it.

Her eyes shifted to the side. Her voice came out a little

breathy as she asked, "Is it true that you're really ah-our...princess?"

I wanted to smack my forehead. Now? We were doing this now?

Granted, her questioning my lineage made sense. I stickily fingered my hospital gown. It was decorated with soot and dried blood. Not what you would call Princess material. My ears turned red. I pushed the feelings away.

Now wasn't the time to go into the cuckoo house details of my life, so I left it with a simple, "Yep," and then, "if you'll excuse me."

Her eyes were the size of sunflowers as she said, "Of course, Your Highness."

This time I did smack my forehead. I'd be glad when these faeries were in Knockaine. Then I could go back to a blessedly simple life where the biggest problems I had were the ones I created for myself.

As if to call b.s. to that thought, Sven stepped into my path. Oh, right. Nothing was ever going to be simple again. I raked my eyes over him like a starving man. Sweet Danu, he looked good. He was pure perfection from his tousled hair to the crease down the leg of his ass-hugging slacks. The cleanliness of him brought me up short. We'd been through hell on earth last night, how was he so clean right now?

"Are you sure you can bring them back there without being caught again?" he asked.

"Of course not," I admitted, throwing my sticky mass of hair behind my head. I didn't get the luxury of being supernaturally flawless. Maybe, that was a vampire superpower. "I'm not sure of anything. But who else is going to bring them back?"

The half-dried blood transferred from my hair to my fingers, and I wiped them down the front of my shirt. I didn't even want to think about the mess that was my wings. How does one clean wings? If I'd ever thought I wanted wings before, I'd changed my mind—what an outstanding pain in the ass.

"You could just let them figure out how to get back on their own." He gestured to the space that was quickly emptying. "This isn't a comic book. You don't have to be the hero."

"Nobody said I was a hero." I bit out.

I couldn't explain the need I felt to make sure the faeries were taken care of. It wasn't a hero thing. It wasn't even a crown thing. The thought of the crown made me turn my wrist. The golden crown tattoo glared back at me, daring me to deny its existence. My breathing grew shallow. I dropped my wrist and forced some deep breaths into myself to even my breathing back out.

It was a little late in the season for a leather jacket, especially a trench coat, but Sven didn't seem to notice as he slid his arms into one.

He zipped the jacket up and popped the collar. "I'm going with you."

I shook my head and dropped it to my chest. Gods alive, how I wished he could. I wished I could waltz him right into Knockaine, show everyone he wasn't what they thought. Wished they all would accept him. Wished they all would accept me. All I'd ever wanted was to be me.

But that wasn't going to happen. It wasn't going to happen any more than Sven being able to continue to bring me into his life. Look what had happened just during our short, whirlwind romance: I had been on the cusp of exposing our existence to the entire vampire race. It didn't matter how careful I'd been. Hell, even with the death of Thomas, there was still the small chance vampires knew faeries existed. It was small, but it was there. Now was not the time to fan that flame with the wrong word dropped in casual company. Can you imagine if anyone got word that faeries existed and that Sven was linked to us? They would do whatever they could to get the information out of him. Then they would come after us, in droves. The fae hunt would be on.

No, Sven couldn't know where Knockaine was, my sweetie or not.

Besides, there was something from last night that had been bothering me. Something that hadn't seemed right. You know outside of the Boogeyman's bogeys without the Boogeyman and there being a faerie blood farm in New York City. Something more...personal. I opened my mouth to confront him about it.

"Your shirt is filthy. You shouldn't put your jacket over that." I said, instead.

Damn it. It was a lie. It was almost as clean as his pants. But it was easier to talk about that than what really had to be said. Way to go, Cy. That was courage.

His response was to strip off his jacket. I worked to keep my eyes in my head as he tore off his shirt right after. His chest glistened in the dim warehouse light.

The muscled tendons stood out on his neck as he threw the shirt on the floor and said, "I don't give a good damn about the shirt or jacket. What I care about is you. And I'll be damned if I just let you go walk into another disaster by yourself."

I blinked at the muscles bulging a mere foot away. I knew he'd let me run my hands over them like a Plinko board if I just said the word, but we really needed to talk. It was too easy to let things go unsaid today and then tomorrow and on and on until nothing was said at all. And this needed to be said. It could change everything.

Blowing out a deep breath, I summoned up my courage and asked what had plagued me all night.

"After we got out of your Uncle's house last night," I paused and carefully chose my next words. "You bit me. Why? Why did you...bite me after you'd just given me blood? You had to have known I didn't have a lot left after almost having been bled dry."

I left out that it had been his Uncle who had been the one bleeding me dry in an attempt to kill me—no sense pouring salt on wounds. But there was more to the bite than just the poor timing. There had been something...more to it. He'd bitten me before. I knew what it felt like. It had been glorious. My face got hot at the admission, but I forced myself to face it. Yes, I'd liked it when he'd bitten me during sex. There. I said it. That wasn't the same as last night, though. Last night had been painful. In fact, I think it was the most painful thing I'd ever experienced. It felt like my soul was being ripped out of my body. I shivered at the immediate comparison my mind came up with. I tried to shake off the thought, but it stuck. What *had* he been trying to do?

He let out a long rush of air like the words had been physical, and he'd been hit by them. His reaction made me go very still. He'd thought I wasn't going to say anything. I thought I was going to let it slide. He was intentionally trying to keep something from me. Unbelievable.

I cocked my head to the side. The words stuck in my throat as I prodded him. "Why, Sven?"

At my words, he looked away. His throat worked as he swallowed again and again.

"I can't risk losing you." He whispered the words.

It sounded more like he was talking to himself than me. He couldn't risk losing me? What did that even mean? Then it hit me. He'd done something to me. Without my permission. He didn't. He couldn't have. What did he do? Did he...?

I couldn't even think about it.

I raised a hand to my mouth, horror crawling over me. "What did you do?"

That was all it took for him to blow up. His deltoids flexed, and then he threw his hands into the air.

"I marked you. Alright? I marked you because I can't lose you. I just can't." His lips curled around the words, flashing his fangs as he spoke.

My nerves crawled. Burned. It felt like I'd been doused with acid. Marked me? As in made me a vampire? My hands came up of their own accord, putting a wall between us. No, way. It couldn't be that. I needed to think. That's not what he meant. It couldn't be.

"Listen. You were a breath away from being Thomas' last night. I couldn't handle that. I love you too much for that to happen." His body curved towards mine, looking for understanding.

I shook my head as if it could make him take the words back. "You didn't. You couldn't have. I've told you from the beginning...you knew."

"Cy, I love you." He said with a shaky breath.

"So what? That gives you the right to mark me? To do whatever you please without my permission?" I wiped my now sweating hands down the front of my jeans. "I don't think so."

Sven's mouth worked, and he took a step towards me. My lips trembled at the need for acceptance in his eyes. I pressed my fist to my lips to stop them. Everything in me screamed to run, to leave. To forget this. But some things could not be overlooked. I moved a few steps away from him and found I could think clearer. When I didn't feel like I was going to fall to pieces by opening my mouth, I started again.

"So what...you marked me when you gave me your blood?" I asked.

I needed to be very clear about this. Being marked by a

vampire hadn't exactly been a hot topic growing up. I didn't know what that meant or how that happened.

He had the decency to look away when he said, "No, blood has to be exchanged for a mark to happen."

The memory of the pain when he bit me last night came back, a sharp memory.

"So since you'd already given me your blood, it was the perfect opportunity to just take a little sip and complete the blood exchange, wasn't it?" I couldn't keep the bitterness out of my voice.

Two long seconds beat in the space between us as we stared at each other. Then Sven gave a curt nod.

It felt like a bomb exploded inside me. My whole being went numb.

"Oh, Dagda be damned, you're kidding me. You are absolutely kidding me. So you could have saved me without marking me, but you marked me because what? You felt like it?" I wrapped my arms around my stomach.

I think I was going to be sick.

"No, because if I didn't mark you, what would stop someone else from marking you later? You are a faerie, Cy. I'd be ignorant to think someone isn't going to try to mark you now that they know."

"So now that you marked me, no one else can mark me?" I asked, trying to understand.

I closed my eyes and rubbed my forehead. This whole thing was so vague. I hated that I knew nothing about this. How could you play a game where you didn't know the rules?

He plucked at his belt loop. "Yes, and no."

The rubbing on my forehead changed to slow smacking. A mixture of a groan and a bitter laugh escaped before I could stop it. I was so done with this.

I dropped my hand and closed the distance between us in

two quick steps. "I need it all. And I need it now. What am I looking at? What am I up against? What is going to happen to me?"

His eyes implored me. "Us. It's us, Cy. I'm not going to-"

My hand came up so quickly anyone who wasn't hundreds of years old might have thought I was going to hit them. I held my hand as still as death and silenced him with a quick shake of my head. He blinked two times in rapid succession and then started again, his voice empty this time.

"A vampire can't mark you. And honestly, that's almost all you will come in contact with. The vampyrs are too comfortable to go out into your world"

I raised my eyebrow. There was more to this story.

"But if a vampyr should decide to eclipse the Claim with their own Mark, they can." He crossed his arms in front of his chest. "You see, since a vampire is so far down the chain on the bloodline, we need three Marks to Turn someone. However, a vampyr can do it in one."

A dry laugh escaped my lips. We were talking about my eternal damnation, and Sven was caught up in bite envy. At least I wasn't turned, but this had to affect me on some level. I closed my eyes. The world had suddenly become too much to bear, its weight hard on my chest. But I had to know.

"So, what's going to happen to me?" I asked. When he looked confused, I gestured to my neck, which felt hot.

His eyes tighten at my inability to find the words. "I didn't brand you if that's what you're asking. A vampire won't be able to tell you're Claimed unless they come close enough to smell you."

I resisted the urge to lift my armpits and see if I smelled any different.

Confident this didn't mean I needed to change to a rare vampire deodorant, I pressed him further. "There's got to be something you're not telling me."

Sven's voice rose. "What am I not telling you? That you'll wake up completely different? That you're going to have to start sleeping in coffins and drinking blood instead of coffee?"

Squeezing my fists at my side, I said nothing. I may be many things, but I wasn't dumb. Sven's eyes bore into mine; I didn't think so much as flinch. I was getting my answers.

After a second, his shoulders slumped. I had to lean closer when he started talking again.

"You might experience enhanced abilities. You might be a little stronger, a little faster. You may heal quicker than you have in the past. You might be able to convince people more easily to things. Your beauty may shine through more. But it's nothing big; I swear. You won't be able to pick up a car or run super fast. And you certainly won't be able to convince people of anything they didn't have half a mind to do already."

I stood there, my heart barely beating in my chest.

"Nothing, Cy. Nothing is going to happen to you. You have my word." He said quietly, stepping closer.

Reflexively, I took a mirroring step backward. I could feel my stomach harden. This wasn't ok.

His face hardened. "What do you want me to do? Apologize for it? Too bad. That's not happening. I'd do it again in a heartbeat if it meant I didn't lose you."

"What about what I want? Does that mean nothing?" I laughed a crazy laugh. Glitter hissed onto the cement below me. "You would think it meant something considering, I don't know, it's *my* life."

His lips pressed into a grim line. He said nothing.

"So I'm that much closer to being...one of you now?" I swallowed past the bile that rose in my throat.

Accepting vampires was one thing. Being one was a completely different animal.

"It's not the death sentence you make it out to be, you know." His head fell back, and he shook it, his dark brown locks falling over his forehead. "Cy, I love you."

The simple way he said it threatened to bleed away my resolve. Panic shot through me. It shouldn't be enough to say I love you and make something like this go away. It was my *life* damn it—my very existence. Words didn't take away what he had done. What he had set in motion. He came to me then —his heart in his eyes. I couldn't get past his selfishness. I couldn't accept his lack of regard for me. He reached for me, his fingertips caressing my arms. It was too much.

"Don't!" I shouted and shoved him.

And to my absolute horror, he stumbled back a couple of steps.

No. I shouldn't have been able to push a vampire. They were too strong. But I wasn't just fae anymore, was I? I had vampire blood coursing through my veins now.

No. This wasn't happening. It couldn't be. I couldn't handle this. It was worse than my nightmares. What was I going to do?

This time Sven stayed where he was, but he wasn't done with me. "You have to understand."

The time for understanding had passed. Too long, I'd been accepting things as they'd come at me. No more. From now on, I was in control. From now on, I made my own future.

"No, I don't," I said, then I turned to leave. "We're done."

I stood there, feeling the weight of my words wash over me. Sven's breath hitched. I could hear all of the unspoken things he wanted to say. They echoed in my own heart. How could we be done? I loved this man. Tremors shook my body. What looked like a choice, wasn't. I couldn't be with someone who thought so little of my decisions to take them into his own hands. And because I loved myself more, I left.

CHAPTER 2

*C*rouched behind the bushes, I parted a small opening to look into the clearing beyond. Three boulders sat in the middle. The Trí Bolláin. The same dandelions and mushrooms waived innocently in the breeze.

It was deceptive. I knew what lay beyond. Capture. An end to my freedom.

"Is this the place?" asked Oren, crouching next to me.

My hair caught in the evergreens as I nodded. I was starting to hate these bushes. Braiden's hand instinctively came up to untangle my hair. I smiled my thanks to him. His hot orange hair bounced as he acknowledged my thanks. I'd never met anyone as helpful as he was. Even during the stress of the rescue of the other faeries, he'd been quick to offer a hand. It was a welcome change when most of the world was lost to its selfishness.

"I can't believe we are so close to being with the others. After all this time," Braiden said, emotion made his voice raw.

The air seemed to waver around him, and then fire flared up to encompass his hand. It licked along his trembling wrist. I knew what this meant to him, but I didn't want to take the chance of catching the whole Catskill Forest on fire.

I placed a calming hand on his shoulder. "Soon, Braiden."

My touch worked to calm him. The fire disappeared. It didn't help as much as I would have liked though, because a couple speckles of red glitter dotted his skin. It was understandable, though. Being overwhelmed was to be expected. They'd been separated from their families for more than 150 years. I turned to the other faeries behind us. The grins on their faces said all that needed to be told as they ribbed at each other. Wendy giggled, and Oren put a finger to his lips. Even he couldn't keep the grin off his face as he did it, though. Their energy was infectious. The end of their torment was almost here. They would finally be able to lead their own lives again, free from oppression. Emotion clogged in my throat. It reminded me why I always found myself helping people. There were times you could do for others what they couldn't do for themselves. Sometimes, they just needed a little boost. It felt good to be able to do that for them. Even if this was an extreme case. It was a rare case that my life was in danger in the process. That reminder of what was at stake went a long way to sober me.

My neck felt tense as I went to speak. I took a few breaths and tried to calm down. The cords in my neck didn't ease much, but I didn't have time to get my shit together. Now was the time for action.

I looked out into the clearing. Nothing. Fuck it. With a thought, I pulled some Kundalini energy. Lightning licked at my hands, inching up my elbows and then shrinking back down to my wrists. I bit my lip to contain it. It took a little longer than usual to hold the ley energy in check. When I was satisfied, I stepped out into the clearing. My movements were jerky as I swung to the left and the right, my hands at the ready. Nobody sprang out from me. Nobody moved. Not even so much as a bird caw. Nothing.

I turned back to the now quiet group. They sat unmoving as if enthralled by a deep freeze enchantment. I'd quite effectively taken away their excitement. The corners of my mouth turned down. I didn't like to be the one to take away anyone's happiness, let alone a whole group. There was no helping it though, now was our chance. I could sit here and feel bad, or I could get them home.

I leveled a hard look at each of them and said, "Let's go."

I looked back at the clearing. Still empty. Thank the gods. I didn't want to see anyone. The fewer people we saw, the fewer chances of being caught.

With a prayer for the clearing to stay empty, I forged ahead. The rustle of feet through thick grass meant the others trudged behind me. Climbing up the boulders wasn't as hard this time, because I had Brock make some other boulders appear for me to use as a staircase.

After I was up, I motioned to the new. "When I am gone, destroy these."

He looked at the boulders, and his brows knit together, but he slowly nodded.

I put my face close to his and said, "Nobody can follow you in here, do you understand? Leaving these will make it too easy for someone to find the mound. Do not forget to destroy them."

His lips compressed, but this time his nod was faster. I'm sure he didn't like being talked to like that, but the group's safety came before spared feelings.

Turning my attention back to the task in front of me, I detailed to the huddled group everything I was doing. I'd be damned if they didn't know how to come home again. "And after you find the glimmer, just keep your eye trained on it."

As if to highlight my point, the glimmer revealed itself at the base of a nondescript oak tree just as I said it.

"There," I said, pointing to the spot.

They all looked at the spot that was identical to all of the other trees and then looked back at me. Some of the more polite faeries kept their faces carefully blank. Others raised their eyebrows and gave disbelieving looks like they thought I might be insane. I didn't blame their skepticism. If they weren't looking from the angle, I was. It wouldn't have looked like anything was there.

"You have to be where I am to see it," I explained.

Wendy walked over to where I pointed. When she walked around the oak, she must have seen the staircase shimmer.

"She's right!" she said excitedly.

As all of the faeries rushed to her, I didn't bother to point out that, of course, I was right. Even though I was the equivalent of a 25-year-old human, it didn't mean I was ignorant. Hell, I'd lived here for almost 80 years.

All of the faeries had gone except Oren. He sat there, staring at me. It was clear he wanted to say something. I was never too good with words, though. I shimmied down the boulder. My boots landed with a soft thud in the grass.

"Just go up to the fourth staircase, knock, and then kick at the knot in the tree." I explained, avoiding his gaze.

"Why don't you come with us?" He said, seeing through me. "You're the Princess. Come be that for your people. You've already proved you are more than cut out for the task."

Part of me wanted to believe what he said. But deep down, I knew better. Saving people isn't what being a Princess was about.

"What happened proved nothing." I said, denying his words.

I counted the faeries as they rushed one by one up the

stairs. The staircase glowed under their feet with each step as they ran. When the last faerie disappeared around the bend, the flight of stairs vanished.

I nodded my head in their direction. "You better go help them figure out how to get in. Gods know they are probably running up to the top of the tree by now. An elf lives up there, and he doesn't take too kindly to visitors."

He stared at me a few more heartbeats before saying, "You take care of yourself, Princess."

"Every day." I said with a nod for him to get going.

I had a very happy life. I argued with myself as he turned and made his way after the others. Sure, I didn't know what I was going to do about Sven anymore. Could I stay with him after he'd done that to me? What else would he do without my permission? What else would he take away from me?

At the thought of him, the strangest thing happened. I could almost feel him as if he were standing there with me. Like I could reach out and touch him. Warmth rubbed around inside me right after the feeling came.

Smacking my brow with my palm, I pushed the feeling away. This was ludicrous. I had to stop thinking of Sven, like that anyway. There was no future for us.

I shook my shoulders and turned to leave. Then I saw something that shot shock through my body. There was no way I could go now.

In my way stood a giant of a man. His black visage blocked out the sun. It wasn't his materialization out of nowhere that scared me to my core. It wasn't his clothes that stood still in the billowing wind or the leaves that swirled in the clearing like the white noise of stark fear swirling through my veins. It was his look of calm.

The Boogeyman was always the calmest seconds before his attack. People said that when he stalked around your bedroom, he started smiling like he had his own private joke.

He delighted in your terror. But as your doom came closer and closer, all humor left his face only to be replaced by a calm that no peace could touch. It was the calm that could only be brought on by the stillness of death. And death was just a day in the life for him. He'd left a legendary trail of death—a depth of gore that was unmatched at any time in history. Nobody stood a chance against the Boogeyman.

I say this, so you understand there was no chance for me as he became the shadows and engulfed me in his darkness.

He was Death. And death was here to claim me.

CHAPTER 3

*M*y face planted into the ground. Correction: wood floor. As the rest of my senses came to, I numbly realized what the grainy texture meant.

"Not quite what I was expecting," said a familiar voice.

Mother. Shit. That, of course, meant I was back in Knockaine. I banged my head on the floor a couple more times for good measure. Maybe I would wake up somewhere else this time.

I opened my eyes. The wood might as well have laughed at me. Nope. Still here. The smell of moss sobered me quickly. Double shit. Wood floor? Moss? That only meant one place.

"You wanted her, did you not?" asked a voice deep as if it came from the hounds of hell themselves.

Instinctively, my head turned to the speaker. You never wanted a dangerous person at your back, whether you were on the ground or not. And the Boogeyman owned that category. Black boots bigger than life loomed at me. The toe itself looked like it would jump off its owner and kick my ass without any provocation. I was pretty sure I heard it growl.

Slippered footfall pattered across the floor, stopping when it reached my side. I didn't turn my gaze from the snarling boots. Soft steps were a lot less likely to go for the throat.

Slender arms came around me, and a disdainful voice said to the wearer of said boots, "You would think you would know how to treat a Princess."

As I rose, the boots bled to black slacks and a tailored black jacket over an unbuttoned shirt that was, yes, black. All of that ended at a dark countenance that made me flinch if I was a lesser fae. A Don't Fuck With Me vibe snaked around the Boogeyman and struck out at anyone dumb enough to get too close. The set of his face screamed it. We were only saved from his piercing glare because of his pitch-black shades.

Even my would-be rescuer's voice faded as she came closer. Now that I was standing, I could identify her. She had been my friend when I was a teenager, Avalynn. My close friend before I'd become obsessed with the idea of leaving this place. I'd had to get out. Her, on the other hand, loved living in Knockaine. She belonged here. It made sense: everyone adored her.

The Boogeyman shrugged his broad shoulders, moving in a massive ripple with his expensive suit. The look on his harsh-planed face was one of boredom.

Without so much as a glance at Avalynn, he said to my mother, "She was not as easy to acquire as I had thought. This erases the debt I owe you."

Debt? I looked from him to my mother. She sat on her winged concrete throne, the ever-present pain in my ass Dian Cecht behind her. She held one of the thrones in the circle of identical 13 thrones held the Fae of the Realm's Kings and Queens. All the thrones were occupied. Except one.

Mother's face remained neutral as she gave a small nod to the Boogeyman and then waved her hand to dismiss him. My mouth fell open. She dismissed him. Like a hired hand. In front of the entire Court.

He sneered something about ignorant faeries, but before his words could collect weight, he vanished in a trail of shadows and spun up then out through the tree branches above.

At first glance, you'd think they were the same trees that were in The Croí. But I knew better. They merely climbed the walls and ceilings, weaving around the stone pillars, in a way that looked organic. They weren't really, though. It was all faerie magic. Not nature. Not the heart of Danu. That didn't make the display any less impressive.

I didn't want to be impressed right now. Impressiveness hinted at power. It was a power you didn't have to flaunt. Power people just understood. It wasn't a power I wanted to be on the other side of.

"Speak for yourself, Princess Cybil Vanguard." said Mother from her queenly perch.

Her words made my insides flinch. I'd expected formalities from the Court's rulers, it was the way of the Court, after all. To be cold-shouldered by her, though? It hurt. She was my mother. I looked to her, trying to keep the hurt off my face. Cecht grinned, a cheshire grin from his domain behind her, and I knew immediately he'd been the one to say it. My teeth ached, and I made myself unclench my jaw. It didn't really matter that he'd puppetted her. She could have stood up for me. How often was she going to prove that it didn't matter one fig that I was her daughter, her flesh and blood before I got it? But did you ever give up hoping your mom would love you? My gut twisted. I didn't know if it was possible, but I was sure as Dagda going to try. Or die trying.

I cleared my throat. Where did one start when explaining

everything that had happened? Being in love with a vampire probably wasn't the best way to start. The faces in front of me said there probably wasn't a good time to bring that up. Ok, so did I talk about the Strange and Wonderful? I scraped the toe of my borrowed boot against the wooden floor. I didn't really want to draw attention to Mrs. Carmichael. She and Charles, the head of the SAW, had been living happily out of sight. Who was I to kill that for them?

I lowered my eyes and ducked a glance at the Queen of the Yōsei. It was said the Yōsei could bring the dead back to life. With her black-rimmed eyes and red shadow bled down to just under her cheeks, I believed it. Her heavy-lidded eyes looked like death was reaching out to me. I shivered.

My heart hammered in my chest. I might not know what to say, but one thing was crystal: time was up.

"Well...I have wings." I started lamely.

Their expressions were understandably droll. From their presence here, it was clear they already knew that. The Fae of the Realm didn't gather unless there was a change in the Courts, the fae of the thirteenth mound made an appearance, or in the event of a crisis. Long story short: they only came around for emergencies. The first two situations were dependent on the death of a faerie and the world's chakras. I'd give you one guess how often those changed. And the first guess didn't count.

I didn't know why I'd worried about what to say. Once I began, the words flowed as if a boulder had been taken out of a stopped-up stream.

"As far as I can tell, we all have wings." I declared in a clear, even voice.

Fabric shifted over the stone as the leaders of the fae assessed my statement. I gauged their reactions. Some reactions were noticeable. The King of the Menehune was one of those. He stood suddenly. His loincloth swayed between his stubby bronzed legs as he began to pace the length of his throne's seat. Some were more subtle. Even the Queen of the Yōsei, whose people prided themselves in their stoicism, had moved. Mind you I hadn't seen her move, but the trails of rubies, dangling in what looked like frozen rivulets of blood from her elaborate raven headdress, swayed. There was no wind here. She was as unnerved as the rest of them. Good. The more I could keep their attention away from my specific predicament, the better. I had to bring this news home to them. That's what they were here for, after all.

Satisfied I had their attention, I walked with measured steps around the circle to look at each of them in the eye. "I think the main difference is mine- as well as probably many of your own kin's wings- are under layers of our skin."

"How can you make such a bold claim?' asked the Queen of the Aziza in her deep, throaty voice.

I turned my attention to her. She was breathtaking with bright flowers woven into her dark braids. She seemed so pure that I answered honestly, much to my surprise.

"Truth be told, Your Majesty, it is purely a guess." Then I lifted my gaze to the ones of the Queen of the Mimis. She was tall and thin, like all of her people. So thin it was said she would break with a gust of wind. This made her head very small. Even though it was slightly larger than her body, it made eye contact almost impossible at this distance. I pretended like I had succeeded though and said, "You all know what I say is true. You can feel it in your chest."

I dropped my hands I'd brought to my heart and leveled a look at the King of the Patupairehe. The speculative gleam in his eyes took me off guard. It wasn't that he was unattractive. His red hair was pulled into a chic man bun, and his pale hands that gripped the arms of the throne were wide enough to give any girl thoughts. But I wasn't interested. It didn't have anything to do with the feathers in his hair or the unfashionably thick chin strap beard. It had everything to do with the broken heart in my chest. With haste, I kept moving.

"But I challenge you to tell me I am wrong. Even though you all do not feel it yourselves, since you all have wings, I know your people have spoken of The Taibhse Géag, of the Phantom Limb. You know how evolution works. Think of the pinky toe. You know things get smaller, subside before they disappear. It didn't make sense that our wings would disappear completely." I banged my hand in my fist.

"So how do we get our people's wings? How did yours come out?" asked the Queen of the Dorset Fairies.

I swung about to her. Her young hands were buried at her sides in her diaphanous teal gown. Gold shimmered in the fabric as it moved ever so slightly. She was wringing her hands and didn't want anyone to see. Queen. What a cut-throat position. What had happened that had made her Queen? She wasn't equipped for the game. That was clear. I wouldn't be the one to out her, though.

The more pressing question was how did I explain how I got my wings? If they knew I'd been bitten by a vampire, there's no telling what they would do. The Queen of the Yōsei saved me from having to answer.

"We cut them out." She said a bored look on her face.

Yikes. I had to admit that it would probably work. Horrific images of mass mutilation crashed through my brain. I locked the thoughts away. No. I wouldn't let that happen. I would admit to the lot of them I'd slept with a thousand vampires before one inch of fae's skin was cut.

But what could I say? How about a version of the truth and just hope they didn't ask too many questions? My mind worked. I could do this. Of course, I could. But why did I have to? Why couldn't I just sit down with a friendly, peaceful cheeseburger instead? It seemed fair given everything I'd already been through.

"I don't think that will be necessary, Your Majesty. When my wings came to me, it was in a moment of joy, a moment of..." As I searched for words, I found myself picking up my pace, "intense happiness. I felt like I was free."

"We've all felt these feelings before," said the King of the Glastonbury Fairies, disbelief scrunching his eyebrows up into his gold crowned helmet.

"It was sudden, acute. It happened faster than any emotion I'd ever had before." The words to make them understand escaped me, but I tried anyway. "It was unexpected. Something that overtook me faster than I had time to think. I think that's the key. I think you have to experience emotion fast and intense. And it has to happen when you aren't expecting it."

His expression didn't change. Shit. They didn't get it. I really didn't want to spell it out for them, but I guess I had no choice. Gathering courage, I took a deep breath.

Before I could speak, Queen of the Aziza did.

"I see it. I see the difference. The unexpectedness of the emotion jolts the wings, which causes them to break free from the skin." Her braids brushed her shoulders as she nodded.

At her words, others started to nod. My knees buckled with relief. Thank Danu. Before more could be said, a commotion sounded outside the room. All eyes turned to the stone archway. A lanky faerie rushed in. His eyes held the look of shock, and he tried to speak a couple times before the sound finally managed to come out.

"Forgive me Your Majesties, but you will never believe this-" He said, his arms doing all the talking.

"I'm seeing the Queen. She needs to know we have returned." said a familiar voice.

Then a line of familiar faeries bustled in. Oren was at the forefront. I almost fell to my knees.

"Pardon the intrusion, My Queen," he said, stopping in the middle of the room and dropping to a knee. He dipped his head in deference and then seemed to notice I was standing there also. "Princess, you decided to come back. I knew you would do the right thing, especially after you saved us all the way you did."

My face flamed. Me deciding to come back? Now there was a stretch, to say the least. I ducked my head to hide my face. It had to be as red as a cardinal.

"Cy saved you?" asked Mother.

There was no mistaking the incredulity in her voice. Wendy pushed forward.

Her pale blue hair bobbed as she said, "She did. She almost died too, she did. Never have I seen someone more deserving of the title of nobility as the Princess."

I ignored the creeping note of hero worship in her voice that made me decidedly uncomfortable.

"Why, I'd say that's deserving of a celebration. Wouldn't you, Queen of Knockaine?" said the Queen of the Dorset Fairies, her young voice surprisingly strong.

My mother had the queerest expression on her face as she nodded. The act looked like it was pulled from her very being. But she couldn't exactly refuse. Court etiquette said you didn't refuse a reasonable request.

"Isn't the Feast of Midsummer Night coming up? You could honor her deeds and her homecoming as part of the celebration?" she pressed on. "I just know the kingdom would love it. She could be a symbol of hope for all of us."

Maybe I hadn't given the young fairie enough credit. She had serious balls to suggest they hail me at a celebration that honored my mother.

After a couple seconds of no doubt wishing the little

Queen was lying dead in a river somewhere, Mother gave another nod, the glass of her hair falling forward. Odd. The locks looked darker than I'd last seen them.

"I think that is an absolutely splendid idea, Your Majesty." she bit out in a tone that precisely what she thought of the idea.

A chill crept across my skin. Mother's tone meant one thing: I would pay for the slight. One way or another.

CHAPTER 4

A pentagram with two slivers of the moon was etched into the purple door to The Poppet Shop. Or to be precise Spells of the Poppet: Potions, Bombs, and Magical Oddities.

Trepidation stilled my hand. I didn't have a problem with entering a witches' shop. I'd met plenty of nice witches. One, supremely kind, witch had given me a place to hide when I was outrunning a bridge troll in France a few years back. However, this witch was not pleasant, or kind. In fact, she would have fed me to the bridge troll and grinned while doing it. Inside was Tristen's grandmother. Yes, the same Tristen I'd dated. The whole thing was absurd. We hadn't gone on that many dates before I got that it wasn't going to work, but that didn't stop him from losing his shit when I broke it off. Crazy is as crazy does, I suppose. He went all Mr. Dramatic and went to live in a different mound, not just the second mound in the two interconnected domes that was Knockaine. That wouldn't have been a big deal. Tor Mór, that would have been too easy. After all, his grandmother's witch shop was in The Oíche. No, he now called the Mount Shasta mound home. At least it wasn't on another continent. His grandmother didn't see it that way, though. She saw it as an abandonment. And blamed me. Last I heard she wanted me dead.

Yep, this wasn't going to be awkward at all. But the death thing might work out in my favor.

Once inside, I saw a door to my immediate left. A quick look put another one at the back of the store. Store was a generous term. The place was barely bigger than two of my living rooms put together. Dried bats, flowers, rats…a whole slew of things hung from the ceiling. It added to the claustrophobia that started to crawl up my throat as my gaze scanned the shop. I shivered as a chill ran through me. We did what we had to do, right?

As I took a step, a puff of dust hit me, and shimmery particles fell around me like snow. I gasped. Powder coated my mouth. Dagda be damned, that tasted awful. Coughs racked my body. My head whipped back and forth. Shimmering remnants of the black powder hung in the air in front of me. What in the hell was that?

Then my body started moving on its own. Not in like a twitch or something that made sense. I started spinning. In a complete, full circle, I twirled. Fuck, it was some kind of witchery.

Round and round, I spun. What in the name of Danu, what was happening? I drug my foot on the ground to stop myself, but I kept going. I reached out to grab the nearest shelf, but it didn't weigh me down. It just came with me for half a turn like a dance partner before I let it go and it went careening—Shop window, kitchen door, shelving, shop window, kitchen door, shelving. I squeezed my eyes close as my insides started to rise. Precious seconds ticked by like centuries. I felt the bile grow. Pressing my lips closed, I held it in.

Dimly I heard a downright chipper voice say, "I wonder...should spin you into a different dimension? Or simply let you go until you regurgitate all of your pathetic weakness onto my linoleum?"

My eyes flew open in time to see a faerie saunter around the downed shelf, a red bucket in hand. Her sagging arms agilely lifted the bucket to the height of her thin chest. Then the world turned and she was out of sight again.

"Iris, we were just teenagers." I ground out as the world spun faster and faster.

Her lips snarled as I flew by. "Tell that to my Tristen."

I opened my mouth to tell her, for the thousandth time, that we'd only been on a few dates, but my insides took my open mouth as permission to relieve itself. Yellow splat-splatted as it spewed across the shop window, kitchen door, and the shelving. Before it got to Iris, I was doused with a thick liquid. I fell to the floor like strings were holding me up, and they'd been cut. My body convulsed the blessedly small remaining contents of my stomach up. A quick sandwich on the way over was all I'd eaten in the last 24 hours. I'd planned on having a real meal when I was done here, but the ache in my stomach had me wondering if maybe fasting was for me.

Acidic breaths were my only connection to the real world. My brain told me I was still spinning. I don't know how long I laid there, but it felt good with the frigid shop floor under me, so I did. It had been a while since I'd done something that just felt good. When the world finally reported accurate information to me again, I sat up. With shaking hands, I squeegeed syrupy liquid out of my eyes.

In front of me lay the shelf I'd tried to stop myself with.

The once careful home to a dozen potions lay, broken, on its side. The bottles were all over the place. Two had tried to run and only succeeded in falling to the floor. One of their lives had ended in a shimmery death. Three others nestled together on the shelf, stubbornly holding onto their lids. Only one had managed to escape to the other side of the room, but it had emptied its contents in a shimmering mess on the floor along the way.

Ignoring my struggle, Iris was splashing the last remnants of red syrup on the potion mess. She set the now-empty bucket inside the kitchen door.

"I never thought you'd dare show your face in The Oíche." She didn't wait to hear my answer as she ducked into the kitchen.

It was insane. I had to admit. Iris didn't know how desperate I'd become, though. I propped myself up on my elbows to keep an eye on her as she came out of the kitchen. Dagda be damned if she thought she was going to be able to catch me unawares again. I pulled a little Kundalini energy into my hand under my back.

She strode back into the room, balancing a baby size sack on her hip. Its top flopped with each of her determined steps. She didn't spare me a glance as she reached into it and fished out a handful.

"I ought to kill you where you stand." Her lips turned down as she tossed a glare at my still reclining form. "Err...sit."

Pulling the powder out of the burlap sack, she said under her breath, "Better yet. I'll turn you into a toad. That would suit you."

Not giving me a chance to respond, she tossed the white and black speckled powder on the shelf. The shelves snapped and flashed like a firecracker, covering the area in dense smoke. I winced. It wasn't the wisest move in a small shop.

Then again, her family seemed to be closer to insane than sane on the sanity spectrum.

When the smoke cleared, the shelf stood tall. The potion bottles shone in the ever-present sunlight Knockaine had during the daylight hours. Gods alive. Forgetting myself, I let the magic seep back into the ley lines. As she proceeded to repeat these steps with the getaway potion, I couldn't help the laugh that escaped me as the trail disappeared. The runaway potion appeared in an instant back on the shelf.

"So what in the name of Danu are you doing here?" she asked as she walked past me.

What was I doing here? Sven, the battle from last night, and the Boogeyman flashed through my head. It was enough to spin your head, without the theatrics of a witch. At the thought of Sven, a weight sat on my chest. It felt more immense than it should have. I really hadn't wanted to end it with him, but what could I do? I couldn't be with someone who didn't respect me. I wouldn't.

A thud from the kitchen brought me back to the here and now. I pushed myself to my feet as Iris walked in. She walked past me again, her chin high.

I opted for the most straightforward answer. "I'm back because I have wings now."

She walked to the far wall and adjusted bottles on the shelf that she had fixed. "I *can* see, you know. Or did you come here just to insult me?"

"No, I came because I need your help." It didn't matter that I had to swallow my pride to admit that. I would have done just about anything to get out of here.

She shook her head. Bitter laughter erupted from her throat as she suddenly left her straightening. With jerky side-to-side movements of her head, she stalked to the back of the store. I followed.

When she made it to the back counter, she plucked a

dried bat from the ceiling. She brushed her teal hair back from her forehead with the bat in her hand. I fought back the urge to gag. You'd never see a dead anything that near to my face. Unless I was eating it. The thought made me think of cheeseburgers again. When was the last time I'd eaten a cheeseburger had it been days? Weeks?

Iris brought the bat back to the counter. She set it on a wooden-checkerboard pig on the counter. With quick movements, she pulled a knife out of her apron. The sunlight didn't reach this far back, and it glinted in the dim interior.

With quick movements, she slapped the bat onto the board. "Isn't that rich? You want my help? You're clearly dumber than you look."

I laughed, a dry laugh. There were very few times I would sit somewhere and be insulted. If I was a lesser person, I'd insult her back and say that if her precious Tristen was such a catch, we'd still be together. I'd storm off and tell her and her whole too-perfect family to go fuck off.

That would just be to hurt her, though. It wasn't true. Before this whole thing with Tristen, I'd like her. And Tristen really was a...decent person; we just weren't meant to be together. Maybe I could make this about the one thing she really wanted.

In case she changed her mind about the knife, I stepped out of her range and continued. "Look, the only reason they brought me back here is because of these damn wings. If I can make them go away, I can split this joint like a bad dream. But short of cutting them off- and no, I'm not into self-mutilation, I can't do that by myself. I need your help."

She brought the knife down with more force than I would have said was necessary because the bat's head flew off and hit the far wall. "Oh, isn't that too bad for you. Why don't-" She stopped her arm in the middle of bringing the knife down again onto the bat and asked, "Wait- did you say you would leave?"

"Yeah," I deadpanned.

"Why didn't you say so?" She said. "Anything that gets you out of my face, I'm all for."

I leveled her an unamused look. It didn't sit well with me that she hated me so much. I liked to think of myself as a likable person. Ok, I was a little rough around the edges, but I was still a good person. Wasn't I?

She ignored my look and dropped her knife onto the counter with a clatter. The dried meat of the headless bat stared at me as she went behind me. I didn't know what she planned until she started tugging at my wings. It didn't hurt, but it grated my nerves.

She pulled and pushed. Just when I thought I was going to have to say something, she stopped. After a moment, she came back around behind the counter. She held the knife, but this time it rested in her hand as if it were an afterthought.

With a grimace, she said, "Yeah, they're on there pretty good, aren't they?"

"Yeah, on as in they're part of my body." I rolled my eyes.

Her free hand reached out to me and then stopped. "You're serious. You have wings."

My wings started to beat with my irritation. I struggled to keep them still, so I wouldn't make a mess of Iris' store.

My jaw was tight as I asked, "Why would I make something like that up?"

She ignored my question. "But how is that possible?"

I laughed and raised my hands. "You tell me."

Her eyes took on a far off look. After a few moments, she focused back on me. Shrugging, she shook her head.

"Yeah, you are never going to be able to leave if you have

those," she said, holding the knife more firmly and going back to cutting. The steady drum of my heart in my chest pounded in my ears. No. I couldn't stay here. The pressure of being Princess with a capital P was too much, never-ending. I wasn't good enough. I never would be. I felt the tattoo on my wrist burn. Danu, forgive me.

"Isn't there anything you can do?" I asked Iris.

I didn't like the way my voice wavered, but I didn't care. I needed to get out. I needed to be free to be me. And that wasn't here. I would give anything to make that happen, including embarrassing myself in front of one of my worst enemies.

At first, she didn't answer me. Then the cutting slowed to a stop. I let out a breath I didn't know I was holding. She set the knife down and then stared into space. A sheer black liquid painted her arm as she stroked it absently. Suddenly, she dropped the blade with a clack that was loud enough to make me jump.

Before my heartbeat had time to slow back down to a just-chatting-with-your-friendly-sociopath pace, she'd disappeared through a velvet moon-patterned curtain behind the counter. Loud scrapes and thumps made me wonder. I debated whether or not to go back there when the curtain flung to the side, and she came back through it carrying a large book. The size of it made me stop. The top of it almost touched her chin, and the bottom of it fell halfway down her thighs. She staggered under the weight of it. She'd just made it to the counter when it fell out of her grasp. It boomed as it fell. Even though I'd seen the whole thing, it still made me jump.

With a frown, she flipped through the pages, mumbling under her breath the whole while. "Forked Tongue…Endless Love…Sonic Split…Where is it? I could have sworn it was here."

Goosebumps ran up my arm, chills sweeping through me. All of those sounded scary as hell. And what exactly was a Sonic Split?

After a moment, the furrows smoothed from her brow. "Ah, here it is. Nevermore."

"Nevermore?" I repeated to make sure I'd heard her correctly.

She nodded, with her head still buried in the book, she read aloud, "Never is forever, but sometimes it is the only solution. If you find you want your troubles to disappear from your mind, never to be seen again, drink me. Never will your troubles bother you again unless you speak from the never. Only then will never be at your door. Otherwise, they will be gone forevermore."

Goosebumps crawled up my arm. Gone forevermore. That's what I wanted. Wasn't it?

The frown crept back onto her face. "Odd. It doesn't say anything about partial."

"Partial?" I echoed, feeling like a parrot.

This time she did look at me. Her expression said she thought I was about as bright as a parrot too. "Right, as in it might make you vanish entirely."

That wasn't something I liked the sound of.

"What would happen if I... 'vanished entirely?' Where would I go?" I tried to wrap my head around the concept. "Would I be able to come back?"

She just gave a shrug and a half-laugh. "I have no idea. This is an ancient spellbook. It's not used much anymore because it has a history of being sort of...unstable. I don't even have most of these ingredients anymore."

Unstable? I didn't like the sounds of that at all. Not to mention the little part about me possibly disappearing and not being able to come back. My wings started to beat in the small space. I took a couple stabilizing breaths. It wouldn't do any good for me to lift off right now. I had more pressing matters to deal with.

I gestured at the giant book she was almost on top of and asked, "Isn't there another...spell we could use in there?"

"Nope, this is all I have that's even close", she said as she slapped the book's page.

Dust plumed up from it, in a beeline straight for my mouth. Staleness gagged me. I coughed.

"What about the...newer books?" I asked around the layer of dust coating my mouth.

She looked at me like I'd suggested there might be a one-eyed monster in the back. "Just how often do you think it comes up that someone wants a piece of their *body* to go away?"

Ok, when she put it that way. But still...did I want out of Knockaine that badly that I was willing to disappear entirely? I didn't even know what that meant. Maybe it meant I would be roving the Earth, invisible to all. I wiped at my upper lip, which had suddenly felt hot and sweaty.

Iris seemed oblivious to my inner turmoil as she scratched flourishes onto a piece of paper. She finished with a dot and tore the list from her ratty pad of paper. She thrust it in my face.

I looked down at the paper. What amounted to a shopping list was scrawled there.

"Thieves' Hair, Goblin Bone, Werewolf Blood, Dragon Scale, and Demon's Hoof?" I asked as I read off the unbelievable list.

Iris didn't bat an eyelash or even say a word for that matter. She just smirked.

"What's this?" I asked, even though I was afraid I already knew the answer.

"It's the ingredient list. Like I told you, I don't have those ingredients." She said.

I laughed and shook my head. "What am I supposed to do about that?"

"Those are the ingredients I need for your potion. If you want the potion, you'll have to go get them." She said simply as she closed the book with a snap.

I laughed some more. This time I'm sure my laugh sounded a tad hysterical. But I couldn't help it. Did I seem like a superhero to anyone? I couldn't just waltz out and grab a dragon scale and a demon's hoof. I might as well just slit my own throat.

"Look, I don't know how you expect me to get these things. They aren't exactly at the corner market."

She waved her hand in the air. "You'll figure it out."

Right, like it was a math problem. We weren't talking about two plus two here. We were talking about what probably equated to life or death. Not to mention there was the little matter of the potion possibly not working anyway.

"But what if it doesn't work...like it should?" I asked, not quite able to put words to the idea that something could wipe me from the planet with such ease.

She shrugged her shoulders as she hefted the book back into her frail arms. "Well, do you want to get out of here or not?"

Of course, I did, but not at the expense of my existence. I adjusted a potion on the counter in front of me.

"Isn't there any other way?" I asked.

I know I sounded weak, but this was way out of my league.

With a grunt, she staggered toward the backroom again. "If there's another way, it's beyond me. Trust me. If I could think of a better way to get you out of my face, I would do it so fast you'd think it was The Mother's birthday."

Trust her. How could I trust her? Ten minutes ago she'd wanted to kill me. My gut told me she wasn't trying to kill me, though. That she really did think this was the best way. Could I do it, though? I could die getting the ingredients. The potion could damn me to a fate worse than hell on Earth. Just how much was I willing to sacrifice to be me?

CHAPTER 5

A little boy balanced a giant ornament in his small hands as he ran past me. His eyes strained to see over it. It was a wonder he could hold it at all.

His wasn't the most oversized ornament, though. Even bigger ones were being hefted into the trees by groups of faeries who were flying them high into the branches. They glittered like small suns in the warmth of the sunshine.

I wandered through the courtyard. My mind phased out the activity. I was numb to it, numb to everything but the thoughts racing through my head. Just how was I going to get out of here? If I didn't do it legitimately and narrowly escaped again, Mother would just hunt me down. Again. I couldn't be on the run forever.

Absently, I passed under a willow tree. My feet carried me as relief coursed through me. Sweet Danu, the shade felt good. My feet crunched on the path as I stared, unseeing. A shift in the crunch of the path to cushy grass beneath my feet made me look up. A clear green pond shimmered in the afternoon sun. I blinked. Somehow, I'd found myself at the spot where Celeste and I had come to talk when we were young. Flowering lily pads and cattails now rimmed the edges of the small pond. Not surprising since it had been some time since it had been swam in. I walked to the pond, drawn to it. I flopped onto the grass at the edge.

I couldn't just sit here and allow myself to be molded into someone I didn't recognize. Could I? That answer was easy: no. I had to be me. And I knew from before, I couldn't do that here. There was no choice but to leave. Being the natural heir to the throne didn't leave me the luxury Tristen had. It simply wasn't allowed for royalty to reside anywhere but the mound of their family. On the surface, it made sense. It kept the chances of a takeover down. Before the peace of the mounds, the fae had been just as intent on expansion as humans were. We'd used all the same tactics too: political sabotage, military conquest, you name it. So I didn't blame them for not wanting me there. It landed me in this impossible position, though. What was I supposed to do? I couldn't exactly go to another mound for help either. It would get back to Mother quicker than pixies fly. Then she'd have me back in the Tearmann so fast my head would spin. I'd heard the only reason I hadn't landed there yet was Court politics. I laughed without mirth. This was the only time Court politics had actually benefited me.

Were my best options really possibly vanishing or being in my own personal hell for the rest of my life then? I swallowed past a lump in my throat.

Pulling the crumpled paper from my pocket, I smoothed out the creases. The words stared back at me, stark and foreboding: Thieves' Hair, Goblin Bones, Werewolf Blood, Dragon Scale, Demon's Hoof.

Talk about a shopping list from hell. How did I even go about getting half of these things? Not to mention I would be lucky if I didn't die just trying to get them. So basically, I could die now, or I could die later. Just great.

That didn't seem fair. What did living mean really? After everything I'd been through, I started to think it had less to do with the beat of a heart and more to do with the way someone felt inside, the person they chose to be.

The person they chose to be. That was a sobering thought. Sven hadn't exactly proven himself to be the most stellar of people. Not by his actions anyway.

And there was the feeling again. A heaviness. It was the same heaviness I'd had when I thought of Sven. It pulled at my heart. I knew he'd hurt me, but the rudeness of it perplexed me. I let it wash over me this time. There was more to it than hurt. There was...worry? That was odd. I wasn't worried. Upset? Trapped? Betrayed? Sure. I was battered by all of those feelings, and a handful more I didn't want to examine too closely. But worried wasn't one of them.

Isolating that emotion, I let myself feel it. Really feel it. I freed my mind, following it down the path. Only then did it hit me. This wasn't my emotion; it was Sven's.

My eyes flew open in shock. I shook my head. But once I'd felt it, I couldn't make it go away. The feeling was so strong, so real. It was as tangible as if he were next to me right now.

I know I looked crazy, but I reached a hand out to the empty space next to me. Not surprisingly, my hand didn't meet anything. He and I weren't together anymore. His presence did nothing but bring me more pain. My chin trembled as I pushed him out of my thoughts. To my surprise, it did go. It left like the removal of a physical thing. I pressed a shaking hand to my forehead.

A shadow blocked the warmth of my sun and shadowed my hands. I dropped them. I watched the black blob shift on the water from side to side. It was a familiar outline. Anthony. A smile twitched my mouth. I was so used to

Anthony popping in and out whenever he pleased, seeing him walk up was strange.

It was so good to have him around. He brought a measure of comfort that was so rare in my life. I turned and raised my gaze to him, grazing over his drool-worthy pecs. I'm pretty sure you could bounce quarters off those. At least he'd put on jeans again.

I looked away. Why was I admiring Anthony? For that matter, why was I happy to see him? I was still mad at him for taking me against my will to Knockaine a couple days ago. Sure, we'd been best friends. But that was a long time ago.

I popped up off the grass. The hurt look on his face almost made me wish I hadn't. Almost. I headed back down the dirt path from my private oasis.

I didn't have to ask Anthony how he'd found me. After Celeste had died, I'd brought him here, to keep my connection to the place alive. My connection to her alive. It was as if I thought that if there was still laughter in this special place that she couldn't really be gone.

When we passed back from under the willow tree into the Courtyard, I faltered. Not really sure where I was going. Uncertain, I shot him a look. His expression was unreadable as he looked down at me. I scowled and shifted my eyes away.

"I don't know why you're even here right now," I grumbled, making sure he knew I was still mad about the other day.

He ignored the comment and looked out over the grass. Following his gaze, I connected with the ever-present group in the dirt circle. Punches and kicks punctuated the air. Muay Thai. It was a different group than the last time I'd come through. There was a rotating schedule. Every faerie in

Knockaine was required to join the groups, at some point.
Even I had.

It was such a silly mandate. A well-placed Superman
punch was all fine and dandy if we were up against a human.
Still, it would be the equivalent to bringing a daisy to a sword
fight when you traded that human for a vampire. And they
were our most deadly predators. Shouldn't we equip
ourselves, so we were protected against them?

Weaponizing our abilities would put us on the same level.
Well, mostly. Ok, it would at least make it a fair fight. I wasn't
faulting anyone for not doing it. Tor Mór, I hadn't even
realized how big of a deal it was that we hadn't weaponized
our abilities until last night. Last night it had been an
equalizer. A big, hairy tarantula of a deal once you realized
any other battle of that size would have ended in a
slaughterhouse.

Sure, we'd barely managed to escape with our lives. But
we'd run. Now that I knew what it could do against
vampires, I'd have to suck it up and have that talk. Whether I
was laughed at or not. Especially since vampires very
possibly knew we existed. They were likely on the hunt right
now. I shivered in the humid air.

Anthony brought me back to the moment when he
started picking grass.

The thin, candy-green blades fluttered as he dropped
them. "For what it's worth, I'm sorry."

I couldn't help the laugh that snorted out.

It would be hard to say there was a single person who
messed my life up to more than Anthony. On the same token,
I would be hard-pressed to find a single person who'd helped
me more in my life than him too. The thought made me
pause.

"Ok, I deserve that." His biceps bulged as he folded his

arms across his chest. "Just know, I was trying to keep you safe."

I inhaled deep and steady breaths. Between Sven's mark last night and Anthony's kidnapping the day before, I'd had enough of the men trying to keep me "safe" without giving a fig what I thought. Mistaking my silence for doubt, he pressed on.

"Yeah, that's right. What I did was for you." He paused and waited for a group to move past our secluded bough before he continued on. "It may have looked like it was for the crown, but it wasn't. It was for you. I just had to make it look like it was for the crown, so the Queen didn't use me as an example. She'd cut me down without a second thought. Sure, she likes me well enough, but no one is above the Queen. Not even her daughter."

The scent of sandalwood floated to me as his steady gaze bore into the grove of trees across from us.

"And you are above her, Cy. Anyone with eyes can see that." He said with a wistful smile.

My stomach clenched. The tattoo on my wrist pulsed. I rubbed my fingers over the raised crown there. Everything in me wanted to get up and run away. I didn't want to be above my mother. I didn't want to have wings. I didn't want to be Queen. I didn't want any of it.

Then a realization hit me.

It wasn't Anthony I was mad at. I would have had to come back to Knockaine. I had wings, and Kittie knew. It would have been all over. I knew that. I think it was all of the sudden responsibility that had been mounting up, and I'd taken it out on him.

Was I upset he'd betrayed me all of those years ago by turning me in when I'd been young and dumb and had broken into the Croí? Yes, but that had been a long time ago. If I was honest with myself, I would have done the same thing now too. You had to stop that nonsense before it started. But young me had seen it as Anthony's wanting to advance. He'd never wanted anything in life but to be Messenger to the Crown. Even his parents had pushed him unmercifully towards the role. So when he'd chosen the crown, and my mother, over me, it had hurt.

He turned to me. I mimicked his body language without realizing it until I noticed I was staring into his deep teal eyes. The sun filtered through the trees to play in the honey blonde of his hair. From the way it hit the strands, it looked like spun gold. Soft gold that you could sink your hands into. That he was too attractive, by far, wasn't what held my attention, though. It was his pencil-straight eyebrows. Sadness and regret etched deep in the lines between them. I wanted to run my finger over them to make him forget all of it. If only it was that easy.

"Look, I'm sorry." He grabbed my hands. The heat of his fingers reached up to melt my heart. "Well, and truly. I only wanted what was best for you."

Anthony must have mistaken my silence for resistance because he continued on. "I want to help you. I want your life to be incredible. I want to *make* it incredible. You've gotten the dirty end of the up-creek paddle for as long as I can remember. I want that to stop. And ok, maybe you aren't completely innocent. Maybe you've caused more than your share of drama. Maybe you've not just walked but splashed your way through more than one puddle of crazy."

I twisted my lips to keep from smiling. That wasn't exactly the most flattering portrait. Should I smack Anthony or laugh? I settled for raising my eyebrow.

He relaxed his shoulders and laughed. I found myself smiling back at him.

His thumb smoothed across my palm. "My point is ... you've just wanted to live your life, be the person you are inside. But being a princess means you're not just your own person. You're an idea, a personification of the power, and strength of the crown."

I winced, all too aware of the gold crown on my wrist. Anthony paused to collect his thoughts. I don't know if he expected me to say anything, but I couldn't speak past the lump that had suddenly formed in my throat. His words pierced my heart like an arrow. He'd pretty much summed up my life in a nutshell. Summed it up like no one else could have because he'd been there for all of it, every last gut-punching moment. I didn't want the weight of being a princess. I just wanted to be me. Forget the responsibilities.

A cool breeze lifted my hair. I took a couple stabilizing breaths and let myself sink into the hum of activity around us. The distraction was what I needed. The weight left rawness as it lifted. One that Anthony filled with a hand on my shoulder.

Awareness blossomed there. I looked into Anthony's eyes. They shone like topaz as they searched mine with an intensity that caught my breath.

"I know you don't want to be here. If I could do anything to undo that, I would. I...just want you to be happy." He finished the sentence in a way that made me wonder if he hadn't been going to say something else.

Before I could give it much more thought, Avalynn walked up. It was so sudden I didn't have a chance to change my expression or body language. I'm sure she could tell that she'd walked up in the middle of something.

She stood there for a second, indecision apparent in the line of her legs. Those balance-beam legs held a quiet strength I'd always envied. Coming to a decision, she put her hands on her hips. She'd decided to stay. That wasn't surprising. When we were younger, she'd stuck around for shouting matches between Anthony and me.

"Hey, guys," she said.

I had to look up to see all of her. The sunlight chose that moment to blink through the trees and blind me.

I held up my hand to shield my eyes. "Hey, Avalynn."

Anthony looked up and nodded an acknowledgment at her.

She tried to swallow a giggle and failed miserably. "I don't mean to break up the honeymoon."

"Well, we *were* just about to make out." I said, dryly.

But a smile crept into the corners of my mouth. Anthony grew still beside me. As I remembered the heat of his touch, suddenly, it didn't seem so funny.

I pushed the feeling away. The pesky thing didn't go as far as I'd like.

Ignoring it, I said, "What's up?"

A few wayward strands of hair caught the breeze and blew into her face.

She pushed them behind her button ear. "Your mom wanted me to come to find you. She has a place for you to stay."

Oh, great. Just what I needed, a reminder that I was here for the long haul.

"What? She doesn't want me to stay in the old house?" I couldn't help but ask.

Don't get me wrong, I didn't want to stay in the old house. It held too many memories. But I had to ask why she had suddenly gifted me with a new place. If it was good enough five years ago, why the sudden move?

"She thought since you had wings now, you might want something...more fitting." She said, searching for the words.

Wings. It all came down to that. Bitterness burned my throat. It shouldn't have surprised me that since I had wings, my mom was treating me differently. After all, this was what she always wanted. And Ainé- Goddess of Fertility, Queen of Fear and Illusion, got what she wanted.

I pushed myself off the ground. "Well, let's go see what she has, shall we?"

Anthony got up after me. I knew we weren't going together, but we would be seeing each other later. I knew that as sure as I knew, the sun was going to rise tomorrow.

"Cy," he said.

I stopped. Anticipation curled my toes. Stop that, Cy. He wasn't mine to have. No matter how much I berated myself, I couldn't ignore how much I liked my name on his lips.

I turned to look at him. His eyes bore into me. He opened his mouth. Then there was a shrill scream. It took me a heartbeat to realize it hadn't come from him but behind me. I turned to look, but the wind was knocked out of me as a body hit mine with enough force to knock me over. Anthony.

CHAPTER 6

*P*rotective hands came around me to cradle my head as we rolled. As the momentum stopped spinning us, an earth-shaking crash came from where our feet had just been.

Dazed, I opened my eyes. Anthony held my head in the palm of his hands like I was fine china.

His shaky thumb came up to caress my cheek. "Are...are you alright?"

I nodded and bit my lip to concentrate on steadying my racing heart. Was that coming from Anthony's touch? Or from adrenaline?

Stomping feet rushed over. Still putting the world back together, it didn't dawn on me that a crowd had gathered until people started speaking at once.

"Gods alive, Cy. I thought you were dead," said Avalynn, her voice shrill.

"Have you ever seen something so horrifying?"

"Such a shock."

"How could someone be so careless?"

I pushed against the protective cage of Anthony's arms.

His body held a slight tremor before he forced himself to let me go. It was an understandable reaction. I was shaken up myself. When I got a look at what had caused the smash, that feeling didn't go away either.

One of the larger-than-life ornaments lay shattered in a million glittering pieces in the exact spot I had been standing. If someone hadn't screamed and Anthony hadn't grabbed me, I would have been dead.

I tried to process it all as I turned back to Anthony with wide eyes. "How...?"

He angled his head at Avalynn. "She screamed and pointed. I didn't have to look to know you were in danger."

Ignoring the warmth at his concern for me. I turned back to Avalynn. She was visibly shaken. Poor girl, it was probably more excitement than she had ever seen. If it wasn't for her quick eye, I would be flatter than a pancake on Sunday morning. I owed her my life. Dusting myself off, I made my way to her side. Her body tremored as I took her in my arms.

"Thank you." I whispered into her quaking hair.

Her hands came up around me to return my hug with a quiet ferocity. She was always looking out for me. Warmth flooded me. I vowed to myself then, and there I would do the same for her. Always.

CHAPTER 7

*T*he door to my room creaked on its hinges as I pushed it open. I wasn't happy about going back to the old place. All of the memories had come rushing back the second I'd stepped over the threshold: the memories of my father's laughter, the memories of Celeste running after me as a child. Then, of course, my mind always brought with those good thoughts the crushing course of events after the pixie raid. Their deaths, Mother being bedridden, my being sent away to Fae Academy, and my returning only to realize Mother had moved out and it was just me alone in the old house. Just me and the ghosts of my past. I shifted my shoulders as if that would remove the weight that I suddenly felt.

I guess it made sense that I had to get my old things. I couldn't exactly go back to my apartment in New York. A pang of homesickness hit me. There was nothing like having a place that was all your own. My apartment made me think of being there with Sven. And there was the feeling again—him, next to me.

It felt like a knife twisted in my gut. I wanted to love the feeling of Sven being close. But I couldn't. We were never going to "go back" to how things had been between us. Things had changed too much since then. His anguish bubbled inside me.

Avalynn bustled in behind me with a box under each arm. I pushed the thought of him away quickly. The feeling went with it. For some inexplicable reason, I felt like I'd been caught naked in the bushes. Like it was somehow wrong. I supposed my connection to a vampire was treasonous in faerie eyes. I swallowed hard. Danu's blessing, there was only so much I could take of that happening out of the blue.

Reaching over, I plucked one of the boxes out of her arms. I appreciated her offer to help me pack up. The sooner I could get out of this place, the better.

Avalynn swung her head from side to side as she surveyed the room. It was a mess. I cringed.

It could have passed for a large apartment, so I was relieved when she said, "It's not as big as I remember, so there won't be much to pack. That's good, at least."

Memories flooded over me again. This time good ones: changing our nail polish in front of the fireplace as we laughed about boys. Hopscotching over toadstools in the thicket behind the house. She was always there, by my side.

"We had some good times, didn't we?" I asked as I took one of the boxes from under her arm.

"We sure did," said a fluffy bunny in the corner.

I looked at her. We both shared a laugh. She was forever throwing her voice when we were growing up. It had gotten us into countless bouts of trouble. It had been a riot. She said as she moved to my dresser and started tossing things into one of the boxes.

"Do you remember when…"

And that was how the next couple of hours passed. Sharing stories and laughing about old times. We hadn't become friends until high school, but she had always been a constant friend. I couldn't say we were best friends because that would have been a lie. But she had always been there. I could always count on her. It had been a world of craziness, some brought on by the crown, some brought on by Mother, and some- I'm ashamed to say- brought on by myself.

I had kind of been a wild child. Looking back, I could tell some of the wildness had been me and some trying to get my mom's attention. She'd all but stopped trying to groom me for the crown when I'd hit my teenage years. And when your mother gave up on you at that age, that took quite a hit on your self-esteem. I'd moved past most of those old insecurities, but I knew I hadn't worked through all of them if I was honest with myself.

Then, as if my thoughts manifested her, Mother walked through the door. I resisted the urge to make a snarky comment asking where her loyal dog Dian was. I was better than that. It took more force than I cared to admit to bite my tongue on that one.

She looked around the all but empty room and said, "Leave the furniture. You'll have more in your new quarters."

Not, hi. Not how are you? No, just come right in and start ordering me around. My teeth ground against each other as I unseeingly stuffed old toys into the nearest box.

Mother turned to Avalynn. I breathed a sigh of relief that I wasn't under the scrutiny of her gaze until I heard what she had to say, "Avalynn, you should be wrapping up soon. Don't you have an Anointed Consult to go to?"

I knew I was asking for trouble, but I had to ask, "Anointed?"

Avalynn flushed at the innocent one-word question, but it soon became apparent as to why when Mother said, "Yes, it's short for Heir Anointed. I invoked the Heir Anointed when you left and didn't come back." At my blank look, she laughed and said, "You didn't honestly think I was just going to go without an heir, did you?"

The color drained out of my face. I guess I hadn't given the matter much thought when I'd left. I had just wanted out. Leaving had been the only thought on my mind. But all actions have consequences. Absently, I rubbed the gold tattoo on my wrist. Sure enough, the bumps of the crown still stood out in a stark contrast to the smoothness of my skin. What did this mean about the tattoo? She couldn't overstep the will of Danu, could she? Granted, she didn't know about the tattoo. Who knows what she would do when she found out. And I rather liked being alive.

When I stayed silent, she added softly. "It's quite common, you know."

I didn't know if that was supposed to be some bad excuse for an apology or what, so instead I asked, "Does that mean Avalynn is heir to the throne then?"

Feeling distinctly uncomfortable, I laced my hand around my wrist to cover up the crown. I wasn't worried that someone would know what it meant. Covering it up just made me feel better.

Avalynn rushed to stand up, "No, it's a group of us. Four, to be exact. Heir Apparent is only selected after the Golden Age of the program has come upon us."

I didn't know or care what the Golden Age of the program was. It seemed so wrong that I would be passed up without even a thought. Would Mother take away everything from me? I refused to let her know she'd bothered me though.

When it became obvious I was expected to say something, I just nodded and turned back to packing.

"I'm happy for you," I said as I snatched a wooden train that chugged and dipped in the air.

It wasn't exactly a lie. I would have been happy for her if

it would have been under different circumstances. Specifically, one where I wasn't being treated as if I didn't matter. Yet again.

Shoving the train into the box I'd wedged under my arm, I moved to collect the cloth butterflies fluttering about the room.

I'd just scooped one off the radiator when Mother said, "Avalynn, take Cy with you. Now that she is back, she should take her place among the Anointeds."

My mind blanked at the news and the terry cloth skimmed over my palm as the butterfly flitted out of it. Avalynn beat me to my question before I even had it formed on my lips.

"She is...to compete for her birthright, your Royal Highness?" she asked. When Mother puffed at her audacity, she added with a low curtsey, "I mean no disrespect to your Majesty. I just want to make sure I know what to tell the Dame."

Mother settled her shoulders at the groveling. "Of course she is. She can't just come back here and expect everything to be as it was. She has to earn her place."

"Yes, your Majesty." Avalynn's voice was muffled from her bowed head.

I didn't bother to even look at them as I stooped down to shovel all manner of childhood toys into the box that was becoming quickly filled. The audacity of Mother choked out all thoughts but one: I had to get out of here. This is why I 'd left in the first place. I was forever being danced around like a puppet on a string. But no more. I'd play her games, but only while I figured out how to get out of here.

"Cy?" Mother's voice came out hushed. Like it had taken an immense amount of courage to say my name.

Her words pulled at me, causing my hand to still as I reached for my ragged bear with the worn velvet heart. His name was T-Bear. He didn't have any magic. He was just a plain, old, brown bear. Ignoring the tugging at my heart, I grabbed him and pulled him to me. I'd loved him fiercely. As I thought back to those simpler days, my fingers drifted through his matted fur: what I wouldn't give for my problems to disappear as effortlessly as they had when I was a kid. Exhaling a long breath, I forced myself to look at her.

"I need to speak with you. Come with me." Mother said, her voice carrying this time. Despite the commanding tone, her voice broke.

I drew back. That was odd. Maybe, she was going to explain herself. Maybe, she was going to apologize. The corner of my mouth pulled up. Sure, she was. And maybe I was going to wake up a cow. Whatever it was, she glided out of the room before I had time to ask. Any other day I'd rather have Braiden set me on fire than be alone with her. But everything in me was dying to know what she was going to say.

Dropping the box, I noticed Avalynn out of the corner of my eye. She had gone back to packing.

Following Mother, I strode into the Solar. Mother sat at the grand piano; her fingers played idly over the black keys. The morning sun kissed the smooth black surface with colors of all kinds as it filtered through the stained-glass window above. Unable to stop myself, my gaze was pulled to the window.

It was beautiful, picturesque, majestic. It was a mural of my father holding my sister Celeste high. Her beautiful ruby stained-glass wings were almost as beautiful as they had been when she was alive. They spanned high and proud, fluttering with abandon as my father bestowed a smile on her that showed her just how much she was loved. It wasn't the white of his smile that drew me, though. Or the cheeky grin of the 18-year-old, who was the equivalent of a 6-year-old as she tossed her head high. Knowing the world was her oyster and she had the love of all, wasn't cockiness. It was as it should be. There was no better girl in the world than Celeste. She was the perfect sister. The perfect daughter.

But none of that held my attention. No, my attention was held by the pale purple hair of my father's. Hair that was just like my own. Sure, I knew our hair was similar, but I'd forgotten how exacting the shade was, like the pale of the moon on a lotus flower. The piano's melody hit a dark note, bringing me back. The music was beautiful. Pulled from the piano like a torn lover, the haunted music drifted up only to get caught in the three-story cathedral ceilings above.

Considering that the sun shone bright outside, it was too dark in this room by far. But this place had always felt dark like a shadow hung over it ever since the death of my father and Celeste.

"He was in this room when they came, you know." She stared unseeing at the distressed wood of the wall opposite her.

My stomach curled at her words. I didn't have to ask to know she was talking about my father.

"We loved each other," she said, her words sitting under the notes being caressed from the keys.

That took me aback. Maybe it sounded cold to say I couldn't think of Mother loving someone, but I couldn't. She had never shown anyone more than passing affection. Since he died when I was three, I didn't remember much of my father, just snippets of his face here and a laugh there, but nothing to hold when I felt alone. Sometimes, I thought it was better that I didn't remember much, didn't have anything to fill me with longing. I had always imagined him as being someone easy to love. It was easier that way. Easier to think someone had cared. Sometime. Even if it was in the past.

Mother nodded to the windowed cathedral above.

"They came through there. Your father was dead before any of us could process what was happening. I suppose it was our fault for being so...lax in our guards. I rectified that when your father died." She stopped to stare at me for a few heartbeats.

Her gaze bore into me, accusing. The silence tormented me. Then she started playing again. But I couldn't let go of the weight that sat on my chest. Taking shallow breaths, I went to sit on the sofas that lined the deceptively bright walls. I sat on my hands. Pinching my thighs, I focused on the pain to redirect my thoughts and calm my body. All the while, Mother played. Her glass hair shielded her face as she bowed over the keys. She coaxed notes from the keys for so long I began to wonder if I should leave. Would she say anything else? Or did she just bring me here to torment me?

After what seemed like an entire lunar cycle, she finally spoke. "He saved you." Her throat worked as her graceful fingers flew faster over the keys, the notes crashing into discordant tones. It was like her fingers were fighting to keep up with the thoughts I could almost see flying through her mind. "For the longest time, it felt like he had died in your place. And I hated you for it."

She stopped playing. The sudden stop to the cacophonous noise was almost as jarring as the melody had been. Glossy strands diffused the light as they moved out of her vision. He lifted her face, seeking mine.

My heartbeat quick in my chest for reasons I couldn't explain. I didn't know why it beat like that. It wasn't like I didn't understand Mother hated me. She'd spent most of my life trying to show that to me without saying as much. She had only said it out loud this time. That wasn't a revelation. So why did it hurt so much?

Quiet filled the space like an expanding balloon as she stared at me.

Then she said the last thing I expected her to say.

"I was wrong." She said.

Sweat broke out on my forehead. I could feel my hands grow slick under my thighs. Wiping them across my thighs, I swallowed a hysterical laugh that bubbled inside me. Wrong? She was wrong? About what exactly? Ruining my life? Practically giving me no choice but to leave? Unbelievable.

A better person would have accepted her apology. A better person would have gone over there and hugged her like my traitorous arms ached to do. They would have apologized the hurts I'd no doubt inflicted on her over the years in a stupid effort to hurt her as she'd hurt me. But no matter how much I wanted to, no matter how much every ounce of my soul screamed to make those amends- to accept her words, I couldn't. My wounds ran far deeper than what a simple, half-apology could heal.

"Thank you for telling me," I managed to choke out past the thickness in my chest.

The truth was it hurt even to say that. I didn't want the gratitude at Mother's words to sing through my body like they were. I didn't want to feel anything but anger. Because tomorrow she would go right back to treating me like the nothing I was. How many times was I going to let her tear me apart?

Her next words lanced me. "I want you to be a Princess, take up the duties of your rightful place."

Ice froze my veins. No, there was no way. Be forced to sit next to her and pretend like our sordid history of pain and torment hadn't happened? I couldn't do it. But would she make me? The thought scared me more than a room full of vampires ever would.

Instead of answering her, I said, "I have to get back. Avalynn will no doubt be wondering where I went off to."

Resisting the urge to drink in her face and savor the

moment we might have been something more, I walked to the door. I wasn't making a mistake. I wasn't. With that thought, fear chased me out of the room. What if I was making a mistake, and I'd just given up the only chance I'd ever get to have a real mother?

CHAPTER 8

"That's right, Stacia. Now, turn. Beautiful." said the graceful woman, her head poised like that of a swan as she twirled her finger over a dark brunette who was treating the stack of books on her head with all the seriousness of a hand grenade.

As if on marionette strings, she twirled in time to the flick of her teacher's wrist.

They were only two of five people in the room, but for the amount of attention everyone gave us- which was a grand total of not a flicker- you would have thought meant no one noticed us.

However, when Stacia's striking features landed on us, I knew that wasn't the case. She zeroed in on me, her expression hardening. She wasn't the only one who noticed because the faerie I assumed was the Dame said without looking at us, "You're late, Avalynn and Cy."

Well, weren't we all in the know? It would have been super nice if I had been. This was a surprise I could have done without. Avalynn and I walked the rest of the way into the large room. The select group sat lined up on one side of a small maple dance floor. From the lack of elbows poking out from the sides of their high backed seats, they were clearly sitting at attention.

With a touch from the Dame to the small of Stacia's back, she curtseyed and went to take her seat in one of the empty chairs. The dame pointed at me with all of the finality of being called on in school for a test I wasn't ready to take and then pointed to her side. I clenched my jaw. I was not someone to be ordered around. Maybe this group was ok with that, but that wasn't going to fly with me. I turned in my tracks, ready to tell her just where she could put that pointer. Then my wings caught on the chair. It was a subtle but clear reminder: I only had to play their game for as long as I had wings, and then I was so out of here. Best not to bring undue attention to myself by bucking the system.

Gritting my teeth, I made my way to her side. I faced the group.

"Everyone, this is Princess Cy." You could hear shifting in chairs at the announcement, which for this group might as well have been cries of outrage. The Dame raised her voice and said, "Since she is back, we will be bringing her into the Heir Anointed. Because she gave up being heir to the throne upon leaving," I raised my eyebrows. That was sure news to me. She continued on. "She will have the same chance at the throne as each and every one of you."

"Now, everyone I'd like you to stand up and introduce yourselves to Princess Cy." she said indicating the mulberry-purple haired man in the first chair.

He couldn't have been more than a year or two younger than me, if that. His purple eyes didn't flicker as he rose stately, with controlled power radiating from his every pore.

"I am Brigad Tomblebeck, Earl of Starling." He talked down his sharp nose at me with an intensity that should have unnerved me, but oddly, I liked.

The woman with more legs than anything else stood up next to him. Hair the color of rust had pooled in the seat behind her and unfurled into a shining curtain as she stood up. She pushed it out of the way with her silkened, ebony hands. Hands that looked like they didn't know the meaning of work, let alone having actually done any of it. "Flora Blesch, Marchioness of Blingenmane. We welcome you to the Heir Anointed, Princess Cy."

When she sat down, it was Stacia's turn. Even though she was positively squat compared to the regalness of Flora, nobody would dare accuse her of being less than. There was a sharpness to her eyes that rivaled the haughtiness of the tilt of her head. "Stacia Ringwol, Duchess of Alluvion."

She had sat back down before the words were out of her mouth. Clearly, she was not happy to see me. Not that I blamed her. This was their future, and my appearance put a mammoth wrench in it.

Avalynn stood up. Somehow, her dress was still immaculately pressed even though we'd been packing all morning. Talk about impressive. Looking down at the pieces of cardboard that clung to my tank top, confirmed that was a level of regalness I'd never be able to obtain. I brushed at the pieces, smiling overly bright at Avalynn.

"Avalynn Dross. Selected. We are pleased to have you join us, Princess Cy," she said as she gave me a little smile.

It wasn't an overly bright smile, just small enough to be considered appropriate, but it made me feel better. Grateful for her acceptance, I smiled back. I appreciated the gesture. This had to be hard for her, especially since she was the only one here without a title. The only one here without prospects if this didn't work out for them. It made me happy that I was leaving and wouldn't be taking this chance from her.

The Dame clapped her gloved hands. "Now, that we have all been introduced. Let's get back to lessons."

I bit my lips to keep a groan from spilling out. Lessons? What was I? Back in Fae Academy? As the next hour bled into two and then three, it became quite apparent this was no regular school. I had my legs, hands, and back snapped with that pointing stick so many times I was a fraction of a second away from ripping it out of the Dame's hand and breaking it over my knee. I slouched. I didn't cross my legs properly. I didn't walk in a straight line. When all of the books had fallen off my head to spill out onto the floor and skid over to stop at Stacia's arrogant foot, I was done.

Turns out the Dame was too. She gave a disgusted snort and a wave of her hand. "I've had my fill. We are finished for the day, Anointeds."

The abrupt send off had my mouth opening and closing like a fist. Humiliation churned in my gut. I would not feel bad about this. They had years to practice; I'd had one day. These were not the teachings Mother, or anyone for that matter, had given me. That might have hurt more than anything. It proved she never wanted me to take her place. The irony of the tattoo on my wrist didn't escape me.

Avalynn was busy retrieving the books that had fallen off my head. Stacia plucked the one by her foot off the ground before Avalynn got to it. Avalynn smiled up at her. It seemed genuine. They both came over to me and handed me the books. That surprised me. I'd never have imagined them friends. I suppose Avalynn had to make friends at some point, though. Considering how many years they spent together, it made sense.

"Those wings must make walking with any sort of decorum painfully difficult. It's understandable that you are dreadful at it." Stacia said by way of greeting, still holding the book out.

I took the book, wanting very much to smash it into that passive aggressive face. Walking away seemed the better option, so I did just that. The two followed me. Lucky me.

"You'll get it. Don't worry." Avalynn said, taking the book out of my hand and sliding it and the others in her hand into a bookshelf before we stepped into the hall. We were in a wing of the Bardais.

Stacia gave a delicate snort that clearly said she doubted it. Then she said to Avalynn. "I'm famished. Let's stop at the Panem Coquere and grab some tarts."

"Oh, I'd love to, but I'm helping Cy move in. Thanks, though." Avalynn said, without batting an eye.

"You're what?" Stacia asked, having a hard time getting the words out of her mouth. "But we always go to the Panem Coquere after a Consult."

It was the first time she'd been anything but an arrogant bitch. I took a second to revel in it. Was it bad of me? Maybe, but I loathed self-entitled people like her.

"Right, but Cy just got back. I have to help her get settled in the Royal Apartments. She's never been there, so it's a lot of extra work." Avalynn said, with exaggerated patience. She brightened. "Grab an extra tart from Tessa for me though, will you?"

I didn't point out that I could move well enough on my own and I could actually use some time alone. Avalynn clearly would rather be with me. And why shouldn't she? We were real friends, with history. Not friends of convenience.

Stacia had stopped walking with us. Her sudden departure didn't sit well with me. I looked back in time to see a look of pure, raw hatred on her face. And she was staring right at me.

CHAPTER 9

The stairs below our feet lit up and faded with each step as we made our way towards the giant oak. I was more than a little relieved when the door at the end of the fifth-floor corridor had led to this golden-railed stairway and bridge. I didn't like to think of myself as anti-social, but I didn't want to deal with the constant ebb and flow of people. I just wanted space to process the quill bomb that had become my life.

We each carried a box, Avalynn and I. I leaned over to take a peek at the ground so far below. This wasn't exactly the most ideal place to try to move everything into. I sighed and shifted the load in my arms. Whoever thought being a princess meant you didn't have to move your own crap had it all wrong.

My mood lightened considerably when we stopped at a single solitary door. At least I wasn't going to have to deal with neighbors. Avalynn balanced her box on her hip as she fit an ornate, gold key into an equally shiny door lock.

She pushed open the door, and I walked in behind her. At first, her lithe frame blocked my view, but I couldn't help but stare when she moved to the side. It was breathtaking. Like the pecan-colored tree outside, glossy wood created a seamless line of beauty throughout the room. Pillars carved like those very same trees, stood in a majestic circle to define the living room. They shouldn't have gone with the very modern double doors that opened to the bedroom, but strangely they were the perfect compliment. Plush couches that looked soft enough to totally encompass you when you sat in them, faced one another. A spray of lavender sat on the low, unassuming glass table that separated them. A red box with a white ribbon sat on the table. A welcome gift? That was unexpected, to say the least.

A look to the left and the right helped me quickly identify the bathroom and kitchen. It didn't have a lot of rooms, but it didn't need them. The place was huge. I'm sure part of that could have been attributed to the cathedral ceiling. I was really going to have to get used to the tall ceilings around here again. I didn't have to pay to heat the place. Thank the stars for that.

Voices came from the bedroom. I cocked my head. Unless Avalynn had suddenly developed a split-personality, it looked like we weren't alone. Cautiously, I walked through the bedroom's double doors. The voice came from a good-looking male faerie I was starting to think didn't have anything better to do than occupy my space.

"Anthony? What are you doing here?" I asked him.

He gestured to all the boxes around him and raised an eyebrow. "Baking a cake, clearly."

"Very funny," I said.

My lips twitched against my will as I walked the rest of the way into the room to count the boxes, tapping each one as I passed them. One, two, three, four, five, six, seven, eight...sure enough, nine. They were all there. The last box I'd touched was in his hands. I looked up.

My eyes drank him in. Tentative excitement skipped along my skin. I ignored the guilt and the thoughts of Sven that rose with it. Then I felt him there with me again. A heartbeat later, I could feel his jealousy vibrate.

My brows knitted together. Why did I feel bad? Our breaking up had been his fault. Dagda be damned, my current predicament was his fault, wings and all. His selfishness had changed me as in forever. Despite knowing how against it I was, he'd bitten me, and what did I do? I forgave him. And what did that get me? Marked, that's what. I'd have to do a lot of life reevaluating if I stayed with someone who didn't treat me like I knew what was best for me. Despite my chastising, my stomach still flipped endless somersaults. How long would it hurt when I thought about Sven? No matter how long it took, I had to do it. I pushed the thought of him away. Clarity returned.

And with it took a flash of recognition to see that Anthony had witnessed my internal tug-of-war and it didn't sit well with him. I dropped my gaze. This wasn't his battle, no reason to burden him with the scars.

"Why are you helping?" I asked Anthony.

Well, I asked the V of his hips. They trailed hypnotically into his pristine loin cloth. My concentration broke when he moved away, and I shook my head to clear the thought. The last thing I needed to do right now was get wrapped up in a rebound.

"Because you two looked like you were making an eternity out of carrying them up one at a time." He said as he set the last box down on the dresser.

Even the dresser was over-the-top, gold handles blinked from the gleaming finish. I tapped my foot on the ground to push down the irritation that rose up. Deluxe surroundings. Presents. All because I had wings now. It was enough to make me sick.

Disgusted, I turned away. Another set of double doors opened to the terrace. I wandered to them. I couldn't stand looking at the luxury around me anymore. It needled me. That frustrated me more than anything. Luxury always made me feel better. I was only faerie, after all. But this was going too far. It smacked of the same thing I'd believed my whole life: I wasn't good enough the way I'd been. But now, unseemingly, I was. It made me want to scream with the unfairness of it. I was still the same hard-headed, smart-ass person I'd always been. The wings didn't make me who I was.

Anthony came up beside me. "Did you see your view?"

Since he knew I had just gotten here, I could have said something sarcastic, but this whole thing made me tired, so I just said, "No."

"Well, come on," he said, walking through the billowy curtains.

Picking my way through the strewn boxes, I made my way to the balcony. The late afternoon sun streamed in. As soon as I stepped out onto the balcony, a soothing wind blew my hair back. Warmth spread over me, and my muscles loosened. Anthony was there already. He looked out over the courtyard so far below. A little fae with long limbs darted through the frame, quickly chased by another flame-haired girl. Laughter drifted up through leaves so green I wanted to touch them to see if they were real.

We stood together in the quietness of the moment. My breathing changed to match the rise and fall of the gently blowing leaves. I sighed, looping my thumbs around my belt loops.

"Yeah, it's pretty spectacular." He said, gripping the railing in his hands and flexing his wings. He dropped them after a second and slanted a smirk at me. "I think you're getting pretty spoiled, *Princess.*"

He was poking fun at me. I looked to the Gods above. Spoiled. Is that what this was? In that carefully orchestrated apartment put together by my mother and her agendas? No. Spoiled by being forced to fight for my birthright? No. But out here with him? Just maybe.

It was then I noticed the leaves canopying us from above. The tender bows waved in greeting.

I giggled and wondered how insane I would look if I waved back. Anthony looked at me and then looked up again. He knew I wasn't laughing at his joke. It was such a relief to be around someone who knew me so well.

I could feel him studying my face.

Finally, he said, "It's good to have you back, Cy."

When someone said that, you always were expected to say it was good to be back. But was it really? I didn't think so. Everything felt like such a lie: my mother's opening up to me, the new digs, how easy everything suddenly was. Hell, the only thing that didn't feel like a lie was Anthony.

I could tell he was waiting for me to say something. Before I could think of what to say, a scream echoed inside the apartment. Avalynn.

Ripping through the gauze curtains, I flew through the bedroom. Before I had a chance to reach her, Anthony popped in next to Avalynn. She was standing over the present on the table, but the ribbon-draped top was in her hands. Her eyes had a hollow look like she couldn't unsee whatever was in the box.

At seeing there was no immediate harm, I stopped running. My heart pounded like a racehorse. Anthony leaned over the box and recoiled, disgust contorted his face.

What was in the box? I was about to find out, determination painted my stride.

Avalynn started babbling when I moved into her line of

sight. "I just wanted to peek. I didn't mean to open it. I didn't mean to. I'm sorry, so sorry, so sorry...sorry...sorry."

Her body started rocking back and forth to the word. She just kept repeating it but getting softer and softer to where it was just a whisper over her lips. The top of the box was still in her hands. A tag was tied to it. It flitted back and forth with her movements.

Anthony pried the lid out of her hands. "It's not your fault. You didn't do anything wrong." He said.

His words were meant to be soothing, but she was past the point of being calmed down. I snatched the tag and flipped the thick cardboard over. There was only one word written on it in block letters. CY.

Dread kicked up my heart again. I didn't want to see what was in the box, but I had to. I knew it was going to be awful. I shouldn't look. But I had to. Whatever it was, I had to see.

I threw the top onto the ground. It crunched under my foot as I strode to the box. Anthony's arm snaked out and caught me right before I made it. Anger shot through me. It felt loads better than the dread and fear I was currently feeling, so I let it stay.

Fury shook me as I said, "Let me go."

"You don't want to see," he said.

His voice was quiet, soothing. The same tone he'd used on Avalynn. It just made me madder. I didn't need saving.

"Why don't you let me be the judge of that," I feinted to the left as I said it and slipped below his arm.

I don't know if he hadn't expected such a quick movement or if he'd just decided to let me go, but he didn't make another move for me as I took the last step to the red ribboned box. His shoulders curled over his chest. His regret was palpable as I leaned over the box.

Inside was a white ball covered in feathers. That's what

my mind told me anyway. As my eyes adjusted to the sight, I saw it was something worse. Far worse.

Big gold eyes sat in the ball, and a slip of a black beak sat just below them. An owl. It was an owl. And then everything clicked. No, not an entire owl. Just the head. Across its majestic brow were two words, written in blood. GO AWAY.

I started shaking at the horror of it, shock rolling through me. Shocked that someone would do this to such a majestic creature. Shocked at its presence in my apartment. Shocked that this twisted message was for me. That's when I noticed more blood was smeared on the inside of the box. I tilted my head and bent closer to read it. The stench of death roiled through me. But that isn't what chilled my bones. It was what the blood said: OR YOUR FRIENDS ARE NEXT.

CHAPTER 10

*A*nthony picked up his pace to keep up with me. Considering he was taller than me, that said a lot.

His words came in short bursts. "Cy, talk to me."

Not breaking pace, I turned around the dark tree that led to the Wiccan's shop. Talk to him? About what? Someone didn't want me here, and they were willing to off my friends to get met to take the hint. I could catch a clue. I didn't have many friends. And I wasn't willing to risk the ones I did have.

Now that I thought about it, how much of an accident had that falling ornament been? What if they had already tried to kill me and decided my friends would be easier targets when that failed?

I dug my heels into the earth and picked up the pace. That wasn't happening. What was the point of fighting it anyway? I didn't even want to be here. I pushed open the same door I'd just passed through a few short hours ago. This time there was no amount of trepidation.

"Iris!" I shouted into the quiet shop.

At the outburst, beads smacked the walls in a hail of

clatter as she charged through a beaded curtain on our left. She stopped when she saw us.

"Gods alive, you silly chit. Are you trying to give me a heart attack?" she asked as she put her hands on her hips.

Without preamble, I said. "I'll do it."

"Do what?" Anthony asked, looking back and forth from the old Wiccan to me.

Heavy, latex gloves went up to her elbows. She pulled them off with a lot of rolling and snapping.

"I knew you would." Making her way to the back of the store where this whole thing had started, to begin with, she talked to herself. "Goblin Bone- ick- goblins, nasty things, but not too much trouble if you stay away from their sticky fingers. Dragon scales- well, no one has seen a dragon for years, have they now. What else, what else? Well, there's that demon's hoof, that'll be the hardest, for sure. What am I forgetting?"

I followed her back.

Anthony was hot on my heels. "What in the name of all that's holy is she babbling about?"

"Ingredients," I said, trying not to dissect what I had signed up for.

But it was hard not to when Iris's words were trickling down my spine. Just how was I going to get all of this stuff? I couldn't exactly go to the corner store.

"Ingredients?" Anthony stopped in his tracks. I looked back in time to see understanding dawn on him. Anger chased close behind. "You're having her make you a potion, aren't you?"

At my non-response, his feet did a staccato over the threadbare rug as he rushed to catch up with me. Iris had disappeared behind the same curtain she had last time, no doubt, to get the book. I wondered if I should mention I had the list still.

"Just what are you getting yourself into, Cy? This...magic is dangerous." He said the last as he looked around the store.

I couldn't help but follow his eyes. All manner of dried things hung from lines strewn on walls: flowers, leaves, squirrels, bats, you name it. I had to admit, it certainly looked like the kind of place that had witchery written all over it. But I didn't see much of a choice.

Iris came back through the curtain. Unsurprisingly, she was carrying the same book the spell was in. I ignored Anthony's warning and gave her my full attention.

She hefted the book on the counter. I was ready for the boom this time. She found the page quicker than before.

"Let's see," she said, skimming her finger down the page. "Ah, yes, that's right- Thieves' Hair, Goblin Bones, Werewolf Blood, Dragon Scale, and Demon's Hoof."

Anthony's head shook in disbelief with every ingredient she ticked off, but with the last, his jaw dropped.

"How in the hell, does one get a Demon's Hoof?" Anthony asked, his eyes wide.

"Well, that is the trickiest one, isn't it?" She said, tapping her chin. "To be honest, I'm not sure how the chit is going to get it."

He leveled his stare at me. Sparks practically flew from his clear, azure eyes.

"Tell me...tell me the Witch isn't talking about you." He said.

I shrugged my shoulders and gave him an extra-wide smile. Maybe the whites would distract him from asking more questions.

"No. Absolutely not. Out of the question." He practically sputtered.

If it wasn't such a disastrous situation, his face would have been comical. As it was, it made my gut knot.

"I have to," I said simply.

He looked like he was about to explode. "Why? Because someone's an asshole?"

Well, that was one way to look at it. There was no use arguing that, though. The best way to get him to see was to go right to the heart of the issue.

"No, because I don't *belong* here, Anthony," I said, anger firing my words. The same outrage left in a rush when I thought about my childhood. I finished quietly, "I never have."

He slammed his fist onto the table. Iris jumped, her ruby crystal pendant jumping against her red apron.

"That's the biggest load of crap I have ever heard. You belong here almost more than anyone. You're the *Princess* for Gods' sakes. And if that wasn't enough, look at your wings. How can you deny you belong here with those glorious things on your back?"

"And how did I get those wings exactly, Anthony?" I said, throwing my hands into the air.

His face reddened. Fury contorted his features. It was cruel, but I continued on.

"Yeah, exactly. Besides, after this potion, these damn wings won't be something I have to worry about anymore." My chin stuck out, daring him to say I couldn't make them go away.

He didn't, though. My words deflated his anger.

A vulnerability clung to him as he said, "You hate being here...that much?"

His vulnerability sliced sadness into my heart. "This isn't *me*, Anthony. The crown, the Court, none of it. I have to leave. It's my only chance at happiness. I have to have the freedom to be me."

He took a few moments to process my words and then let out a defeated, ragged sigh.

"I thought you were here to stay this time. I thought..."

His lips compressed, and he took a second before he continued. When he did, his words were steadier when he said, "But if you are truly that unhappy, I will help you."

His words blew me away. I knew what he thought. I'd have to be an idiot not to. The unspoken words trampled across his features. He thought we would have been together. He thought this was our time. I let that knowledge sift through my head. So many emotions swirled inside me; it was hard to identify them.

How I felt about him didn't matter, though. I couldn't stay here. There were so many reasons why- the rationale didn't matter. The real issue was I'd be damned if I risked one more friend with my selfish behavior.

"That is not an option," I said, turning to him.

"Last I checked, my decisions are my own." He said, leveling me with a stare.

Heat flooded my cheeks. Was I really trying to do the exact thing I had accused others of doing? My gut hardened. Putting myself at risk was one thing, but to put him at risk was something else entirely.

"This is going to be dangerous, Anthony." When his face deadpanned, I added. "You know, as in life or death type of stuff.

"And you would be doing it alone otherwise?" He countered.

I tried to look confident as I said, "Of course. I couldn't ask anyone to risk their lives for me."

He just shook his head with a wry smile on his face. "If you don't think that makes me want to do it a million times more, I don't know what to say."

That he cared about me so much pricked my eyes.

"Besides," he said his gaze locked mine with its intensity, "I failed you before. I won't make that mistake twice."

Iris took that unfortunate time to pipe up. "You do

remember this might not work, right? That you might simply just disappear?"

"This could make you disappear?" Anthony asked, his voice rising as high as his eyebrows.

If his pitch had left any doubt, his face clearly said it: I was insane.

I didn't pay him any mind, though. He'd thought I was insane for a long time. That was nothing new. What I was paying attention to, though, was Iris. She had been standing quietly while we had spoken. I didn't trust the quietness. Or her body language. Her arms were crossed, tight across her chest. She was thinking of something.

No, not thinking, scheming. I could see the wheels turning behind the steel of Iris' eyes. It was a look that would send most people running- a look you shouldn't trust. It made me wonder if she really thought this spell would work at all. If this wasn't just a ruse to get rid of me once and for all. After all, if I was gone for good, there was a chance her son would come back.

A shiver ran through me.

I didn't want to think of that because there was no other way to get out of here. And I had to leave. I couldn't be in this place, nothing about who I was belonged here. And if that wasn't bad enough, to be a threat to my friends on top of that? Well, that just wasn't happening.

I nodded. "I remember."

Anthony shifted from foot to foot. He looked ready to burst. "I don't like this. It feels too much like black magic."

Iris rolled her eyes. "Since when does the color of magic matter? Do you really think you can mess with the Natural Order and not have anything be affected? Such ignorance will be the death of you, Messenger."

I'd never thought about it like that before. That made me like what we were about to do even less.

CHAPTER 11

"Just snip it," Anthony whispered into my ear.

At least I'm sure he thought he was whispering. I bit the inside of my cheek to keep from swearing. Why did he have to be one of those thinks-they're-whispering-but-they're-so-not type of people? His voice echoed around the small cell. Just perfect.

The big guy's chest paused in his bright orange jumpsuit before it continued its labored up and down movements. He really was the fattest man I had ever laid eyes on. More importantly, though, he was still asleep. Thank the Gods.

"Shut up." I hissed back.

I focused back on clipping some of the chin hair from the tattooed man on the bed. I prayed for quietness as I snipped the scissors. The slice of the scissors was deafening in the small cell. I breathed a sigh of relief as the sizable clump of hair fell into the bag I held under his chin.

I turned to Anthony and mouthed, "Let's go."

But he wasn't paying attention to me, his eyes were locked on the behemoth on the bed. Crap. I turned back in what felt like slow motion, already knowing what I'd find.

His face was the same as when I'd left it. If you didn't count the bloodshot eyes that were open and narrowed on me.

I let out a screech as I leaped away from the bed. His hand swung out to grab me. Air from the weight of the swing breezed past my arm.

Anthony closed his wings before the beast of a man was able to heft his huge mass out of bed. I slid underneath them just as the winds started to move. And we were gone.

We popped back into my apartment back in Knockaine. Naked. Again. How splendid. This really needed to stop.

"Do. You. Have. It?" Anthony's voice came in spurts like he'd just come back from a long run.

Glad for the distraction, I uncrumpled the bag from my death grip and held it up triumphantly. "Sure do. Thieves' Hair."

He stretched wide and exhaled, finally regaining his breath.

"How do we know for sure he was a thief?" He asked, apparently determined to pee on my parade.

"I used my work's system and pulled his profile from the database." I tried not to say it too smugly.

There were perks of being a bounty hunter.

Ever the pee-er, he had to say, "That's so reliable too. Wasn't he supposed to have hair?"

That had been an argument we'd had when we'd first popped into the thieves' jail cell. The previously well-maned man in the picture had apparently decided to shave his head. We'd been lucky he still had the beard.

"You can change your hairstyle but not the fact that you've committed over a dozen counts of grand theft," I grumbled.

Anthony was reaching into the Spaces Between and pulling out another loincloth as he said, "Yeah...let's just be careful."

Him getting dressed made me realize I was also naked. Possibilities flicked through my mind. I pushed them away and picked my way through the boxes to the one labeled CLOTHES. I bent down to tear it open.

"That's the plan," I muttered into the pile of clothes tossed in the box.

What did one wear when you had wings anyway? Up until this point, I'd been having luck with other people giving me clothes that accommodated them. I didn't have anything stitched to fit around them. That meant getting creative. After a few seconds of searching, I found a jersey cotton halter. Bingo.

"Gods, Cy. Have some mercy, would you?" said Anthony in a strangled voice.

I looked back to see what he was talking about. He was staring right at my ass. My body tightened as I realized he could close the few feet between us. What would I say? What would I do? His gaze burned into mine. My whole body felt the heat.

What was wrong with me? After a few seconds, I stood up, keeping my back to him. It felt less vulnerable than if I faced him.

My face burned, no doubt it was as red as the cherry top I slipped over my head. I tied the back as quickly as possible before sliding on the first pair of jeans I saw.

I took the time to move the boxes out of the pathway and line them against the wall. It seemed senseless to unpack since I wasn't staying here long.

When I heard boxes being shoved across the floor on the other side of the room, I looked down. Anthony was wordlessly helping on the other side of the room, mimicking my actions. He had always been so helpful. Well, not always.

"Don't think any of this means I've forgiven you for that

bullshit with you choosing my mother over me," I called to him.

I could see him roll his eyes as he hefted up a box and stacked it on top of a larger one.

"Oh, hey. You're welcome for the help with moving." Then he held out a hand like a stop sign. "No need to thank me. The pleasure is all mine."

I smiled despite myself and shook my head. He was such a dork.

He stopped and turned to me; his eyes tight as they searched mine.

"Look, I was stupid before. I know that. I let my ambition get in the way of what was most important when we were kids. I'm older now and know better." His lips thinned. "Trust me when I say that will never happen again."

I believed what he said. We all had actions from the past we regretted, things that we learned from. Logically, it made sense. Emotionally, it hurt more than being stampeded by a herd of stags.

"It better not happen again, or I'll have Iris turn you into a toad," I said, sticking my tongue out.

"Remind me not to eat or drink anything you give me, would you?" he said, picking up a pillow and bouncing twice as he sat on my bed.

He looked too much like he belonged there among the crisp down comforter and goose feather pillows.

"So…what's next on the list?" he asked, throwing one of the pillows at me.

Feathers puffed out as I caught it. "Goblin bones."

"I don't suppose there's a Goblin Museum we can steal some from?" he asked, hope high in his voice.

I set squishy the pillow on the dresser. "I wish."

A strong musk floated up to sting my nostrils. It didn't take long to realize it came from me. I needed a shower, like yesterday. I made my way to the boxes. Thankfully, they were all labeled. KITCHEN. LINENS. I swung a couple more boxes around to see what they were. Where could we find goblins anyway? The last I'd heard they were in the Orapa mines in Africa. But that had been decades ago. Bingo. BATHROOM. The box looked pretty big if all it held was shampoo and the like.

"Do you think there are still goblins in those diamond mines?" I asked around the weight of a box as I lifted it.

Tor Mór, what was in this? A baby giant?

Anthony lifted it out of my hands. "Yeah, I think Moreanna still has her kingdom there."

It was gratifying to see his face register the shock of the weight of the box. He set it down on top of the dresser just as a knock came at the door.

"Who's that?" I asked him.

He shrugged his shoulders. "Beats me."

Turns out, it was Avalynn.

I breathed a sigh of relief that it wasn't Mother and leaned against the doorjamb, "What's up?"

"Hey, Cy." She said. Right then, Anthony walked into view. She paused for a second and added. "Hey, Anthony."

"Hi, Avalynn." He said, smiling.

From her look back and forth between Anthony and me, you could tell she was wondering about us. It took everything in me not to groan. Really? We were going there already?

She turned to me with an unsure smile and said, "I saw the lights on and thought you might want some company..."

The awkward way she finished the sentence filled in the obvious point that I already had company. Still, it was nice to see someone cared enough to check on me.

"Thanks for thinking of me, Avalynn. That was really sweet of you." I said, and I meant it.

She smiled a sheepish smile in return.

With a nod and a shrug, she said, "Of course." Then with an awkward curtsy-bob, she added. "I really can't stay anyway. I just wanted to see how you were doing."

"Come by anytime, ok?" I said, realizing I really did enjoy seeing her.

She stopped, and her gaze roved over me.

Then a smile spread over her face. "I sure will."

We waved our goodbyes, and her feet lit a blinking path as she made her way down the long, suspended staircase. We watched her leave.

"I like her," I said.

Swinging the heavy oak door shut, my mind immediately turned to goblins and their wide, ugly mouths and too many teeth.

"Maybe we'll find a dead goblin," I said, lying to myself more than Anthony.

He knew better. Hell, I knew better. Goblins were wretched, vile, and wily as the devil.

CHAPTER 12

*P*itch-black blanketed my vision. Revulsion crept into my veins. It reminded me too much of when I had been kidnapped by Thomas. From the occasional curse in front of me, it sounded like Anthony wasn't handling the dark much better.

Rock crunched beneath our feet as we crept through the tunnel. My foot caught a rock, and I fell forward. I caught myself with a hand on the wall of rock to my left. Not that which hand I shot out mattered, either the wall to my right or my left was close enough to catch me. But lucky for me, I just happened to pick the wall with the insects. I felt something crunch under my palm and then goo when I pulled it away.

"Oh, Ewwww. Are you serious?" I whispered to no one as I wiped the grime on my pants.

"What happened?" Anthony whispered back.

I bit back a hysterical giggle and said instead, "What happened? What happened? I'll tell you what happened. We're in the middle of gods-know-where Africa, in Dagda-knows-how-far underground- which I'm pretty sure could fall in and crush us at any moment. And why? Because we're looking for trouble, that's why."

I tried not to focus on the underlying fact that my selfishness had landed us here in the first place. Why had I ever slept with Sven? Because he had been a beautiful possibility. Correction: a beautiful lie. At my thoughts, his presence started to encompass me. Oh no, he didn't. I didn't have time for that nonsense. With a mental door slam, I pushed the thought away. Now was not the time.

Despite the pain of my ex, it's what I needed to do anyway. I hadn't been exaggerating: Goblins were mean, nasty, and just downright evil. To even be here, uninvited was like ordering Chinese torture and driving to the location where they would torture you.

So that's why we'd come up with the idea to sneak in. The problem with "sneaking" was it meant no light. And I was done with that plan.

I focused and snaked some energy into my left arm. A soft light came from my arms, lighting up the narrow space. Jewels, embedded in the rock, sparkled and danced in the sudden light. I held out my hand like a flashlight, lightning coiled, and licked around my bare forearm.

"What are you doing?" Anthony closed the distance between us and grabbed my arm and yanked it down. "I thought we said no light."

At his interference, my concentration broke. The lightning flickered then died. My jaw ticked. I took a breath to tell him exactly what he could do with that part of the plan when his hand shifted. Swallowed by the dark, the touch was heightened, and it felt...different, more intimate. His was more firmly around my wrist. Was he holding me? Or was that my imagination? And his breath. I could hear it in the small space as if it were my own.

I shook myself. Now was not the time. We had to find a goblin bone and get out of here before we were caught.

I focused and lit energy into my other hand. The light grew until it lit up the planes and hollows of Anthony's face. There were so many places on his face that I could have looked at him all day and still had not seen them all. The most disconcerting part was he was studying my face just as intently. It was hard not to do in the soft light. It made everything feel like a dream. The diamonds winking behind him didn't do anything to dispel that feeling.

"Our chances of success will be much higher if we are alive," I said with a raise of my eyebrow, daring him to contradict me.

I don't know if he even heard what I said. His eyes followed every punctuation of my lips as I spoke. If I moved my lips closer, would he finish closing the gap?

I had to snap out of this. Stepping back put tension on Anthony's grip. His gaze sharpened. The movement brought him back to our current predicament.

He dropped my hand like I had leprosy. "Yeah, maybe that wasn't the greatest idea."

I stuffed a frown that tugged at my lips back down. The quickness at which Anthony dropped me felt too much like rejection. My ribs tightened. With effort, I pulled my gaze away from his. Not the time.

Lifting my chin, I breezed past him, giving his bicep a pat. "Great. Then we're keeping it."

If I noticed his arm's firmness beneath my palm, that was nothing I had to think about.

Taking up the lead, I held my forearm in front of me. The light flickered and danced along the narrow passage as I hedged forward. Uneasiness inched its way into my consciousness. I tried to ignore it.

After all, the gleam of diamonds cradling me on all sides

was breathtaking. Bugs the size of my palm skittered along the pitted surface.

It didn't take long to feel like the creepy things were all over me too. I resisted the urge to slap myself. Dagda be damned, every time I looked, there was nothing there, but I still couldn't convince myself they weren't crawling all over me. It was time for a little distraction.

"So what's been going on at Knockaine while I've been gone?" I asked.

As far as distractions were concerned, it was pretty weak, but I was a little preoccupied. I wasn't going to be too hard on myself.

"Nothing really that different from when you were there." He answered.

I could practically hear him shrug. That wasn't helpful at all.

"Nothing?" I prodded.

"Nothing." He confirmed. "We still have the same festivals, the same torturous traditions. The only difference is Avalynn usually is in charge of them instead of your mother."

"Avalynn?" I asked, feigning surprise as I came to a fork in the tunnel.

I wasn't. Avalynn was forever helping out with everything. She'd pitched into every cause thrown her way as long as I'd known her. I used to tease her for it. Now, I secretly envied her.

Which way should I go? Eenie, Meenie, Miney ...that way. I steered us towards the one on the left.

"Yep." He said and then popped his lips.

I had no clue how far down we were at this point. Thank the Gods Anthony could pop in and out wherever he liked. Or else I might worry we'd get lost and die down here. I pushed that thought back down where it belonged. I didn't need to get panicky.

After a second, he blurted out. "Honestly, Avalynn and I haven't seen eye to eye on a lot of things since she started spending more time with the Queen."

"I'd imagine that would change now that you are here," Anthony said as we rounded yet another corner.

My brows knitted together. A small headache bloomed in the spot.

"But I'm leaving," I said, not believing that I had to point that out, given our current predicament.

"We'll see." was all he said.

The light cast in swirling shadows and spotlights over the jutting walls as my hands waved around in explanation. "Come on, Anthony. That's why we're-"

As the words left my lips, my feet slipped on the downward slope of the path. The suddenness took my breath away.

My heart dropped as my body dropped backward. A space of a heartbeat passed as Anthony's arms skimmed around me. His own feet slipped on the rock before he could catch me, though.

I'd almost hit the ground when his legs shot forward. The hardness slid under my thighs. I squeaked in surprise as I dropped onto his lap. I didn't have time to feel anything about having him pressed so intimately against me, though. The tunnel's slope had turned into a full-fledged drop, a drop that the momentum from Anthony's "rescue" now rocketed us down.

When I realized what was happening, I threw my hands to either side of the narrow corridor to stop our quickening descent. Pain lanced up my hands. That was a dumb decision. Instinctively, I pulled my arms back. We shot down the incline.

Diamonds passed by in a blur like shooting stars in the night. The passing air snatched my hair and threw it into

Anthony's face. Despite the hair, he didn't let up his grip from my waist. He held onto me like I was his last lifeline.

The tunnel took a sharp turn to the left. We careened into the corner, buckling as our hips smashed into it. That did nothing to slow our momentum, though. The racing of my heart bled into the jostling from the rocks underneath us. Pain ripped through me as we kept dropping down this slide of death. Screams were pulled from my throat. Anthony's hand came up to cover my mouth.

"Goblins. Must. Be quiet." The words barely came through the pain in his voice, but I caught them before they were ripped away by the rushing wind.

His obvious pain sobered me like nothing else could. With a hard swallow, I resolved to not make another peep. No matter what happened.

Just then, a red glow appeared on the ceiling farther ahead. Dread blossomed in my stomach. I reached up to try to pull Anthony's hand off my mouth. The move tilted us, and my shoulder hit the wall. I screamed a sister scream into his hand as pain lanced up my shoulder. Ok, I wasn't doing that again.

As we slid, the red expanded until it took on the unmistakable shape of a door. That couldn't be good. Out of options, I threw my hands to the side once more. The heat came first. Scorching seconds burned by before my mind registered the stinging. This time I was ready for it. I gritted my teeth against what felt like ice picks slicing through my skin. It paid off, though. Our drop slowed.

Anthony had to have seen the ominous glow too. His hands joined mine on the walls. Our rocketship slowed like a ride at Disney, still moving but enough to show signs of stopping. Would it be enough, though? The rocks broke my skin, and hot blood splattered down my arms as I prayed to the Gods that it would be.

It seemed like they were listening. Just as we reached the doorway, we slowed to a stop. It turned out the door had turned into a ledge, though. Our legs dangled where the sloped edge opened into a cavern. Bright lava swirled and popped at the bottom of the cave. Intricate staircases and doorways peppered the walls around the lava pit.

Sweet Danu, what now?

My arms shook with the effort to keep us in place. My pressed lips together. I couldn't let go. We'd hurtle to our deaths for sure. I didn't have to look down to know the same lava was beneath us. Its heat blasted us, even from our high perch above.

The harsh hiss of our breaths mingled together, ragged as we wrestled with it and our beating hearts. How were we going to hold on? My arms were already so tired.

"Can you let go and climb over me?" Anthony asked through gritted teeth.

I blinked a slow blink. I almost couldn't process his words. "You want me to climb...over you?"

"Yes, climb over me. There's a ledge above us. If you're careful, you can use it to make it back to the entrance to the tunnel." His voice was becoming more urgent, the longer we sat here.

The weight was clearly becoming unbearable for him too. Then it hit me that he wanted me to leave him. I shook my head. Once I started, I couldn't stop. I wouldn't leave him here. That wasn't even an option.

Then an idea hit me, and I wondered why I hadn't thought of it before. "Why don't you wrap your wings around us and poof us out of here?"

"I tried. I can't move the left one. I think it's broken. If you could somehow wrap it around me, we could try that, but..." He let out a shaky breath. "I don't know if I can hold on that long."

My arms shook with a visible force too. This was insane. He was willing to sacrifice his life to save mine. My throat thickened. With effort, I swallowed. I couldn't do it. I couldn't leave him here to die.

"Anthony, I am not leaving here without you," I said, tasting salt as I realized I was crying.

"Cy, for the love of gods, don't argue with me on this." He said, each word coming out sounding like its own sentence. "Now's not the-"

He never got to finish his sentence because we started to slide again like a string had been snapped. Either his arms gave way or mine did. I didn't know which. But what I did know was that we were slipping. I worked my legs for purchase on the wall and flailed my arms, desperate to catch something to stop us.

But it was too late. Within seconds my arms and legs were hitting nothing but air. I tried to move my wings, but they were trapped under Anthony's weight.

Hot air burned my face as we hurtled to our deaths.

CHAPTER 13

I slammed my eyes closed. Not like this. Gods, not like this.

Seconds later, my body hit something. I braced for searing pain, but none came. I didn't have much time to contemplate it before Anthony was jolted off me on impact. My eyes flew open. I was staring at lava, but it was from between the holes of a giant net.

Laughter bubbled inside me and came rushing out in a wave of gratitude. We were alive. We weren't dead. Relief rushed through me in delirious tears. Anthony? Was he safe too?

I sniffed the tears away. Rope bit into my hands as I pushed myself onto my knees. Sure enough, Anthony was less than a foot away, as safe as if in Sunday School.

"Anthony!" I crawled over to him, laughing. "We're alive!"

He moved each muscle slowly before sitting up. The tears started again when I threw my arms around him. I was so grateful he was still alive.

"Yes, you stubborn girl, I see that." He said as he hugged me close.

I sat up and pushed him. He fell over, unsteady on the mesh.

"You better be quiet before I push you over that edge after all," I said, wiping my tears and nose on my shirt's underside.

He looked over at me and smiled. My insides warmed at it. Then his smile froze on his face as his eyes focused over my shoulder. I turned and looked. And promptly wished I hadn't.

Beady eyes peered out of a door that was carved into the cave. Red eyes glowed from the dark. Fear stilled my body. As they came out of shadows, the rest of their bodies became clear: ears like taught bows stuck out of the wrinkles on their gray heads, broad foreheads crinkled as their skeleton-like noses sniffed the air. Goblins.

Then the slightly taller one bared its razor-sharp teeth and said, "Faeries."

Disgust was evident in his voice. It boiled the blood in my veins.

Before I could stop myself, I said, "Look who's talking, Gobbie."

"Cy," Anthony warned under his breath.

I knew I shouldn't be taunting them when we were clearly trespassing on their territory, but I couldn't just sit here and be insulted.

"A cocky little thing, aren't you?" He pulled a staff out from behind him and rolled it in his hands. "Let's see how cocky you are when you're taking a lava bath."

His hand moved to a ring at his feet. Worn cords were tied in an intricate knot to the ring. The same cables made up the net that kept us from being Cy and Anthony Stew. As if the ties had already been cut, my stomach dropped. My eyes flew to his. A feral smile twinkled in his eyes. He knew I saw what he was going to do.

My mind raced: How were we going to get out of here?

Could I carry Anthony with my wings? Considering how new I was at using them, I didn't know how likely that would be. I didn't have much choice, though.

I grabbed Anthony around the waist and beat my wings with all of my might. We lifted off the net. My wings quivered and pushed as we rose slowly but surely. By the gods, I was doing it. I don't know how, but I was. Then there was movement beneath us. A branch of a hand wrapped around my ankle and pulled.

The added weight was all it took to bring us down. We fell back to the net. It bounced under our sudden weight.

But the goblin wasn't done. He grabbed my ankle and started to drag me towards the edge of the net. My body seized up. He wanted to kill me. We only made it two steps before I grabbed the rope like my life depended on it because it very much did. The hold stopped him in his tracks. Nasaled grunts punctuated his jerks as he tried to dislodge me. No, way. I wasn't going down like that.

"You fool," said another goblin from the doorway. "That's Princess Cybil from Knockaine. Do you want to start a war?"

The goblin that had me by the ankle dropped me. I tried not to look too relieved as my heart resumed its I 'm-not-going-to-die-this-second pace. I don't know how many more times I could be on the verge of death today and still sleep with my sanity tonight.

The goblin spit. His belly jiggling with the force of it. "Well, how am I supposed to know that? They all look the same. And who's keeping track of all those princesses from those damn mounds anyway? I'm sure they have more. Might as well do them a favor and get rid of one."

Despite his harsh words, he sheathed the staff behind him again. Taking that as a sign that we might actually get out of here alive after all, I affixed a smile onto my face. It felt a little too bright like my face was stretched a little too high and long, but I went with it.

I reached a hand to them in the universal sign of help. "It's so good to meet you. If you would be so kind as to-"

"Stuff it, Princess. You know very well you're trespassing on goblin land. And for that, you're going to have to pay." The goblin at the door rubbed her long fingers together. "Moreanna is going to love this."

I swallowed hard. That is what I was afraid of. I'd almost be willing to take my chances with the lava.

CHAPTER 14

*H*eat hit us like a wall as we entered the chamber. I staggered but was prodded forward with a crack of the staff against the rock under our feet. Pulling myself up, my gaze immediately went to the Moreanna. The goblin queen slouched back in a jagged throne. It was formed, crude, from the pile of rocks it sat on. Spits of lava jumped from the pool behind her. That's when her eyes lit upon us. She lumbered into a sitting position. Her long breasts moving in globed unison atop the mound that was her belly. Thankfully, most of the view was concealed by masses of jewels jumbled around her neck. But that didn't stop a coal nipple from jumping out when she leaned over to brace those twiggy arms on her knees.

She opened her mouth wide. A laugh wheezed out. Then two guards on either side of the pile of rock started laughing too.

I pushed their mockery aside. With a deep breath, I focused on what lay before me: Queen, throne, a pile of rocks, guards around the throne, lava pit in the background. I brought my scope back. High ceilings, stalactites, and stalagmites throughout the room. Goblins that caught us on the left and behind us. Ceremonial altar to the right. Upon laying my eyes on the altar, I froze. All of my attention zeroed in on it.

The altar was set back in a carved out section of rock. Light from the lava bathed it in a warm glow. It had been smoothed down to a revered canvas. A larger than lifelikeness of a goblin was painted onto it with what looked like coal and dried blood. Considering the primitive design, it was breathtaking. That wasn't what held my attention, though. It was the carefully laid out set of bones beneath it. Bingo.

"Lost your way, little faeries?" Moreanna sing-songed in her gravelly voice.

Little? I almost laughed. We were twice as big as they were.

"No, Queen Moreanna," I said, dropping into a low curtsy, hoping to buy time while I thought of an excuse. Just when I thought I had been down too long, one came to me, and I rose back up.

"We are here to get a paltry diamond from your bountiful caves. I've grown weary of the ones brought to me and wanted one of your fine specimens to call my own. Legend tells of the Moreanna diamonds, and it does not disappoint." I said with an incline of my head.

From the assessing look on her face, I could tell she was weighing the truth of my words.

One of the thick-legged guards at the base of the throne said, "So you aim to steal from her royal majesty?"

From the outraged look on Moreanna's face, she had come to the same conclusion. And she was royally pissed about it. To be honest, I didn't think that it would have been taken like that. I thought my choosing her mines would be a compliment, but it did look like stealing, didn't it? Well, crap.

How did they prosecute would-be thieves here? I had a feeling I didn't want to know. We had to make our exit out of here before things got out of hand, like now.

Thankfully, they didn't know me. So that was on my side. I laid a hand to my breast in feigned disbelief about to give the performance of a lifetime.

"Me? A common thief? The mere thought makes me shudder." I staggered back and bumped into Anthony.

I'd jostled him on purpose, but he didn't know that. I pretended I hadn't known he was there and whirled around to face him. All of the goblins in the room stiffened at my movements, but they relaxed again when I threw myself into Anthony's arms.

I projected my voice and said, "I can't believe they think I would steal. Me. Princess of Knockaine. A common thief... I...I just can't!" I bowed my head, and then I lowered my voice to where only he could hear me and said, "I'm going to grab one of those goblin bones over there, and then we're going to split like a sundae."

He gathered me into his arms and said loudly, "There, there, Princess."

Our acting skills were awful. It sounded like we were part of the worst acting troupe in history. It would be a miracle if they were buying any of this.

He lowered his head and said for only my ears, "But my wing is broken."

I reached up to grab the sides of his face and kissed both cheeks while barely moving my lips and saying, "I'll hold the one like we talked about earlier."

"I said I thought that *might* work." he hissed through his teeth.

But I was already moving away. It had to work. It was our only chance at getting out of here- bone or not. Understanding wasn't a known goblin trait.

When I turned back to Moreanna, she looked slightly pacified by my display. Obviously, the theatre wasn't a past time of the goblins.

"But isn't she a bounty hunter? I thought I heard she was a bounty hunter. Why would a bounty hunter care about what diamonds she gets when she gets paid in paper?" Said the female goblin who'd recognized me earlier.

My heart thundered double time at her words.

"Bounty hunter? A princess? Just what nonsense have you been listening to?" her companion said, turning to her.

"Isn't her name Cy? Yeah, I think I heard the same thing," said one of the guards.

"Her? That slip of a thing? Catching people." Piped up the other guard. "You've lost your mind."

And the bickering started. Moreanna's eyes darted from one goblin to the next, clearly trying to decide which side to believe.

The idea that I couldn't possibly be a bounty hunter was highly offensive. Still, it wasn't a notion that was utterly foreign to me. People had been telling me how impossible my being a bounty hunter was for years. I didn't care about that right now, though. With everyone distracted, this was my chance to get the bone.

Quick. I thought. Then I ran. I dug my feet into the uneven rock floor as I pumped my arms and continued up the two steps to the altar. Moreanna's shouts behind me signaled they'd spotted me. I snatched a random bone. One was all I needed; I wasn't a total heathen.

I turned around. Anthony's eyes were the size of saucers. I don't know what he was so wide-eyed about, but this wasn't the time. *Now.* I mouthed to him as I ran down the steps. He ran to meet me, curling his wing like he usually did to start the engine, so to speak. His other wing predictably didn't bow. I reached my arm up to grab the veined expanse.

The membranes felt flimsy in my hands as I pulled it around us, like butterfly wings. I had a split second of panic to wonder if I would rip it. Then a stake crashed into my hand.

I screamed as pain throbbed across my knuckles. The cold shock of wind rushed around us as the goblin grabbed my hand. I took the bone and smashed the wrinkled goblin head peeking above the wings.

He fell back the exact moment we disappeared.

CHAPTER 15

"What in the hell was that?" shouted a very naked and very angry Anthony.

His shoulders heaved from the exertion of having zipped through the Spaces Between. I was so glad we were shouting from the comfort of my apartment, I didn't even care.

"Which part exactly?" I asked as I went back to the clothes box and rummaged through it.

It was probably too much to hope that there was another halter top in there. If these last two little adventures had been anything to go by, I would probably make all of my t-shirts into halters. Or maybe Anthony still had some clothes that would work with these wings.

"Hey, you don't happen to have any more of those dresses that I can use with my wings, do you?" I stopped rummaging to look at him.

He was so upset he looked like his head was going to pop off. "Are you serious right now?"

"I'll take that as a no. Got it." I went back to wading through clothes.

Irritation stretched my nerves—still nothing. We only had three more ingredients to get before my wings would be gone, and then I'd get to wear my own wardrobe again. Life being easy? The hell you say. That was if the potion didn't make me disappear entirely. It was a sobering thought. Pushing that little tidbit to the side, I continued my quest.

I could almost hear Anthony rolling his eyes from where I crouched.

"And which part? Oh, I don't know. How about the part where you moved faster than any faerie I've ever seen. That's no small feat, Cy."

"Maybe living on the outside isn't so bad after all," I shot back as the Gods graced me with another halter top from the box.

I pulled the halter over my head.

"No, that isn't it." Anthony started to pace.

He moved from the bed to the dresser and back again. "The last time I saw someone move that fast, they were...a vampire."

Realization and horror chased across his face. "You were marked, weren't you?"

And just like that, my happy mood disappeared. I pressed my lips together. Why couldn't anything be private? Why couldn't I just keep one thing for my own? Did someone always have to know my secrets?

Anger radiated from his every pore as he strode over to me and gripped my arms. "Weren't you?"

His fingers sunk into the soft flesh of my arm. It hurt. I don't think he realized it, but I didn't want to say anything because I knew how much this knowledge was hurting him. I didn't want to hurt him. Gods knew what was stopping me, though. He'd hurt me in the past. I don't know why it bothered me so much to do the same to him now. Maybe on some level, I felt like I deserved to be hurt for putting our race at risk.

He shook me. His body curled towards me as if he was in pain. "Answer me, damn it."

There were so many emotions welling inside me. Anger. Hurt. Betrayal. And guilt. Sweet Danu, the guilt was the worst.

"Yes, ok. Just yes!" I pushed his hands away.

They let go only to come around me in a hug.

He pulled me to him, crushing my face against his chest. "God damn it, Cy."

I wanted to be thankful that he wasn't pushing me away. Grateful that he accepted me for me, regardless. Vampire blood or not. Unconditional acceptance: it's what I'd always longed for.

But now that I'd started to open up, I couldn't seem to stop.

"It's not like I had a choice, Anthony. It's not like anyone asked. It's not like anyone ever asks what I want." I struggled against his embrace as I wrestled with the tide of emotions churning through me.

To my horror, I could feel my lip start to quiver. I hated it, but I couldn't stop it any more than I could control my feelings.

"I didn't want any of this. None of it. Not a single bit." Sadness and bitterness welled up inside me.

I hadn't chosen this. I hadn't asked to be this: Princess, marked by a vampire, you name it. But what could I do now? A big fat nothing, that was what. Nothing was going to change those facts. The best I could do was try to escape it all before I lost even more of myself.

"Shhh, shhh," Anthony said as he moved his hands up to gather me to him. He trapped masses of my hair against my head as he turned my face up to his. "It's not your fault. I'm so sorry this is happening to you. I can't even begin to imagine how hard it is for you. I wish I could take it all away. Everything."

He seemed to be wrestling with what he wanted to say. His lips worked, lips that were a brassy-red from being in the sun. His eyes had a sadness like the blue-green depths of a lake you could step into and never come back from. It had to be hell knowing the girl you wanted was ruined.

"Cy, I just want to give you peace. I want to give you everything you deserve. Love, affection, security. I've wanted it for so many years." He said the last in a harsh whisper like it pained him to say it.

All I could do was stare at him, my heart raw. What I wouldn't give to have what he offered. To be able to grow in the warmth of pure love. One unstained by fears and betrayal.

My mouth parted, to say something, I'm sure. But I didn't know what to say. Hell, I didn't even know what I wanted to say.

Anthony's eyes dropped to my mouth. He groaned and inched his face towards mine, unsure. The world slowed to a mind-numbing halt as he came to me. Did I want this? No. Yes. Gods, for so long, yes.

I felt my pulse quicken in anticipation. Anthony saw me not moving away. Saw me waiting with bated breath for his lips to touch mine. My eyes dropped to those familiar, delectable lips. Then they were on mine.

His eyes fluttered into the back of his head. I squeezed my own closed as his lips touched mine. It was tentative at first and then grew bolder. The world spun. His hands cradled my head, and his lips slanted over mine, deepening the kiss. I'd dreamed about this exact moment for so long. I'd envisioned it, acted it out even. Yet, nothing compared to the real thing. He was hot and cold all at the same time. Yielding and demanding. Hard and soft. He was a perfect paradox of sensations that had me reeling.

And just like that, it was over.

He pulled away. All I could do was stare up at him. The room's soft light seemed to create a halo around him. Then he smiled. It was a radiant smile, and just then, I knew how he felt. It made me want to make everything ok for him too. I just wished it were that easy.

His eyes said he loved me, but it was his next words that showed he cared. "So how many more ingredients do we have left?"

After such a beautiful shared kiss, it would have been so easy for him to press home our obvious attraction and try to keep me here by his side. He could have ignored my wishes because my leaving would clearly hurt him, but he didn't. Instead, he showed me that my needs mattered to him. I wanted to tell him how much that meant to me, to thank him. But things were so tenuous right now. There was an undercurrent of emotions that buzzed between us. One wrong word could snap it.

So I played it safe and answered his question.

Because I was a big chicken.

"We have three ingredients left." I ticked them off to give my suddenly fidgety fingers something to do. "Werewolf Blood, Dragon Scales, and Demon's Hoof."

He blew his cheeks out and shook his head. "Gods, that's quite a list."

"Yeah, not exactly things you can get at the grocery store either," I said.

"No kidding," he agreed with a laugh.

It felt more like things used to be, and I appreciated that.

The lack of tension helped me think. I smiled wide as the perfect solution for the next ingredient dawned on me.

"Well, next on the list is Werewolf Blood." I said, leaning against the dresser with a smirk. "My bouncer friend just happens to be a werewolf."

Anthony laughed and said, "Good luck finding him anywhere but with his pack on a full moon."

"Why does it have to be a full moon?" I asked, crossing my arms over my chest.

"Because their were cell counts rise when they shift. It's highest at the full moon." he said, sitting on the bed.

I narrowed my eyes at him. "Just how exactly do you know something like that?"

He just raised an eyebrow. "Did you pay attention in school? Like at *all*?"

I glared at him. He made a face back at me. He was right, damn it. I do remember a lesson about werewolves when we were in Fae Academy. I also remember skipping that class to sneak out of the mound and look for wandering human boys to steal kisses from because when were we going to need to know about werewolves? Boys were so much more interesting. Especially the human ones. They were off limits, so they were intriguing to 15-year-old me. I blew out my cheeks and then let the air out with a deflated sigh. Fat load of good that did me now.

"Didn't the test say something about on the full moon you were required to communicate directly with the alpha of the pack because they had the most control over the turn and were less likely to eat you for dinner?" I asked, struggling to remember.

There wasn't much that was coming back to me. Wasn't my memory helpful?

To my surprise, Anthony nodded, "That's right. And I can tell you right now, your friend isn't an alpha if he has a job.

The pack takes protection of their alphas very seriously. They don't have jobs."

I scrunched up my nose. I couldn't decide if that was a good or a bad thing. Having all of the power but not being able to go anywhere. Now that I thought about it, that sounded suspiciously like here in the mound.

Popping my lips, I pushed off the dresser. "Well, seeing Marc is out. The next full moon isn't for another week and a half, so we've got time."

"Do you want to try to get one of the other ingredients in the meantime?" Anthony asked, pulled his legs to his chest.

"No, I'm exhausted. Let's get you to the healer. We can figure out what we want to do from there." I said, with a noncommittal shrug.

Honestly, I just wanted to get out of here. The last thing I wanted to do was sit around with Anthony in a room all alone. I so didn't need him to get any fancy ideas.

"What time is it anyway?" I asked, scanning for a clock in the still packed away room.

Anthony pushed out of the bed and stepped onto the balcony.

Through the billowy curtains, I saw his head tilt up. The sun kissed his bronzed features.

"About two. Who knew that almost getting killed would take such little time?" he said as he came back in.

"It does feel like it should take longer, doesn't it?" I picked up the goblin bone I'd been eyeing earlier and smacked it into my palm.

He made a face and pointed at the bone. "So...uh, whose bone do you think that is?"

I could feel my face heat up again at being reminded of where the bone had come from. I never thought I'd steal a bone, let alone one from an altar.

"I'm not sure..." The more I thought about it, the more it

creeped me out, so I set it down with a hollow clunk onto the dresser. It looked out of place on the cheery yellow surface.

He gave me a lopsided grin and said, "You stole from an *altar*. You are so going to hell."

"Tell me something I don't know. Where else but hell are we getting a demon hoof from?" I quipped.

CHAPTER 16

Not surprisingly, healers weren't on every street corner. So we were heading to the Bardais. Its stately crystal columns looked almost ethereal in the late afternoon sun.

We were almost there when I spied another group in the corner of the courtyard practicing Muay Thai. Again. Irritation stopped me in my tracks.

"Why do we continue to do that year after year?" I asked in disgust.

Anthony stopped too and looked in the direction I'd been looking.

He apparently didn't see anything to be too concerned with because he looked back and asked, "Do what?"

"That," I said, throwing a vague hand at the dirt circle and its occupants. "Why do we continue to practice Muay Thai like that?"

He looked at me like I had said I was going to take up kitten wrangling.

"Because we need to be able to protect ourselves?" he said like he was fishing around for the right answer.

"How to protect ourselves." I couldn't help but stutter it out. I was beside myself. "Why don't we use- I don't know, maybe our abilities?"

He crossed his arms over his chest and looked at me. "Right. And what about the faeries that don't have magical powers?"

"Everything can be weaponized," I said matter-of-factly.

It wasn't an exaggeration either. Everything could be. You just had to get creative about how you used it.

"Is that right? Ok, then what about Oren. How are you supposed to weaponize the ability to melt things?" He asked.

I shrugged. "That's easy. Have him melt the weapons of his attackers."

He nodded around the thought. "Ok, what about Elder Elspeth. What good could flower petals be in a fight?"

Oh. That was a tough one. You couldn't deny that flower petals weren't precisely fighting material. Still, ...there had to be a way. I firmly believed this was the way we should be fighting. Then it hit me.

"You could use them to blind the opponent," I said with a dismissive wave.

He took a second to mull it over then held his hands out wide.

"Ok, I've got nothing. You might be onto something." He conceded with a laugh. "But it isn't me that you have to convince. You'd have to start at the heart of things."

At first, I didn't get what he was referring to. When he pointed to the practicing group, it clicked. He had a point. If I didn't convince the person heading it first, I wouldn't convince anyone else. That "anyone else" being Mother and the Court, of course.

Part of me said I should go and talk some logic into them. It really didn't make any sense to be doing that with the powers at our disposal. There was no reason we had to try to suppress them or use them as cheap party tricks.

Why did I care, though? I was going to be out of here as soon as my wings did their presto-chango act.

I don't know why that thought sat wrong with me. I wanted nothing more than to get out of here. It probably bothered me that I'd battled vampires and had barely escaped with my life. There would be no hope for the rest of the fae if they only used Muay Thai to defend themselves against vampires. If they didn't use their powers.

That was the only reason I could justify why my feet started moving in the direction of the dusty circle.

I could see Anthony from my peripheral. He stared at me like he was trying to figure me out before I heard his footsteps behind me.

As we came upon the group, a male faerie took down a confident, strong female. Dirt puffed from the ground at her impact. After a few seconds, it drifted back down around the startled woman. The man flexed his muscles. It was a cocky move that made me dislike him instantly.

"Good, Harmon. Very good." Said the instructor from the sidelines. "Jasmine, tuck, and spring back into a fighting position when he takes you down like that next time. It's more advanced, but with practice, it will come with ease."

Then the instructor turned to me. Sansonite. His weather-wrinkled skin seemed to soak in the sun. He brought his tan hands together to bow to me. He had been the instructor for ages, easily as long as I could remember. He had salt and pepper graying his brow. It never ceased to amaze me how he was always so serene, yet his quiet presence demanded respect.

"Princess, such a pleasure to be graced with your company once again." He said.

The use of "princess" made me cringe. I pushed my discomfort away. He had always made a point to call me that, despite my asking him not to.

"The pleasure is mine, Sansonite. May I speak with you?" I asked.

There must have been something in my tone that made him pause.

"Is it of a personal nature?" he inquired, his brow never puckering.

It took quite a bit to ruffle Sansonite.

"Not in the least," I said, then when it was clear he wasn't moving, I added. "It's about the practice of Muay Thai."

He looked at me for a second, assessing. Then he waved a hand to the group in and around the rough circle. "Then please do say it now, as I am sure my students would be most interested in what you have to say." He said.

I wanted to smack my forehead. I'm sure there was an ulterior motive Sansonite had for staying here, but I wished he wouldn't insist on it. This was going to be a touchy subject. It was going to make them feel awkward with a capital A.

I decided to approach it with the same level of tact I gave everything, which was none.

"Muay Thai isn't effective. It won't work against...those that matter. It needs to go." I said as I cut my hand through the air.

Gasps came from the clustered students. Everyone looked at me just like Anthony had: like I had clearly gone round the mound. Sansonite's face remained still, despite the unsettled students around him. His gaze assessed me.

"And just what would you propose we use instead, Princess?" he asked, cocking his head to the side.

"We can use our abilities," I said simply.

"How could we do that?" asked a girl in the back.

I could just make her out in between the bodies of the other students who'd started to gather around. Anticipation lit her face up.

I gave her a little smile of encouragement and said, "You willfully manifest your ability and direct the energy into something or someone."

"Direct it into someone?" Scoffed, Harmon, the winner of the match from when I'd first walked up. "What does that even mean?"

"It means you hold it in. Then you focus on an object and direct the pent up energy into that. You just don't want to hold it too long, or it can get dangerous." I warned, directing the comment to the girl who'd asked earlier.

Harmon scoffed and rolled his eyes. A frail faerie to his right chuckled, her lips turning up in a jeer. A quick look around the group showed more people shaking their heads. It wasn't surprising. Nobody liked to do things differently. I'm sure the idea of harnessing something that had the power to be volatile was pretty intimidating. They didn't realize how much better they would be able to protect themselves this way. It would be so much easier to walk away right then. To let them keep doing what they'd done all along. I couldn't, though. It wasn't in me. Let's not even talk about that vampires might know of our existence. That weighed heavily on my gut as it was.

"I know it seems scary, but trust me. With a little practice, you will be able to make weapons out of your abilities. It's such a better method of protecting yourself. Farther reaching, more damaging. It's damn near perfect."

"B.S., you mean," maintained Harmon with a twist of his lips.

I'd had about enough of him.

"Look, I know a thing or two about it. I was on the

outside for 5 years, and it was hands down the best way of protecting myself when it was a life-or-death situation. And that's what we're preparing for, isn't it? In the event, there is a breach in the shields, and we have to defend ourselves?" I asked, directing this question at Sansonite.

Before I had a chance to respond, Harmon piped up again.

"Yeah, I know you. You're that washed-up, joke of a princess. Why did you even bother coming back here? We were better off without you." Harmon said, shaking his head.

It was a low blow, and he knew it.

Anger heated my collar in the space of a heartbeat. Just who was this punk? Never mind the fact that he put a voice to all my fears. That alone singed my nerves. But for him to talk to me like that? Who was he that he thought he could do that?

"Let's not go throwing insults, choir boy. I've seen better moves from a 6-year-old, so you should watch yourself." I warned in a quiet voice.

It was his turn to turn progressive shades of red. They were fascinating, but I didn't think that's what he wanted to talk about as he stood there sputtering.

"Not a chance, *Cybil.*" He said, spitting on the ground.

Cybil. My blood started to boil. That was crossing the line. I wondered if being a princess meant I couldn't punch him in the mouth. Because I wanted to. Sweet Danu, how badly did I want to.

Then a thought came to him a lot like I imagine an STD came to a whore, slow and painfully.

"I know." He said with a cocky smile. "Why don't we test your little theory? My skills against your...abilities."

He punctuated the last word with a spit.

Anthony leaned close. He knew me far too well to think I'd let something like that slide.

He whispered in my ear, "Uh....he's the Muay Thai champion, Cy. As in champion of all the mounds. I don't know how good of an idea that would be."

It took me a second to remember what he was talking about, but after a second, I remembered. The mounds held yearly tournaments for Muay Thai. It was more of a PR move than anything, but everyone took the games pretty seriously.

Well, that changed the dynamic of things, didn't it? But then again, it could be the perfect arena to prove my point.

"Ok, you got a deal." I said, then I paused for dramatic effect before adding, "But let's put a little wager on it. If you win, I'll drop the issue. But if I win, then we bring it to the Queen and see if she will allow the weaponization of powers...alongside the continued practice of Muay Thai."

I'd added that as an afterthought. There was no way they would make weapons out of our powers and stop Muay Thai entirely. However, I might be able to convince them to add it *to* a faerie's training.

Anthony's sigh reached my ears even before Harmon's self-assured laugh.

Harmon rubbed his hands together. "Oh, you've got a deal."

There was only one more approval we needed to get.

I looked at Sansonite. "You're the one in charge here. What do *you* say?"

He looked between the eager champion and me.

After a moment, he gave a quiet nod. "It sounds fair to me."

I fought the grin that threatened to break over my face. At least one thing was looking up.

With a crack of my knuckles, I stepped across the worn barrier of the tight circle. "Perfect. Let's do this then, shall we?"

Crossing the small border felt like stepping back into another lifetime. My pulse slowed. It felt...good. I shook out my muscles, but this time it was for show. They felt loose and ready the second I'd stepped into the circle.

Harmon was clear on the other side of the circle when I came into it, but that didn't stop me from raising my hands and letting energy seep into my arms. Lightning licked out with the barest whisper of power. Heat flowed to the tips of my fingers and danced up my forearms to stop at my biceps. Adrenaline washed over me in a buzzing rush, and I giggled. This was going to be fun. Electric white shot out of my hand and hit his foot.

He let out a little scream. It brought another smile to my face. I should feel terrible, but I couldn't stand the arrogance. He shook his foot for a second before putting his weight on it again.

This time he advanced as he said, "That's not playing fair, *Princess.*"

There was a darkness to the way he said the last word that put all of my bells on high alert.

"No, it's totally fair, and I did it for a reason," I said, trying to keep the smugness out of my voice. "You see, when you use your abilities in combat, you can easily gain the upper hand when it comes to distances."

"Handy, maybe, until your opponent is in your face," he shouted, picking up the pace.

He was coming toward me in leaps and bounds, so when he said the last word, he brought his elbow down. His goal was clearly to smash my face. I brought my arms up in a quick V and was able to catch the blow. Thank the Gods because the force of it alone sent me down on one knee.

He didn't let up, throwing a knee into the mix. I danced my midsection back and flowed a little lightning to where our arms connected. Heat and light flared at my forearm.

He let out a louder scream this time. I wish I could say I felt terrible for hurting him, but violence was the only thing some people understood.

I had no sooner stood back up when a knee connected with my midsection. Pain flared in my gut. I gasped for breath. Then he windmilled his arms and brought his other leg around to smash into me. My world rang. The force of the kick struck me down. I fell like a tree.

My whole body throbbed. I caught myself with my elbows before my head connected with the ground. Before I could get up, he was on me, pinning me to the dirt.

The weight of his body trapped my arms underneath me. That was when the first breath of panic hit me. I couldn't use my ability without my hands. Glitter sifted from me at the realization. It pooled around me until his knees started to slide in it.

But he didn't fall off me. Instead, he gripped my sides tighter with his legs and started to pummel me. I wriggled and moved, but the most I was able to do was turn till I was facing him. His fists shot into my midsection. I bucked, but he didn't budge. He just continued to slam his fists into me.

Stabs of pain hit me one after another. My entire stomach melted into a blanket of searing pain. I could feel my body start to give up as my struggles to unseat him became weaker and weaker.

I turned my head to see Anthony's petrified face at the sidelines. Fear was etched into his face like a rock. Then I saw a decision melt it, and he crossed the two feet to Sansonite. He started to say something, and Sansonite held up a flat palm. Red blossomed onto Anthony's cheeks, and it quickly turned to an angry purple. His hands waved fervently in the air.

Then I shifted my head to the left of the arguing pair and

saw a beautiful faerie with long, ice-blue hair. She made a small tap on her legs. And just like that, it clicked.

I gathered what little physical effort I had left and rocked my legs into the air, swinging them forward. The first attempt I missed, but the second time they wrapped around Harmon's torso. With as much energy as I had left, I twisted my legs and sent him sprawling to the ground. My head reeled. I blinked the feeling away.

He sprang back up, but I managed to bring my hands up in time in those precious few seconds. With a prayer, I shot lightning into him. I shot surge after surge of energy into him. His body convulsed with the amount of electricity being pumped into him. Only then did it dawn on me I had to stop. I let out a guttural cry as I forced the Kundalini energy out of my body. When I did, he slumped to the ground. And he lay still. Shit. I turned and crawled the couple of feet to his prone body.

Please let him not be dead. Cocky ass or not, I didn't want him to die.

As I reached his side, I saw the air draw into his lungs with enough force to raise his chest a few inches. I collapsed onto my knees, my effort spent. I buried my face in my shaking hands.

My body burned as I sat there. Something had to be broken. I almost didn't care, though. Danu's blessing, that had been close. Too close.

I pulled myself together and reached down to check his pulse. No sooner had I touched his neck that his eyes opened, a slow aching flutter. He saw me right away and narrowed blue daggers at me. Reaching up a hand, he grabbed mine and tossed it away. I didn't want to point out that it was a weak toss. He looked soundly beat and not too happy about it.

Sansonite must have agreed with my assessment because

he said, "That's enough. I think the Princess has proven her point quite effectively."

The beaten champion propped himself up on his elbows, panting with the exertion.

There was malice in his eyes as he said, "All you've proved is you don't belong here. Those wings on your back don't make you a faerie. You're no more faerie than that little whore that was tracking you."

Anger lit inside me quicker than a match to gasoline when I realized he was talking about Kittie. My gut burned, and I couldn't tell if it was from my injuries or my anger, but I stood up. I opened my mouth to speak, but Sansonite beat me to it.

"I think that is enough for today. Princess, I will meet with the Queen regarding this matter." He said with a nod.

There were so many things I wanted to say to the jerk at my feet. Logic prevailed, though. I should leave while I was ahead. I started to do just that when a hand wrapped around my ankle like a snake. Startled, I braced myself. When nothing happened, I looked down.

The champion's eyes held a cold hatred. "You better watch yourself, *Princess.*"

Again with the sarcasm. I'd had about enough of it. The best way to handle people like that was to just ignore them, so that's what I did. With contempt in my eyes, I kicked his hand off my foot, and this time, I did walk away. My pride wouldn't let me limp, though. I kept my spine straight even though my injuries grew worse after the adrenaline had left my body.

Anthony met me at the sidelines. He was a wreck. When I got close enough that he could see the pain in my eyes, he shook his head. I walked past him, and he fell in step behind me.

He took a shaky breath to calm his nerves and said in a

voice that only I could hear, "So this is how we're doing it, huh?"

"You bet your sweet ass," I said as I walked across the terrain. It had looked so smooth before. Now it seemed rife with valleys and hills. Much like my life.

CHAPTER 17

*C*rackling and crunching erupted from the giant tome in front of me as I wrestled with turning the massive page. The waxy paper sounded like a sail catching the wind when I finally got the thing turned.

"Shhh!" shouted an angry hush from the librarian station. The station sat raised in the center of the library, a mountain of knowledge to be revered.

My cheeks turned bright red. Why did they have to make the book about dragon breeding habitats big enough for an actual dragon to read? Did any dragons plan on showing up? I mean seriously. At this point, I almost wished they would. Then I could ask them where they kept their eggs. It was a good thing I'd decided to do the research on this while we waited for the full moon. I had no idea such a seemingly simple fact would be so hard to find. This was the second day I'd been here, and already I'd been here for an hour. Not that I was any closer to finding out where dragons lived. The most I had found was that it was on another plane. Well, duh. Dragons weren't wandering around our world. That would have made the news.

Since Anthony could manipulate the Spaces Between, that meant he could go to any plane. Ok, so we could get to where they lived. But where was that? There had to be a better way than going to each plane and doing the equivalent of bird watching until we finally spied a dragon. So I kept searching. Twenty minutes later, I had it. Fireborne. Bingo. I looked back at the oversized book. It mocked me with its hugeness. Dread stayed my hand. I suppose I should put that back.

I'd just put a hand on the worn spine when the librarian laid a weathered hand over my own.

"Why don't you let me get that. This was dropped off for you," she said handing me a slip of paper with a reedy smile.

It was clear her patience was on its last thread. Maybe not helping was a form of helping, in this instance. With a nod of thanks, I took the paper and uncurled it. *Anointed Consult, Enchantette, 7:00 pm.*

Just great. Another Anointed meeting, just what I needed. I tossed the paper into a nearby trash bin. After I'd talked to Avalynn about it, it seemed like the meetings were about once every other month. I thought I'd be able to squeak by without having to suffer through another one of these. Looks like I wasn't going to be so lucky. Darting a look at the clock, my heart jumped. I only had 12 minutes, and I knew how the Dame felt about tardiness. My knuckles ached at the memory of the smack of her pointer stick against them.

I made it to the Croí. I plopped down into the brocade chair, praying the Fitting could be done in record time. I only had 3 minutes until 7:00. To my absolute relief, it took less than 2. It helped that the will of faerie hadn't tried to give me the queen's crown again. There wasn't time to argue with it.

Picking up my beautiful sheer overlay skirts, my heels clacked down the hall as I ran the last few steps to the white thorn trees that formed the intricate door to the Croí. With a breath of relief, I burst into the doors, pretty damn proud of myself.

That pride was wiped from my face as I looked at the spectacle before me. It wasn't a private tea party for the Heir Anointed. It wasn't the Enchantette. Whoever had written the note had deliberately wanted to make me look like a fool. And I had a damn good idea who that someone was. Well, mission fucking accomplished.

Don't get me wrong, everyone from the Heir Anointed was there, but they were all dressed for cleaning, not socializing. Flora was plucking dead blooms from the winding roses above. Under the direction of the Dame, Brigad was repairing part of the ring that had caved in. Avalynn was sweeping the blooms off the floor. And Stacia was cleaning out smashed blooms from the floor, like the snake that she was. Anger clenched my fists.

My bursting in had gotten everyone's attention, and they all stared at me with big eyes. Everyone except Stacia, that is. She had a satisfied, snarky grin on her face. My fists ached to go snatch it off her face.

Avalynn rushed over. Dipping her head low, she whispered, "I am so sorry. When Stacia offered to send you the note about the Consult, it didn't even occur to me that she might do something to embarrass you."

Fury clenched my jaw. I knew it was that little witch. That's ok. I wouldn't give her the satisfaction of knowing it bothered me.

Waving Avalynn's apologies away, I laughed and said loud enough for everyone to hear, "Are you kidding? It's been so long since I had a Fitting. It felt good to have one done again. I do so love what the will of faerie does for us. What are we doing here anyway?" I asked, changing the subject as I walked over to grab a bucket.

Avalynn took the buckets I'd grabbed and separated one out for me.

"Oh, service to our community is one of the tenets of good leadership. So we're here to clean up these sacred grounds." Avalynn said, putting the other bucket back in the pile.

"Oh, dear. You're all dressed for the tea party. And didn't you just have a Fitting like a month ago? That's not long at all. This must be horribly embarrassing for you." Stacia cooed as she came over to grab another bucket.

"You know, now that you mention it. That's right. I did have one recently. It was the same Enchantette where the will of Danu gave *me* a throne, didn't it?" I asked, not bothering to keep the smirk off my lips.

Everything in me itched to tell her about the crown, but I stopped myself. Whispers got back to Mother. And if the Queen of Munster found out about that, she'd have my head. Her eyes blazed daggers at me.

Her hot breath fanned my face as she stepped closer to me. "You better watch yourself, *Princess*. You don't know who you're playing with."

Suddenly, pieces came crashing together. She was the one threatening my friends. It all made sense. She didn't want me here. I had taken her friend, and in her mind, I was taking her crown. There was no doubt from the set of her shoulders that she considered herself to be the next Queen of Knockaine. My coming had killed all of her chances, crushed all of her dreams.

I threw the bucket on the ground, "No, *you* watch yourself. If you harm a single hair on anyone I love, I promise you, you will wish you never set foot on this Earth."

"Big words with no way to back them up," she said with a sneer and then laughed in my face.

Rage boiled in my stomach. That was it. I'd had enough of

her shit. My hand shot out before I even knew I'd made the decision to hit her. The sound echoed with a crack before I remembered where we were. We were on holy ground. Lighting crackled over my closed fist and Stacia was out cold on the mossy floor. Shit.

CHAPTER 18

"I can't believe you knocked out Stacia," Avalynn said from where she lounged on my crimson sofa.

She had it coming didn't seem like the appropriate thing to say when you'd laid someone out cold for just harassing you. Was it really only harassing, though? I was beginning to think she might have something to do with the threats against me* If that was the case, she deserved a lot more than being knocked out cold. She deserved to be locked up. And if she was indeed the one doing it, she'd be locked up with the Department of Truth a million times faster than my fist had been.

"*And* you fought Harmon," she added with a shake of her head. "You better cool it or people are going to start thinking you are here to cause trouble."

Word had gotten back to her about the fight last week, and she'd come over to get all of the gory details. Nestled in like she was, she looked every inch the Heir Anointed., especially with her diaphanous gown flowing over the side of the couch and spilling onto the floor the way it was. I was jealous of the way she seemed so content there without a care in the world. What I wouldn't give to be able to have that. Instead, here I was preparing to go tango with some werewolves. Tonight, the full moon was upon us.

"Hey, you were there. Stacia started it. And as far as Harmon is concerned, how else was I supposed to get my point across? We shouldn't still be practicing ancient arts when we have real powers we could use instead. It's like using sticks and stones when we have a bazooka," I said, not bothering to sugar coat it.

She was my friend, so I shouldn't have to sugar coat it. Besides, the sooner people accepted how much sense this made, the better. I looked up through the high ceiling of my living room and admired the carved designs there as I stretched my arms high and my wings far out. A girl could get used to living here. Too bad I wasn't going to be staying.

The stretching wasn't because of sore muscles. Anthony and my visit to the Bardais and their healers had me feeling better than I had in years. No, I stretched to mentally prepare myself for what was to come. If the last round of ingredient gathering was anything to judge by, this wouldn't be a stroll through the woods. Thankfully, Anthony and his wing had been healed at the Bardais too. That's what had taken so long. Bones were harder to knit back together than muscle tissue.

Avalynn sat up. The movement made me look over. She leaned forward, a look of earnestness on her face.

"You better be careful, Cy. There are a lot of people who like the old ways. People who are desperate to keep them that way and frankly don't like that you are back. Not everyone is like Anthony and me." She said concern etched into her regal features.

My mind immediately went to the last time we were in this living room and the gruesome warning that had been left here.

"Don't worry about me. I don't scare easily." I said with a smile. When I saw the frown pull at her face, I added. "And don't worry; I will make sure you aren't hurt either."

The smile I gave her had more confidence than I felt. Truth be told, there was always the uncertainty underneath the smiles: uncertainty in what I'd done, uncertainty in what I was about to do, hell, even uncertainty that I was doing the right thing. It was a hard truth to admit to myself, let alone anyone else. It was easier just to act like I knew what I was doing like I had all of the answers. I didn't.

"So are we going to chat like old housewives all night, or are you and I going to get out of here? There's only one full moon a month, you know." Piped up, Anthony coming out of the bedroom.

I opened my mouth to tell him that wasn't always true, but Avalynn piped up from the couch. "Where are you guys going?

I could tell she was curious but had been trying to hold it back. Politeness, it ground at me. She always had a habit of being overly polite. In the wrong situation, that could get you killed. With the gods' blessings, she'd never know that.

Pushing the uncomfortable thought away, I turned towards Anthony. "Just waiting for Your Royal Slowness."

"Oh, haha." He said with a roll of his eyes walking his muscled torso over.

The soft light of the recessed lights played across his chest. Shadows farther down his torso, let me imagine the rest. I shook myself. Had he always been this good looking? I found myself walking over to meet him halfway. My cheeks flamed. Had I been staring at his chest the whole way over? I pulled my eyes up and stared instead into the topaz of his eyes. My mind immediately went to our earlier kiss. From the way, his eyes darkened, and his nostrils flared, I could tell he was thinking the same thing.

As if things weren't strained enough, Avalynn added to the tension by walking over and standing next to us.

"Where are you two off to?" asked Avalynn again.

I turned and cocked my head. Maybe she wasn't so polite after all. Good for her.

"We're going…" his eyes caught and held mine. It almost took physical force to pull away from their snare. Distracted, I finished the sentence, lamely with "out."

"Ooooo, like a *date*?" she asked, wagging her eyebrows.

I wanted to laugh, but the idea wasn't as laughable as it would have been before this afternoon.

I settled with rolling my eyes and saying. "No, nothing like that."

"We are going into the forest." Anthony elaborated.

"Right, a romantic stroll in the woods." she said with a wink.

Oh, brother. The last thing I needed was for it to get out that I was dating Anthony. I'd look like the whore of Babylon after just being with Sven. I'm sure that was common knowledge in the Court by now.

"No, really. We're-" I tried, but Avalynn was already at the door.

She turned and raised her eyebrows and smiled.

"Enjoy your non-date, you two!" she said."

I shouted across the living room, "It's not-"

She shut the door with a wave.

"-a date," I said to the back of the door.

Anthony smirked. I rolled my eyes at his non-help and smacked his arm. My fingers warmed at the momentary contact.

"What?" he said with a faux innocence that earned him a punch in the arm this time.

"Oh, I found something for you to wear." he said, bringing

his hand out from where I didn't realize he'd been holding it from behind his back.

Two scraps of cloth held on with ease to the two fingers he held into the air. One was yellow like the moon and the other a black like midnight. Yeah, that was not going to happen.

"Maybe you found something for you to wear." I countered back.

He laughed. "No, I have to pop back to get my clothes from my place."

"It better be just as bitty." I said, though I was doubtful anything could be as bitty as the loincloth he perpetually wore. When he shook his head with a grin that was as big as his face, I shook mine. "No way."

He shook it at me to take it, a cheshire smile on his face.

"What do I need to dress like that for anyway? And where did you even get that from? I don't dress like that. I'm not a piece of meat."

He grinned a devilish smile I didn't like the looks of and said, "Well, today you are. Oh, and wear your hair blonde."

Since when, in the name of Dagda, did you have to dress like a bleach blonde slut to fight werewolves?

a cold breeze blew through the dark trees, shaking the leaves like bones of a skeleton. A shiver ran down my spine. I pulled my tube top farther up, trying to cover as much skin as possible. Not surprisingly, it still didn't cover much. I was tempted to pull my skirt higher to cover my stomach, but I stopped myself. I didn't need my ass hanging out. I shot Anthony a dirty look. Him with his blue jeans and fitted T-Shirt, loincloth mysteriously missing. Somehow, this didn't seem right.

"Tell me again why I'm dressed like a Brooklyn hooker?" I asked, pulling my stiletto heels from the moist earth with each step.

"The local Alpha likes blondes." He said as he looked up.

I pushed a hand to his ridiculously understated outfit. "Then why aren't *you* dressed like a Brooklyn hooker too?"

He laughed. "Actually, I'm wearing what you might call the werewolf dress code."

"I don't know why I couldn't have worn the werewolf dress code," I muttered as I prayed Marc wasn't in this pack. I would shrivel up the size of a witch-doctor's head if he caught me in this outfit.

The full moon came around a cloud to light up the creases around his eyes as he studied the stars. I had the overwhelming urge to reach out and run my hands across his face. I shook myself. This wasn't going to get us anywhere. I had to focus.

I looked up and tried to make out where we were based on the winking constellations above. After a few seconds, I gave up and looked back at Anthony. I'd never been good at that.

"This way," He said, changing directions.

"So, how do you know where we're going anyway?" I asked.

He shrugged, but then after a couple of steps of silence, he said, "I stopped by earlier and asked if they wouldn't mind some company."

"You what?" I stopped.

The sudden stop combined with the heel's angle threw me off, and I tilted back. I waved my arms to steady myself. I wasn't going to fall, but before I could move another inch, Anthony was there and had me in his arms.

With all the skin I had out on parade, my brain became confused when his hands slid over me like a feather. The light pressure had me reeling as I looked up. I was having the damndest time keeping the world in focus as his hands slid to my lower back. Logically, there wasn't any other place he could put them with my wings in the way.

But logic had nothing to do with the way my hands found their way around his shoulders. They were sturdy, square shoulders. There was no denying the solidness of the muscle beneath his cotton-blend shirt, either. My traitorous hands gave a small squeeze.

Gods, they felt good. I wanted to touch the rest of him to see if he felt just as good.

"Are you ok?" he asked.

It was a silly question. I had barely even wobbled on my feet. Anthony probably didn't realize it, though. From the way his voice came out breathy, I could tell he was thinking of other things. Things like softness and heat and the tightening down low.

I looked at his lips. They were red in the light of the moon. A dusky red that reminded me of dark cherry Kool-Aid before you mixed it. Come to think of it, his kisses reminded me of Kool-Aid too. Not how they tasted, no. The act of kissing him. It mixed up my insides, stretched my emotions to the breaking point until I felt all liquid inside.

A growl came from the trees. All thoughts of kisses fled in that second, My breath hitched in my throat. We turned our heads in horror-movie slow motion to see what had made such a blood-curdling sound. A pair of eyes glowed in the underbrush. Then slowly, it unfolded itself from the darkness, a rippling mass of corded muscle.

It was a gray wolf. His coat was just deep enough to make it hard to keep eyes on him in the dark. I was in full, freak-out mode. Anthony, on the other hand, had different plans.

He stepped towards the wolf.

Of all the idiotic moves. I had half a mind to strangle the cocky Messenger's tanned neck before the wolf had him for a snack. I grabbed his arm and pulled him back. Thanks to the vampire blood in my veins, the force pulled him back.

"Are you crazy?" I hissed.

"Relax; it's one of the local weres." He said, brushing my hand off his arm.

I balled my fists by my side in an effort not to grab him again. When he got a few feet from the wolf, I bit my lip to keep from calling out to him. He was a big boy if he wanted to be an entrée, that was his choice.

Now, if I could just convince my rioting stomach of that.

"How do you know?" I blurted, unable to help myself. "Besides, so what if he's a local. He can eat you anyway, you know."

At this, to my astonishment, the wolf stood up. Before you could say, "We're not in Kansas anymore Toto," his body bunched, folded, and Rubick' S-Cubed its way back to a person.

Since I'd never seen a shifter…shift, I knew my eyes had to be about as big as the moon as he said, "I assure you, he's not my type Miss Cy."

'Miss Cy.' Not 'Princess' just Cy. My whole being relaxed. Well, as much as one could around a newly naked stranger, that is. Were or not, it was bizarre to see someone hanging out for all of the gods' creations to see.

"This way. The Alpha expects you," he said right before he turned and disappeared back into the brush.

I shot Anthony a not-a-word look as we followed him in. Was it just me or was the forest thicker on that side of the brush? Limbs reached out like hands to grab at us. I told myself that it was silly and focused on not getting a branch in the eye. That must have been the reason I was taken aback when we came upon the pack.

At first glance, you wouldn't have guessed they were anything but a bunch of people out in the woods for a party. I searched through ripped jeans and T-Shirts for Marc. When I looked closer at the clusters of people, you could see that each person seemed to be engaged in a discussion, but not. They waited for something. Expectant energy hummed underneath it all, belying the seemingly casual get together. There was no sign of his burly, spiked-blonde self, but I was starting to wish there would have been. What he thought of me paled in comparison to the hum of suppressed violence around me.

And it was all centered around one woman. She was sitting on the fallen log at the center of it all. Well, sitting was a tame way to put it. She sat on it like she was the roots holding it into the ground. Her knee was bent, making her blue jeans ride up her leg. It exposed a tanned shin. Her legs ended at a pair of red high heels that flashed in the moonlight. They almost distracted me from the naked men resting on the ground below her. Almost.

Her eyes were already on us. When I met her eyes, I just knew.

She was the Alpha.

I shouldn't have been surprised. She was very Amazonian in her frame and movements. The weres at her feet swung their heads in my direction in unison—their elongated faces evidence of the moon's call.

"Princess Cy, so good of you to join us." She said.

Her voice was rough around the edges like the change had started to affect her too. I wasn't surprised, considering the full moon was already out.

"I am Shiloh." She rested her hand on the bark of the tree and leaned towards us. "We've heard about your need and are willing to oblige."

They were willing to give *blood?* I about fell down. How did we get so lucky? Maybe Anthony had been right to come ahead of time.

I didn't know how to thank her for such generosity, but I sure was going to try. "Wow, I don't know what-"

"However, you will have to earn it." She said smoothly.

So much for thanks. I didn't like the sound of that at all.

"And how do you propose I earn it?" I asked, keeping my features expressionless.

"We like a little warm-up to our feast." She said, her eyes

roving over my outfit in a way that said she approved. Then she shifted her hand out to caress the man at her feet. "My pet suggested you be a part of the hunt. The idea has...appeal to me."

Well, that didn't sound so bad. Hunting animals for sport was way different than out-thinking a criminal. Though I didn't have much of a stomach for hunting animals, there were way worse things than running around the woods with a pack of dogs for the night.

"I can do that," I said, then I patted my skirt- which was clearly lacking pockets and said. "You'll have to give me something to hunt with though. I didn't bring a knife or gun, and I don't have those pretty teeth you all get when you shift."

She laughed at that. It was a deep, throaty laugh that floated up into the star-filled night. She reached down to trail her fingers over the blonde below her again. His control wasn't as good as hers. The moon's call erupted hair all over his body in a slick burst. He was young and eager, leaning into her caress.

"Isn't that cute?" she said. The way she tilted her head, it was clear that she was speaking to the pack. Then she focused back on me and said, "No, you won't be hunting. We will be hunting you. If you can outrun the pack, we will give you the blood you desire."

Anger and fear chased each other down into my gut. This was so not what I signed up for. Someone had some explaining to do. Like now.

Anthony.

I pulled him down to mouth level, so I was pretty much whispering into his mouth. "You better explain and explain quick."

"This wasn't the deal," His words strained because of the death grip I had on his arm.

My jaw clenched. "Just what *was* the deal?"

He opened and closed his mouth before he slumped in my grasp, "She just said something could be arranged."

Perfect. I let Anthony go. Well, she hadn't been lying. Apparently, the deal was me being the appetizer. Don't think it had escaped my notice that nobody had said anything about leaving me alive after they caught me.

But...if I could somehow avoid being eaten, we could get out of this pretty much painlessly. My eyes went to the pack of wolves around me, all in various states of The Change. What are the chances I could win? Better question: what were the chances of me getting werewolf blood any other way that didn't send us into an all-out war.

My gut hardened as I kicked off my shoes. This was such a bad idea.

"I'll do it," I said before I could change my mind. I kept my tone light—no need for the pack to know how every bone in my body screamed to leave this place.

Her wolfish smile and the eager looks on the faces around us confirmed how bad of an idea this was. I pushed down the doubt and worked on psyching myself up. I could do this.

Anthony grabbed my shoulders, turning me to look up at him. "Don't do this, Cy."

I peeled his hands off me. "Anthony, it's the only way."

Denial worked his throat. Finally, his face twisted and he said. "If anything goes wrong, just-"

"We're running out of moonlight, Princess. If we're going to do this, we need to do it now. Unless you've changed your mind that is..." Shiloh trailed off and crossed her legs. The red of her heels winked in the moonlight.

The insinuation was clear: I couldn't handle it. I wasn't good enough. That fuse was a short one, let me tell you. The muscle in my jaw ticked.

I faced the ragtag group, square on. "No, I'm ready. What are the rules?"

She grinned, a model-worthy grin. The smile expanded her face. It stretched out to almost a clown's face until the front of her face elongated. Then the smile fit into a wolf's muzzle.

"Run." She said with a thick, darkness that raised the hair on my arms.

Adrenaline shot through my body.

"What?" I said, not sure I understood her correctly. Not wanting to hear her correctly.

Then, as fur knit itself down the expanse of her throat, the rest of the people milling around her started to change. Muscles folded themselves in to make way for huge frames. One man that looked to be a total of 18 years old raised his human head to the moon and howled. At first, it sounded human, and then in a split second, it wasn't. It darkened to be the embodiment of the monsters that crept in the shadows. His jaw fell open to reveal a mouth full of huge teeth that could slice your flesh with the ease of a knife to warm butter. I froze at the sight.

Anthony moved to me. Fixated on the horror show in front of me, I was slow to see it, but when I looked up, I saw his face had become a sheet of panic. That didn't do anything to make me feel better.

His hands were on me, pushing me to the darkest parts of the forest. "Just run."

He was right. I had to get out of here.

So I ran. Through the trees and brush, I ran. The branches I'd tried to avoid so hard before now slapped at me, clawing and scratching at my exposed limbs. I ignored them and focused on running. I don't know how far I'd gone before I felt wetness oozing thin lines down my pumping arms and legs.

My heart beat a staccato in my chest. Anthony's words shouted in my head: just run.

And I did. I ran faster than I ever had before. Sure, the trees didn't blur by, but I was quick like no fae before. Maybe, I had a chance.

As if to remind me of reality, I heard the excited yips and howls behind me. They weren't at my heels, but they were close enough to set my stomach into knots.

How fast could wolves run anyway? I scoured my memory as I ducked under a thick branch that popped in my path. Frustrated, I grunted. I couldn't remember the exact number from my Life of the Wolf were history class, but I was pretty sure they could run faster than the fae. What about a vampire? Could werewolves outrun a vampire? Any other time I wouldn't be wishing I had the full powers of a vampire, but with wolves hot on my heels, I'd let myself be ok with it. Just for now.

I heard the yips getting closer. My heart slammed into my rib cage. The sound had come from right behind me. Was panic twisting my imagination? Or were they really that close? I couldn't spare a second to look back and see. There was no way I was going down like a horror movie chick. Even if I did look the part at the moment.

I don't know if it was the wind, but I swore I felt breath across my bare ankle.

If I didn't do something soon, this cat and mouse game would be over. Over for me, specifically. I had to change tactics, like now.

Think. I had a brain; I wasn't a rabbit being mindlessly chased. Options. What options did I have? I could use lightning to try to stun them. My mind flashed back to the group that had been milling around their Alpha. There were too many of them; I didn't have a chance in hell of being able to pick them off one by one. Then an idea hit me. If I could reduce their flow to a manageable number, I could pick them off. But how?

Then, like a message from the Gods, a branch hit me across the face. It wasn't big enough to stop me, but it did sting something fierce. I didn't care, though. I knew what I was going to do. I laughed into the cold night, feeling better for the first time since this nightmare had been sprung on me.

I eyed the trees ahead. It only took a second to spot my target, a giant sycamore tree nestled in the grove over the ridge. The branch at the bottom looked close enough to the ground to grab. I ran full tilt towards it.

I'd get up the tree and start picking them off as they circled the base. It was brilliant. This was actually going to work.

Excitement boosted me. Before I could blink, I was there. Right before I hit the tree, I leaped and reached up. I managed to hook my arm around the branch I'd been eyeing just seconds ago. Good thing too because no sooner had I pulled my legs up when I heard the unmistakable snap of teeth. I sucked in a breath between my teeth as I dug my feet into the branch. Bark bit into my feet as I climbed higher and higher.

After four branches, I leaned over to look down on the weres below. They circled the base just like I'd thought they would, but that's where the similarities to what I thought was going to happen ended.

Moonlight reflected off their eyes. The very human emotion of rage-filled them. I blinked as I tried to process it. Had they thought they were just going to make quick sport of me? Apparently, the answer to that was yes, and the monkey-wrench I'd thrown into their plans infuriated them. Their legs grew before my very eyes. Fear vibrated through me as the wolves grew and changed shape. They only stopped changing when they were half-wolf, half-man. The difference was their legs retained the same massive muscles of a wolf's hindquarters. They could shift parts of their bodies? Holy Gods, were they the scariest species in the world, or what?

That wasn't even close to the worst of it, though. My breath caught in my throat as one by one, the beasts stood up on those massive legs. The legs made them a full foot taller than logic said they should have been. My heart skipped when the one closest to the tree reached up to wrap a paw around the branch. Its claws came out, their whiteness was unmistakable in the shadows. Each one looked like a curved dagger embedded in the coarse hair.

They were coming.

"Move, Cy. Move!" I said to myself as I talked myself back into action.

Reaching up, I grabbed the next branch. And the next and the next. The creak of branches said they were still coming, but I was far enough away to be ready this time. I turned around and held out my palm as I gathered energy into myself. It reverberated inside me, coming to a dull thrum as I peered into the branches for signs of life.

When I saw a muzzle appear from behind the branch, I let out a little zip of energy. Lightning shot from my hands. I wasn't quick enough, though, because the wolf's muzzle disappeared behind the branch before the lightning hit. Black singed the tree, bark curling away on impact. It was ok that I hadn't hit the were. All I needed was for it to stay away.

Shiloh hadn't said how long I had to outrun them for, but I was pretty confident the hunt would be over at daybreak. Didn't werewolves hunt during the full moon?

The wolf head came around the bend of the tree again. Its teeth were bared. Great. I'd pissed it off. These things were scary enough without them being pissed off.

It was ok. I could do this. The coarse bark bit my butt as I pushed against the trunk for leverage and aimed again. This time I hit him. A very dog-like yelp echoed into the forest as he fell back again.

Elation shot through me. Bingo. Nothing to it.

Ok, maybe that was a lie, but it certainly wasn't impossible. For the next five minutes, I played pin-the-lightning-on-the-doggy. And overall, I was giddy to report that I was winning.

The sight of them falling away from the tree like ants sat in my gut. Was I hurting them? Then I saw one with a white patch of fur on its brow come back. The damage I was doing clearly wasn't significant enough. I stopped feeling bad.

But then, suddenly, they stopped coming. The silence was thunderous in the damp darkness. It was far too quiet. The butterflies in my stomach didn't like it. Making a decision, I climbed higher, keeping a wary eye out for them.

I was right to be worried too because then two peeled around the trunk like a Rorschach test gone wrong. My pulse jumped. Fuck. I couldn't aim the lightning with any sort of accuracy at two things at once.

Just below me was a V in the tree. They disappeared behind it. I was wondering what side they would come out of when they appeared from each side at the same time.

I bit my lip to focus. A tiny prick of pain helped clear all thoughts from my head. Then I shot off a zap of lightning. One yelped, and the mistakable sound of branches breaking a fall snapped through the night. Score. A second later, I turned and shot the other one. Yip and thump. Score two. I was feeling pretty good about myself when two more came immediately after them. My heart flipped. No, it was fine. I could do this.

I think the pep talk worked because I picked off the other two with just as much ease. Well, at least it was that easy now. The beginnings of a slight feeling of dizziness started at the top of my head, warning me that all of this repeated turning from left to right wasn't an ideal option. What else could I do, though? They came faster and faster around the fat trunk. The night became a blur of purple staccatos of lightning and the acrid smell of singed fur.

Then a movement in my peripheral drew my attention. Never stopping the shots to the attacking swarm below me, I turned just in time to see bared teeth strobe towards me. The sharpness of his mouth full of teeth made the blood freeze in my veins. It was only through years of training that my body reacted instinctively and ducked.

Huge paws wrapped around my thigh as it sailed past. The sheer weight of its downward momentum ripped me from the tree.

Leaves slapped my cheek. Pain exploded, but I didn't have time to decipher if it was just from the leaves, or it was a more damaging hit from a branch. Another branch slammed into my chest, knocking the air from me seconds before I was airborne.

A scream ripped from my lungs as I dropped. Panic threatened to overcome me before I remembered I had wings. I beat them furiously.

Relief tightened my throat as my descent slowed. Soon I was rising instead of falling. The pounding of feet on the packed earth thundered below me. The most massive wolf I'd ever laid eyes on leaped at me with a giant bound.

I kicked down. I felt its wet nose sponge in right before it dropped back down with a howl.

I beat my wings to steady myself while my heart reacquainted itself with my chest. It didn't take me long to realize it wasn't too much of a struggle to stay up here like this. It was the equivalent of treading water.

Could I stay up here long enough? The sky was lightening

at a rapid rate. Hope rose in my chest with it. Maybe, I could actually make it.

Then I saw the eyes. They glowed like a thousand tiny fires in the trees on either side of me. A shiver skittered down my spine. This couldn't be good.

Who knows what plans they had. My gut screamed to get above the trees. To put as much distance between me and the glowing eyes of my demise. I pushed my wings faster. Gritting my teeth with the effort, I inched up more quickly. There was no relief with the knowledge though. It wasn't fast enough. It was like moving through molasses. Too long, my wings had sat uselessly. Now, they were weak. Gravity pulled at me. Not enough. Talk about the story of my life. I needed to get out of here. Like now. There was no explaining how I knew that. I just did.

A massive wolf sailed past me. While I stared at it in disbelief, it landed, quite ungraciously, in a tree on the other side. Thank Danu for the tall trees. They bent with ease this high up. My attackers couldn't have any real accuracy.

That didn't stop the eager weres, though. It only took a handful of seconds for more to follow on its heels. Soon they were jumping at me from all directions in a deadly aerodance. I couldn't possibly dodge them all.

Fear made clams of my hands as gusts of air from the wake of their jumps jerked me around in the air. Falling back on instinct, I blocked out the leaping wolves and concentrated on my wings. Up, down, up, down. After a few beats, I realized there was a press of air when I pushed them all the way down that shot me up faster. I focused on that, using short up motions and long down presses. Press, press, press the feathery softness of my wings stroked my lower back. The steady beating pushed me higher quicker than I'd ever gone before. It was working.

A paw the size of a frying pan caught my wing. Its knife-sharp claws sliced a hole from the top of my wing to the bottom, seizing on the bone.

I don't know why I was shocked when pain blossomed, where he'd ripped me open. Fear overrode the sting as the were's claw caught on the bone. A second's worth of a pause blanketed my body right before we plummeted to the earth. No, no, no. I beat my newfound limbs to stop falling. Wind whipped the shreds of my wing.

A triumphant growl roared from the wolf before its teeth tore into my shin. More pain came. This was a burning, stinging pain. Saliva dripped down my leg as I kicked at the jaw. It took a couple of times to smash the bottom of my foot into its wire-haired snout, but his teeth finally dropped their death grip on me. Fiery pain blazed. Blood poured down my foot.

Any relief I felt was fleeting as the ground rushed towards me. Shit. Thinking quickly, I twisted my body. Reaching an arm out to the wolf, I'd just pulled myself from, I grabbed ahold of its shoulders and piggybacked on top of it seconds before we hit the ground.

My head snapped back with the impact, and all of the air left my body in a whoosh. A ringing overshadowed all other sounds. But I knew there must have been noise because I saw wolves all around dropping to the ground from the trees. The predatory gleam in the eyes of the one closest to me was unmistakable.

My heart started beating double-time as I realized just how many of them there were. There seemed to be so many more now that they were all in plain sight. I had to get out of here. I rolled off my sorry excuse for an impact pillow and stood up to run.

My legs gave out from under me.

Needles jammed into the flesh of my knees as they crashed into the packed earth. That didn't have my attention, though. No, that was hopelessly glued to the wolves advancing around me.

I could've tried to get up again, but running was useless at this point. They were too close. My jaw ached with the effort to push back tears that threatened to escape. So after everything, this was how I was going to go? Well, I'd be damned if I went out alone.

Bitterness curled lightning into my palm. I aimed it at the were closest to me and let it go. She yelped, but I was already on to the next one. I plunked a shot into the next and next, but the circle grew smaller and smaller with every small victory as they came closer and closer. I just couldn't shoot everywhere at once. They knew it too. They were playing with me now. No longer were they rushing me. They were prowling in an ever-tightening circle, the set of their mouths seeming to smile mockingly.

They were probably imagining how they were going to tear my body to shreds. Saliva drooled from one wolf's mouth in a thick glop. Fear shuddered through me as it dropped to the ground. I wasn't going to make it out of here alive. They were going to eat me.

I wasn't giving up without a fight. I took a few breaths to calm down. At first, they were rapid breaths, and then they slowed. I could do this. Resolve shot energy into my fists. The craziest thing happened then. Lightning arced between them.

Surprise took away the energy, and the arc disappeared. I tested it again. I curved my fists towards each other and leaked more sparks into them.

Sure enough, lightning arced between them. I opened my fists, and the line of energy thickened. Could I use this? I spread my fingers wide, and the thick cord splintered into five threads. Hope tingled my limbs as I spread my arms wide, and the ropes arced around me like a rainbow. What if I could use this as a shield?

I didn't have much time to give it thought, though. Apparently, my actions were starting to make the pack wary because they stopped circling and were heading straight for me. Making a split-second decision, I dropped back to the ground and curled into a ball to make myself as small as possible. Then I closed my eyes to focus and thought about the energy wrapping around my entire body. Elation rose inside me as the heat of the energy did just that.

It must have been just in time, too, because I heard a yelp behind me. Now that I had the energy focused, I opened my eyes. The wolves circled, anger showed in their precise movements. It beat at me in waves.

My heart was in my throat as one unfortunate, brave hound came right up to the cage. Dread danced down my spine as I was reminded there was the intelligence of a human in there. Purple light lit his gray fur as he tilted his head and maneuvered it between the bars of energy.

I kept praying he wouldn't be able to reach me. That it would be enough. When he got close enough to where I felt the heat of his breath on my face, I knew I had to do something.

With a push, I sent even more energy into the cage around me. The bars flared brightly as they grew. It was so fast that the dog never had a chance. There wasn't even a yelp as he fell. Dirt puffed up and snaked into his throat when he hit. The energy felt like it was rushing out of my body as I coughed to get a breath. When my head went down, I realized he'd fallen right into the line of energy.

I wriggled backward, the sweat on my body mixing with the dirt as I moved out of the path of his body.

When the cords flared again, I knew I'd moved far enough. Sweat slicked my hands. Glowing bright and then dimming, the waves faltered. Too much magic was flowing out. Teeth clenched, I narrowed my focus. I couldn't let the Kundalini energy go. If I did, that would mean another wolf could get in, and I couldn't see behind me to know if any of them poked through there. All I could do was pray that I could hold out long enough. It was my only chance.

When my hands started to shake, my whole body soon followed. My eyes pressed shut. Hopelessness scratched at the surface of my resolve. This wasn't how I was going down, damn it. I'd be damned before I let them see me break. My chin hit my chest as my head fell forward, heavy.

I don't know how long I sat there for, crouched in my ball, unwilling to let the world win. A sound brought my head up. It wobbled, weak with the effort, and the cage flared and faded. Gritting my teeth, I went to scrape the last of the power from the base of my spine when I saw a shadow shift and elongate from the back of the circle. One of my attackers had knitted themselves back to human form. Then the circling wolves parted. The Alpha sauntered through their snapping ranks.

As she passed each of them, they came to heel in the morning light breaking over the horizon behind her. She walked through their deference, her eyes trained on me. My brows lowered. I wasn't stupid enough to let down my guard.

Those red pumps flashed back white from the fading light of my makeshift cage as she stepped into a wider stance. She could easily breakthrough at this point, and there's nothing I could do to stop her. I rolled my eyes up to watch her, blinking the sweat out of them. To my surprise, she crouched low. She cocked her head, her long blonde ponytail trailing on the forest floor as her eyes roved over me.

"My little faerie princess...my, my. You are quite a surprise, aren't you?" She said with a nod and a small smile.

I wanted to tell her to bite me, but the most I could get

out with a grunt. It felt hoarse in my throat. I settled on giving her a glare that I hoped said the same thing. She tossed her head back. The slender line of her throat shone in the pinkening light as she laughed.

She focused her attention back on me, a light of respect in her eye. "Very well, my little Princess. You win. A deal is a deal. You may have your blood."

"Swear you won't kill me." I bit out through chattering teeth.

"You will not be killed by any of my people...not on this night." She added with a little purse of her lips after some thought.

I didn't like the answer, but it was probably the best I was going to get. Not to mention, I don't think I could have held my electric prison for another second.

Like cutting a vibrating cord, I released the energy. The bars disappeared with an audible snap. I uncurled my body and spread out in the dirt. I just laid there, my body twitching. I wanted to feel good about winning, but all I could do was try not to be sick.

CHAPTER 20

The sun hit me as soon as I walked out of the Bardais. I threw up a hand to protect my eyes. The world focused again. My stomach flipped at Anthony lounging against a storybook sized oak that had decorations weighing its bows down.

Telling myself I wasn't happy to see him, I stalked over to the tree.

Those beautiful lips framed perfect teeth as he smiled at me as I reached him. "You're looking better."

I would love to run my tongue over those lips, just to feel how soft they were. That wasn't helping. I scowled at Anthony.

"You know if you keep looking at my lips, I'm going to have to kiss you." He said with a little pucker.

Embarrassment flamed my cheeks.

"I should punch you," I said, trying to continue to be mad at him through the embarrassment.

He gave a little shrug of those tanned shoulders. "I've never had it rough, but I'm willing to give it a shot."

This time I did punch him. A dull ache blossomed on my knuckles, and I shook my hand out. He deserved it.

"You could have at least told me." I chided, despite the smile curving my lips.

He rubbed his arm. "I know. I'm really sorry-"

Had I really hurt him? I cupped my hand over my mouth. This more powers thing was going to take some getting used to.

"Why are you, sorry? Did you do something on your date?" Avalynn asked Anthony, walking up beside me.

Her bubble-gum pink hair teased the regal set of her shoulders. She definitely looked the part of a queen, more than I ever would. I ignored the little jump in my chest at that realization and the gold tattoo on my wrist that suddenly itched. Danu had to find someone else to be Queen. Avalynn would be a great candidate for the position.

"It's fine that I'm leaving. It is." I whispered to myself as I stared behind her into the kaleidoscope of colored hair that was the fae, unseeingly.

Avalynn's tone lost its bright tone. "What did you say?"

Snapping my attention back, I made a show of rolling my eyes. "It wasn't a date."

She gave me wide eyes and then a little wink. "Whatever you say."

"We had quite a heart-pounding time," Anthony said to her with a leer at me.

The need to kick him itched my foot. Despite his playful words, his eyes collided with mine. I couldn't get over the way he looked at me. His eyes held me like a spell.

The last time he'd given me that look, we'd been in my room. My pulse clipped at the memory. We'd both been naked. And when he'd taken me in his arms, ...his lips had been a dream come to life. Was he really, though? I pulled at my ear, uncertain.

Avalynn gave an uneasy laugh and cleared her throat. She shifted on her slippered feet and then said, "You two are too funny. I have to go get ready for The Enchantette. I'll see you there, right, Cy?"

I chewed the inside of my cheek. Attending The Enchantette was the one real thing I loved about being in the mound. The tiny little treats danced out by vines and elaborate outfits everyone oohed and ahhed over was only a small part of it. What sprung from the ground was the very will of the fae. Their manifestation was a decree by the Goddess herself. Any other time, it brought joy to my heart. It felt like coming home.

There was no way I could attend, though. Danu was legendary for her patience. I rubbed the gold crown on my wrist. That's why I hadn't been back to The Enchantette since coming back to Knockaine. If she dressed me as Queen and presented me to the Tea Party of the Rose Crown, Mother would have no choice but to defend her title. She wouldn't care that I was working day and night to leave this place. To fae, what I wanted didn't matter. The will of the Goddess did. It wasn't all in my imagination, either. This wasn't the first time Danu had forced her will onto someone. My eyes burned at the thought of being like them. Dagda be damned if that was going to happen to me. I was in charge of my own fate.

I made myself calm, even though my insides rioted, as I said, "No, I think I am going to pass this time. Give everyone my regards, though."

After a long pause, she frowned and gave a small nod. "You'll be missed. See you two later."

As we watched her regal posture weave in and out of a crowd of darting faeries, my brow knitted together.

"It's fine, right?" I asked Anthony, never taking my eyes from her.

"Sure, nobody needs you there. They'll be just fine at the Tea Party of the Rose Crown without your presence," he said mockingly. He didn't understand. How could he? It's what he said next though that chilled my bones, "It's not like you're Queen, after all."

I swallowed hard. Anthony was right: I wasn't Queen. Not yet.

Shaking myself, I reminded myself this was for the best. As soon as Anthony and I collected these last two ingredients, I was out of here. I shouldn't tie myself to anything here. To the Crown, to Anthony, to none of it.

I leaned forward and poked his chest.

A red spot appeared where I'd poked him. I wasn't going to get used to these heightened abilities anytime soon.

He rubbed his chest. "Hey, what was that for?"

I refused to feel bad. He'd purposely let Avalynn think we were sleeping together.

"You know what it was for. Quit being cute." I shook my finger at him for emphasis. "We don't want people to think we are sleeping together."

His grin faded as he gave me a possessive look. The wind died and took my breath with it. I didn't know if it was the temperature or his intensity that made my whole body heat up.

I decided it was him when his muscular thighs corded as he rose. He never took his gaze off of mine. He stopped when he reached his full five foot ten inches. I had to look up to hold his eye. Mere inches separated us. I felt each one as if it were a physical thing.

"Do you still want to do this?" He asked, his words a quiet caress.

I had to blink a couple times to process what he was talking about.

He wet his lips. "The ingredients."

The act made me draw a breath.

"Of course," I said, running a hand through my hair.

It was hard to feel 100% about leaving when he was so close to me like this. It wasn't something I wanted to admit because I really did have to go. It just made doing what had to be done that much harder. Yes, I loved my life outside of Knockaine. It was more than that, though. On the outside, I could be who I wanted to, who I was inside. That kind of freedom and acceptance I would never get here. I was too different.

My throat closed up, and it suddenly became hard to breathe. Inclining my head, I started walking. He fell in step next to me. We needed to focus on getting that potion. On ending this. Standing here, thinking about a childhood fantasy future wasn't going to do me any good. That wasn't my path anymore. Everything had changed. I had to give my attention to the now.

"Where are we going to get the dragon scale and the demon's hoof from?" I asked the perpetual sunshine warming my skin.

The Latha, the second in the interconnected domes of Knockaine, was where I'd spent most of my life. When I reflected on my childhood, it made my chest tight to think about how we took the sunshine for granted after seeing it day after day for our entire lives. That seemed to be the way of so many wonderful things in our lives, didn't it? We took them for granted. Until they were gone.

Anthony took up my change of subject without flinching. "Let's try to get a scale from a dragon's nests.'"

That made me laugh. Next to me, a faerie stopped in surprise at the sudden sound, her delicate hand on her throat. I nodded to her, and she blinked before nodding back, her bustle bouncing back and forth as she hurried away.

"Oh, I'm sure they wouldn't mind if we waltzed into their nest," I said with a roll of my eyes.

"Miss Naysayer, hear me out." He said with a scrunched nose. "They shed scales during the nesting process to help keep the egg warm. If we find an abandoned nest, we wouldn't have to get even close to a dragon."

I cast him a side-eye. "I don't know. Your last plan was supposed to be simple, too, and it almost turned me into an appetizer."

He had the grace to pull a face, "Yeah, sorry about that."

I shrugged it off. "Don't be. What other options did we have?" Which brought me to our current predicament. It really did seem to be the best-case scenario. After a moment, I slapped my hand on my thigh. "Fuck it. Let's do it. What's the worst that could happen?"

My feet had been walking on their own as we'd been talking. I found I'd brought us back to my place. Thoughts of our shared kiss tightened things down low. I bit the inside of my lip. Going upstairs with Anthony probably wasn't a good idea at this point. Since when had a dear friendship turned into a thing I didn't recognize anymore? Something I couldn't trust?

As I wondered where else we could go and rounded the corner to my apartments, I pulled up short. I reeled at the sight before me.

"No," I whispered, numbness filling my body.

There, between the weathered, split shake sided apartments in the emerald grass, was Avalynn. She was sprawled, face down, on the ground. I choked out a gasp and ran to her.

Anthony reached her before I did. By the time I'd caught them, he'd already snatched up her shoulders. She crumpled, limp in his arms.

Black dirt streaked down her shimmer-pink dress. Only after I looked closer did I see the rips in it too.

The whites of Anthony's eyes were wide around his azure pupils. "Avalynn? Avalynn, are you ok?"

His fingers white as he gripped her, he shook her shoulders vigorously. Her head lolled back and forth. No, no. This couldn't be happening. My mind flew to the gruesome warning that had been given to me. I pushed the thought away as Avalynn's eyes fluttered open. Her hands smeared dirt over her face as she clutched her head.

I dropped to my knees, wet grass soaked my knees. "Gods, Avalynn. What happened?"

With a shaking hand, she pointed to the trees. The movement took obvious effort. My heart constricted.

"He...he jumped out and...and put his hands around my throat until...until the world went black and you were here." She said, wincing as she managed to get the words out.

Anthony rotated her arms and moved her feet gently. Anger roiled through me.

"Who attacked you?" I asked.

It was hard to keep the anger out of my voice. I didn't want to put Avalynn through more than she'd already been through, but my insides vibrated. She was beloved by all who knew her. Whoever did this had to be the biggest piece of shit.

"I don't know. I was attacked from behind." Her shaky voice came from beneath her disheveled hair as Anthony turned her head from side to side to inspect it.

The thought crept back into my mind again like a Moray Eel. What if this was because of me? Everyone knew we were friends. My pulse thundered in my ears. I don't know how long Anthony took to check her over before I finally got up the nerve to ask what I feared most.

At least that's what I tried to do. The most I got out was, "Did they...say anything?"

She closed her eyes. Her eyebrows turned down, and her lips pressed together like she was going to cry. I placed a hand on her back for comfort. I felt terrible for making her relive it, but I really needed to know. Needed to know it wasn't what I thought it was.

"The voice was hard to hear, but it...it said 'your friend had better think about what I said if she doesn't want to see you six feet under.'" Her overly bright eyes opened and found mine. Her voice tremored as she asked, "Do you think...?"

My breath came fast at her words. "It's got to be the same person who sent the threat. They think that I'm going to stay and are trying to make me leave."

What if it was Stacia? Would she attack her friend? If she'd thought Avalynn had abandoned her for me, she just might. I didn't want to put that on Avalynn right now, though. There was no sense in upsetting her any further.

Avalynn seemed not to notice my preoccupation. Her teeth chewed the words as she said, "That's right- the...box at your apartment."

I hugged her seemingly-fragile frame to me. "Right. But don't worry. I'll make sure they don't hurt you again."

"But how can you do that?" She asked, tears thick in her voice.

That was a good question. How exactly did I keep Avalynn safe? I couldn't be her bodyguard. I'd have to pay Stacia a visit is all. I couldn't tell Avalynn that, though. I didn't want her worrying or, worse yet, telling her friend.

I focused on the question I could answer. "Well, I'm leaving, so ultimately this problem will go away. We'll just have to figure out a way to keep you safe until I get a chance to get out of here."

"You're ...leaving? But you can't do that. The Queen

would never allow it." She asked gently with a meaningful look at my new shining appendages.

Self-consciously, my wings bobbed once. Concentrating, I steadied them.

"I have to. For...many reasons." I shrugged off the why. It felt too personal. I focused instead on the facts, "The wings won't be an issue soon."

Despite my words, I could see her struggling with the fact that I was leaving.

I added gently, "It's not just because of this."

After a searching look, she bit her trembling lip and gave a short nod.

Her hand came up to find and squeeze mine. "For what it's worth, I'm sorry that you're going."

My stomach fluttered at her words. It did feel good to be here. Wrestling with the butterflies in my stomach, I pushed the thought away.

I scooped her up into a hug. "Thanks. That means a lot to me."

She returned the hug.

"Why don't I go stay with Jessamine until you can leave. That way, you don't have to worry." She said.

All the breath rushed out of my body, grateful this was one answer I didn't have to come up with. It still sat, uncomfortable in my chest, that my friends had to make such sacrifices for me. But that she was willing to go to such lengths for me, overwhelmed me.

"Thank you," I said, blinking back tears of gratitude.

Avalynn braced a hand on the ground to get up and then stopped, "Oh, I forgot earlier, your mom wants to see you."

Of course. Things could never just be without Mother having to put in her input.

Anthony asked Avalynn, "Are you sure you're ok to walk?"

"I think I can manage, but help me up, would you?" She lifted a hand to him.

He laid her arm over his shoulder and pulled her close. She shook her skirts out. Anthony and my eyes caught each other. His kindness never ceased to touch me. That was the kind of man you wanted in your life. He could be yours, my head whispered.

Avalynn inhaled deeply before letting it back out in a steadying breath, "Do you want some company to your mom's?"

Something about my leaving this time felt so...final. My shoulders tensed at the thought. I found myself saying yes before I could tell myself Avalynn should be resting. My throat tightened. I can't believe she'd been attacked like that. I should have been with her. Then I could have stopped it. But what was I supposed to do? Follow her and Anthony around until I was able to get out of this hell? There was no way. I couldn't handle this on my own, though. That much was painfully apparent. Maybe, I could enlist some help.

"Let's get you to the Department of Truth to report this first though," I said, smoothing a hand over her shoulder.

"Well, you girls enjoy yourselves. I think I'll sit this one out," Anthony said with an exaggerated grimace.

His eyes rested on me for a second, and all the joking left his face. I could tell he didn't want to leave me. As crazy as it was, I wanted him to stay too. Then he gave a little wink. Ignoring the way my stomach flipped, I looked away.

"No, I'm fine really. All that fuss for nothing seems incredibly silly," Avalynn said with a wave of her hand.

Two children running down the lane pushed between us. Tinkling laughter trailed after them. I barely noticed them. All I could do is gawk at Avalynn and her rapidly pinkening cheeks. It was clear she was uncomfortable with my reaction to her declaration, but I pushed on anyway. It was important to be honest with friends, even when it made them uncomfortable.

"What do you mean it seems silly? It's your life we are talking about here." I dropped my hands when I realized I had them clutched at my temples like I thought she was insane.

Avalynn twisted her hair in over and over again in her hands as she contemplated me. After a moment's pause, she started walking again. "Listen, I can't jeopardize my chances at the Heir Anointed like that. I'm not doing it. Let's just forget it happened, ok?"

Standing my ground, I watched her walk away. Finally, I made a disgusted grunt in my throat but walked after her. Forget about someone trying to kill her? How was I supposed to do something like that? What if they succeeded next time?

When I caught up with her, I knew the conversation was over when she turned towards the royal apartments. What could you do when people wouldn't listen to reason? A fat load of nothing. That was what.

Turning my thoughts to something that didn't make my stomach turn with dread, I brought my mind back around to the puzzle that was Anthony. I really had to get a hold on that. I was leaving. What was he going to do? Pop in for a booty call? That wasn't Anthony. And I wasn't in the business of playing with people's hearts.

I didn't even know how I felt about him. All I knew for sure was that I cared for him. How could I not? For all his posturing, he was a great person. That didn't mean I loved him, though. You could be attracted to someone, like them as a person, and not want to be with them...right? I shook the thought away. I don't know why I thought I was qualified to answer a question like that, just look at how I'd messed up things with Sven. I'd believed I loved him. My heart tugged at the image of him that came to mind. At the thought of Sven, that same feeling of his being next to me popped into my consciousness. Regret and sadness radiated in me. I blinked at the suddenness of the emotion. Then it hit me that the thought wasn't mine. He should feel bad for what he did to me. Tor Mór, it changed who I was. It was part of the reason I couldn't stay here. How could I? I couldn't, not when the very thing that had driven faeries to the brink of extinction now ran through my veins.

With no little amount of force, I pushed the thought of Sven away. The feelings of guilt and sadness went with it. At least most of the heavy-heartedness did. What was left was the constant heartbreak I'd lived with since this whole nightmare had started.

Avalynn turned a corner, bringing me back to the present. Heat pricked my ears. Here I was lost in my thoughts again. I shook myself. For the love of Gods, someone was out to get the ones I loved. I really needed to be more aware.

With a subtle shift in my eyes, I assessed the people around me. More than a few of them had stopped what they were doing to watch us. Most of them didn't even stop gawking when they noticed I was staring back. A few of them even started to whisper behind their hands.

Avalynn noticed the stir too. She leaned towards me and then paused. I wondered if she knew what was going on. She seemed to know everything.

After a breath of indecision, she patted my arm. "Don't pay them any mind."

"What is it?" I asked and narrowed my eyes at the gawkers.

One woman bounced at my scrutiny and hurried to shut the top half of her wooden door. The slam made me jump.

Avalynn shrugged as we turned into the tall doors of the

royal apartments and out of their view.

I shot her a look. She looked like she wanted to say something. The way she worried her lower lip between her teeth set me on edge. There was more going on here.

After a second, she said in a babble, the words pouring from her, "I didn't want to tell you- you shouldn't have to deal with this on top of everything else."

"Just tell me," I said, wishing she would get to the point already.

We turned down the long corridor of the royal apartments. I'd had enough of couched feelings to last a lifetime. I wasn't prepared for what Avalynn said next, though.

"Nobody is happy you're back," she said like she couldn't stop the words once they'd started.

My feet rooted to the ground. All I could do was stare at Avalynn's back, stunned. I knew I didn't belong here, but was I such an atrocious person that *everybody* hated me? Granted, I had been a little rough around the edges growing up, but still.

She noticed I'd stopped and rushed over, her gossamer gown bouncing in her haste.

"Oh, honey." She grabbed my arm, misunderstanding my shock. "Not me. I couldn't be happier you're back. I've missed you. You always know how to make me laugh."

At my still stunned expression, she rushed on. "And Anthony. He's talked about nothing else since you came back."

The memory of his lips on mine took some of the shock away. If Avalynn only knew. That brought me out of my reverie a little bit. My feet started to shuffle again. She took up my lead, and we continued on our way to Mother's. My mouth opened and closed as I tried to work through this new, impossible information.

"I know you guys care. I guess I just...didn't know that so many people didn't want me here." I finished lamely.

"What do they know?" she said, in a blatant attempt to comfort me. "People hold awful feelings in their hearts for the strangest of reasons."

When I didn't respond, she gave me a comforting smile and continued on. "Oh, honey. I didn't want to tell you. Like I said, pay them no mind. They don't know the real you."

Though I appreciated the thought, I didn't think them getting to know me would help. People just didn't want my kind of thinking around. All they wanted to do was sit in this old-world mound having their old-world celebrations having old-world viewpoints. They didn't want to change. They didn't want anyone who bucked the system. They didn't want me.

My throat swelled. I was so grateful for real friends.

We walked through a door that led us to a staircase that was very similar to mine. The difference was this was a spiral staircase that wound us upwards. As we stood there, the air became thick and floated around us in black tendrils. Then stars appeared all around us, between us.

It meant so much to me for her to try so hard to make me feel better. To stand up for me when so many others just stood by ridiculing. Judging.

Gratitude at her kindness overwhelmed me. "I appreciate you saying what you did back there."

She looked at me. The stars floated in and out of the soft pink of her hair.

"I meant it." She said, then she grabbed my hands and squeezed them tight. "Don't you dare forget us."

As I returned her squeeze, the pressure of her hands on mine was nothing compared to the pressure in my throat.

"Never." I said back in a harsh whisper.

And I meant it.

CHAPTER 21

T pushed in the two-story black door that led to Mother's apartments. My muscles flexed with the effort. Let it never be said going to see my mother was easy.

I stepped inside. Blood dripped down the walls in sticky chunks: half-dried rivers of horror. Vampires hung from the ceiling like humanoid bats. Their eyes red, and their expressions slack. They wanted blood. My blood. I could feel their hunger pulse. Could feel them looming ever closer.

Terror raced through my veins, turning me into an immovable statue. It was my worst nightmare.

Avalynn slanted me a look. "What is it?" She asked.

Then it hit me: she couldn't see what I was seeing. It was all a trick. Damn it, Mother. Would the games never stop?

It took everything in me to grit out, "You should go."

She searched my face, her eyes unsure. With effort, I nodded. Everything would be ok. Now, I just had to believe it. Her brows knitted together before she slipped me a quick hug. Focusing on breathing, I continued into the room. The door closed with a soft whoosh of air.

It took a few seconds of knowing she was gone before the

knot in my gut loosened. Just a little. Until my eyes settled back on the vampire closest to me, that is. His long talonlike fingers crossed over his chest. They were fingers that could rip my chest open with barely a thought. My pulse jumped in my throat as their hunger beat at me.

Years of practice kept my voice even as I called out. "Mother?"

One of the vampire bats swooped down. He came at me like a dark angel of fury, the power behind his flight, making my knees quake. His feet hit the decadent, thatched floor with a whisper.

In a second, he was at my side. He hulked over me, his dark gray flesh stretching over grotesque muscles as he bent towards me. I held my ground as his mouth stretched wide; his hot breath slid across my neck like the devil's snake.

I wanted to throw up a hand to stop its descent, to push it back. The worst thing you could do was battle it, though. I'd learned that long ago, the best thing you could do was remain impassive.

Fear of being killed by a vampire was nothing new. What was new this time was the fear of becoming one of them. As the realization hit me, I brought up my hand and watched it turn gray. My fingernails grew to claws.

Keeping the fear out of my voice, I said, "Mother, do you want to talk or not?"

And just like that, the illusion vanished. Cold relief washed through me. I wanted to gulp it down. Instead, I took a shallow breath. Evenly, I let it out, so Mother couldn't hear me. You never wanted to let Mother think she'd gotten to you. It made things worse next time. I knew.

My shoes whispered across the thatch as I crossed to the main room. Mother was standing with her back to me, her full crimson skirts brushing two trees that wound around each other. Dian Cecht was by the window, his attention out the arched window, bored with my presence already. Emptiness caverned inside me. It was just as well. I didn't want or need his attention. If only his actions weren't so representative of Mother's, I could more easily dismiss him.

It took me three more steps to realize Master Sansonite was there with her. He sat, serene, belying how uncomfortable her baroque couch was. I'd had the displeasure of sitting there before, so I knew just how unpleasant it really was.

Her stance didn't even move a fraction. She said, "Master Sansonite says you have the absolutely obscene idea to do away with Muay Thai."

Why did being around her always make me feel like working on my deep breathing skills?

I knew very well, Master Sansonite hadn't said it like that. He was an excellent communicator. However, he also had enough sense to not correct my mother.

Too bad I didn't have that same sense. "I didn't say we had to get rid of it. But what could it hurt to teach our people to have more than one way to protect themselves?"

This time she did turn to look at me. Seeing her head on, made me take a step back. For the first time in my life, she looked...less than perfect. If I'd have seen her complexion on anyone else, I would have called it sallow. Her green eyes held no sparkle and her hair...was it actually limp? At the very least, it lacked her trademark shine. It looked less like glass and more like...well, hair. What had happened to her to make her like this? To take away her beauty? Could it be me? It couldn't be. Could it?

Unaware of my inner struggle, her gaze sharpened and looked me up and down with more disdain than I'd seen on her face since I'd been brought back. The glare was a cutting thing. I rubbed my arms.

Her features twisted as she said, "Clearly, like much of

your life, you haven't thought this through. What about faeries with flower gifts? What would you have them do? Pelt their enemies to death with petunias?"

A derisive snort came from the window, where Cecht still sat, steadfastly ignoring my very existence. My eye twitched. Fuck him. Fuck all of this. I could just walk away right now and not have to deal with any of it. Everything would be better. For me, anyway. Who it wouldn't be better for is our people. Their safety was tantamount. I'd potentially put the devil at their door. I couldn't leave them with no way to defend themselves. That would be the end of us—this time for good.

Chin high, I glided into the room with all of the regalness I could muster. I refused to let her get to me. "I have thought about it. Every power would have to be used to its distinct advantage. For example, flower faeries could use petals to blind their enemies then they could finish them off with Muay Thai. It would give them a huge advantage."

It was clear that she hadn't expected an actual answer from me. Her eyes narrowed.

"The Princess has a point," said Master Sansonite.

Silence crackled through the room. A dark presence moved towards us. I knew it was Cecht before I looked up and saw him there. "Were you spoken to, *Master*?" Disdain dripped off the last as if it were the greatest of insults.

"You are excused, Sansonite." Mother said, not bothering to look his way.

For the first time since I'd known Sansonite, hesitation quieted his features. Then he gave a stiff bow. As he turned and left, my body vibrated with rage. I couldn't believe Mother was going to stand by and let Cecht suffocate the advancement our entire race, like he'd done to his own son, Miach. When Miach had gone into the healing arts, he'd been called to reconstruct an arm that Cecht had replaced for

Nuada, the first king of faerie. He'd enchanted the solid silver arm and within a matter of days flesh had knitted itself back over the metal. In a fit of jealousy, Cecht had killed Miach. All for the sake of power. Importance.

Mother started to circle around me like she was a predator, and I was her prey. I held my back rigid, refusing to be swayed by her scare tactics.

"You think you're so clever." She snapped, whipping her skirt so hard it made a crack like a whip.

I didn't say anything; I just let my eyes follow the tree pillars up to the ceiling.

"You desert your people, and now what? You think you know what's right for the very people you abandoned? More like the outside world has poisoned your mind. A vampire slut does not have all the answers." Her acidic laugh curled my stomach.

The top of the pillars, five of them, dissolved into a fan of white leaves.

"Little Miss Know-It-All. And you even have wings now, don't you?" I could feel her gaze rake over me. "You must think you're pretty special."

"She always has." Added Cecht, his derision clear from the arch of his back.

The leaves were shaped from plaster and clung to the ceiling. It must have taken forever to do. Maybe they'd had to listen to Mother talk too.

Her tone took on a feigned tone of indifference. "Nobody's buying it, you know."

Letting my gaze drop back to her visible bitterness, I swallowed a sigh and took the bait.

I tried not to sound like the thousand-year-old I was beginning to feel and said, "Buying what?"

"This image of perfection you're trying so hard to portray." The smug look on her face made me feel crazy.

My teeth ground against each other as my stomach churned. Then I realized that the Queen of Knockaine, my mother, was trying to bait me. She must be pretty pissed off to be spoiling for an argument like this.

I decided to cut to the chase. "What's really the matter, Mother?"

Her face flamed, and if she wasn't the perpetual ice queen, I'd have said she sputtered. She'd never been a fan of my calling it like it was. Time, it would seem, hadn't changed that.

"What's the *matter*? *What's the matter?* I'll tell you, 'what's the matter.' We have existed like this for over 250 years. And now you traipse back, having fucked a vampire no less, like you have the answers to everything. Like it's nothing to change everything we, as a people, have worked so hard to maintain."

Despite my resolve, my blood started to simmer. We as a people. That was rich.

"Oh, sure. When's the last time anyone asked anyone but the Elders and the Court what they wanted? You're leaving out whole generations of fae, and you don't even blink."

"Things will remain as they are. As they have been. As they always will be." She bit out.

"But what if that isn't the way things are meant to be. We have a real chance. You didn't see how we fought against those vampires. We were doing some real damage."

I don't know why I was trying to reason with her, but she had to see how big of a deal this was.

"You think you 'did damage,' do you? Are you really ignorant enough to think vampires don't have more of those faerie farms out there? That maybe you'd come across the only one?" She let out a bark of laughter. "I can tell you for a fact there are more of them out there."

I blinked at her, unable to want to hear what she was

saying, but I couldn't stop myself from asking, "Are you telling me you know of more...farms out there like *that?*"

Dian added from his new seat on the couch, "She wouldn't be much of a Queen if she didn't know what went on in the outside world, would she?"

I had no doubt he spoke for Mother. What he knew, she knew. He was her right hand man for a reason. "I can't believe you would let that stand. We have to save them. We have to-"

"Enough! We will do no such thing. This is the end of the discussion. In fact, this is the end of *every* discussion I've had the displeasure of hearing today. We will not jeopardize our race to save a few faeries. Furthermore, we will not change our ways with our powers. You will appear when required. You will be a model princess. You will be an *obedient* princess. And nothing more."

Laughter bubbled in my chest. There was nothing funny about what she was saying. It was crazy. She had lost her mind if she thought I would actually do that.

"No way. You can't honestly expect-"

"No? *No?*" She laughed. It was a maniacal laugh.

The world seemed to get darker. Or was it just Mother? Her hair darkened, her skin ashier, not her eyes though-those grew pale like the eyes of a ghost. Goosebumps raised on my skin. My heart slammed against my chest.

"Oh, really? You think not? Well, try this on for size. As the only female faerie of your generation with wings, it is your duty to help reestablish our race's greatness. As such, you have one of two choices: you are either required to breed with a male from your generation with wings, or you will be held in the Tearmann for observation and testing. Indefinitely...and by force, if necessary, until we can find a way to make someone else like you."

Anger tossed in my gut. It didn't take a genius to realize

two things. One: Anthony was the only male faerie in my generation to have wings. Two: By 'observation and testing' she meant they were going to go Dr. Frankenstein on me. So I could either breed with Anthony or be torn apart. Alive.

She was insane. She truly had lost her mind.

"So, what is your decision?" She asked.

The fevered look in her eye only reinforced the thought that she had lost her mind.

"There isn't much of a choice, is there, Mother?"

The arrogant smile on Cecht's face made me want to smash his face in. Mother simply shrugged. Indifference while she off-handedly ruined my life. What else was new? I swallowed a hard laugh.

"You know what my answer is." I bit out, bitterness coated my words.

She tilted her head in acknowledgment of that fact. At that, the darkness around her lightened. Seemingly, she was normal. If there ever could be normal for her. Bile rose in my throat.

What might have been called a soft light entered her eyes as she walked towards me and said, "I think once you have seen how good it is to have children with one of your own kind, you will understand. Maybe you will even grow to understand what I've gone through. Understand why I do what I must."

She stopped in front of me, brushing my hair behind my ear. My heart thumped in my chest. Long ago, in a time I'd almost forgotten, she'd done that when I'd fallen out of trees or gotten into fights. It was almost like she was saying, 'You are strong. Everything will be ok.' Seconds passed like minutes. What did this mean? Was she trying to say everything would be alright now too?

Finally, she broke the touch and stepped away. "Besides,

Anthony loves you, and he is faerie. You belong with your own kind."

Fury ate at me. She'd tried to control my entire life. Now, she was manipulating my love life? No way. And how could she say such a thing in a way that pretended like she cared? It was just proof I would never understand her. That I'd never be like her. I'd die first. With that I went off to make one of the two statements true, and it wasn't being like her. Instead, it had everything to do with dragons and death.

CHAPTER 22

*I*t was the dead of night. This was long overdue, but it was the first time I had a chance to get out here undetected. Crickets had been chirping all around me, but when I'd come up through the tall grass to stand outside Stacia's window. At least that's what the maid I'd slipped a toadstoole to had told me. Curtains billowed into the night from the bright recesses inside.

The light inside flickered out. Still I didn't move. To be safe, I waited twenty more minutes. Sending a silent prayer to Danu, I beat my wings to fly up to the third floor. These things sure did come in handy sometimes. By the time, I reached the third floor, I was slick from the effort. Ok, they were handy but a lot of effort.

No matter how much the strain pulled at me, I didn't stop beating them until I'd grabbed a hold of the window sill and got both my feet inside. Catching my breath, I listened for the steady rise and fall of breath. When I didn't hear any, my heart sunk. A click of a light confirmed my suspicions. Tor Mór, was this really happening? I turned around to find

Stacia in her nightrail with her arms crossed in front of her chest.

"What didn't kill me last time? Come back to finish the job?" She asked with all of the regalness of a queen addressing her Court rather than a Duchess in her pajamas catching someone breaking into her house.

I hopped into her bedroom. I didn't dare come further in than that, though. The last thing I needed was her waking the rest of the house up.

"I came to tell you to stay away from my friends." I said, hoping it was just as menacing as I'd imagined it would be across the room like I was.

"I don't give a shit about your friends." She scoffed.

Either she was a great actress, or she was telling the truth. I was betting on the former because anyone who succeeded in the Court was a master liar. And being Heir Anointed, she had to have Court success.

I stepped closer. "I mean it. My friends are my family. You leave them the hell alone."

"Listen, you freak. I'll do whatever the hell I want to with whoever I want to. You can't stop me. And if you don't get the hell out of my house this second, I'll have your ass jailed, Princess or not." She said the last with a slight tremor.

She was nervous. As well she should be. Nobody messed with me or my friends and got away with it.

I leveled a finger at her face. "Just remember, touch them, and you're a dead woman."

And with that I hopped out into the cold night air, praying it was enough to keep my friends safe. Why did I have the terrible feeling it wasn't?

CHAPTER 23

*D*read made my foot heavy as I tried to find a place to wedge it. This was a terrible idea. After a couple attempts, I gave up. I almost felt relieved that it wasn't going to work.

With a sigh, I stepped back and looked up. Way up the dragon's nest. Thick branches and logs were stacked and woven together as far as I could see. I might have even admired the skill it required to build such a fortress of a nest if I didn't have to scale it.

"Why don't you just fly up there," said Anthony with a painfully-logical point.

Embarrassment crept up my neck. Not at his words. At the words that had echoed in my head every time I laid eyes on him now: required to breed. Mother's words. It was single-handedly the thing I didn't want to think about and the thing I couldn't stop thinking about. Him and I, together. Every second near him was a distraction.

And that would be why I hadn't thought of flying to the nest instead of climbing.

He came over. The heat of his body burned next to mine.

Instead of saying all that, I snapped and said, "Do you want to get the scale?"

He gave a shrug. I frowned. I wasn't going to make him go up there; it was bad enough to accept his help. The whole thing made me grumpy. Who could blame me? My life was being turned upside down, turn after turn.

"How do we know there's not an egg up in this one?" I asked, my stomach telling me I wasn't so sure I wanted to go up there.

"It looks pretty old." He said noncommittally. At my look, he shook his head, "Look, if there's an egg up there, just come back down. We'll find another nest."

That didn't make me feel any better. I'd never seen a dragon, but if dragons were as big as this nest, I didn't want to be anywhere near one if they thought I was out to harm their baby. Being fae dinner wasn't on my To-Do list.

My muscles tightened in anticipation, and I said, "Right, be back in two shakes of a Bakeneko."

Crouching low, I inhaled deeply and jumped into the air.

I tried not to be surprised that my wings actually lifted me up. A little thrill of accomplishment went through me. I think that was the first time I'd flown from the ground. From the steady pace that I rose with, I could tell I was doing pretty darn good. Not only that, but it was, dare I, say fun even.

So much so that I had to slow down and put myself on guard as I reached the top of the nest. I had to be careful. I didn't become a dragon snack. With a cautious eye, I came over the crest of the nest.

Two things made me happy right away. First of all, there were so many scales that they lined the whole nest in a shimmering, iridescent blanket. Second, to my relief, an egg was nowhere to be seen.

There were plenty of scales below me. My feet did a

happy jig. I'd just touch down, grab one, and be off. Maybe this could actually be over quickly, Gods forbid.

The branches weren't as cleanly laid here, so it was harder to find a place to land. They jutted out in every direction. Turns out they were looser here too. That critical piece of information I didn't know until I landed. In a flash, the wood shifted, and I went down.

Before I knew what had happened, the wood was rolling down the steep slope of the nest. I grabbed at the nearest limb. It dug into my hand as I squeezed my fingers around it in desperation to hold on while the logs continued to roll beneath by flailing feet. A snap of the twig in my hand threw my stomach into my throat right before the landslide of branches carried me in a blinding ride. Stinging lit up my arms as I struggled against the tide. It was no use, though. More logs rolled over my head as the world somersaulted. Covering my head, I miraculously made it to the bottom of the nest unharmed. Until my descent was stopped by my knees, smashing into something that was as hard as cement. It jerked me back. My teeth ground together as I struggled not to scream.

My chest heaved in and out as I took deep breaths to calm my fast-beating heart. Tenderly, I touched my knees. They were tender, but alright. Pushing limbs off of my, I stared at the sky and blinked the still spinning world back into focus. When the world stopped turning, I tried to push myself to my feet. I must have whacked my legs harder than I'd thought because they screamed in pain. I put my hand on the mound of sticks and logs to my right. My hand pushed through the first two sticks to touch something warm. I stopped, half to my feet. It wasn't just toasty. It was smooth. Shit.

Branches surrounded it. The more I looked at the mound of sticks, the larger the pit grew in my stomach. I pushed them out of the way with quick movements. The first peek of blue and green swirling into magenta confirmed my fears. No way. How could it be here? The nest was too old. Wasn't it?

"No. No, no, no." I said as I moved the sticks with larger, sweeping movements, willing my eyes to unsee what I was seeing.

By the time I'd uncovered it, fear was dancing in my veins.

"Well, shit," I said.

Shiny and beautiful, the colors danced and mingled in the sun. It was a dragon's egg.

And then I heard the number one sound you don't want to hear when you are sitting next to a dragon's egg.

A bone-shaking roar.

I looked up so quickly it was a wonder I didn't give myself whiplash. Only the light of the clear blue sky greeted me, but another earth-quaking roar confirmed that wouldn't be the case for much longer. The dragon would only come to one conclusion when she saw me here: that I was after her egg. Frantic, I pushed the sticks back over the egg. Not that it would do me much good if the mama dragon saw me. It was more likely going to be a case of roast first and ask questions last.

I looked around for somewhere to hide. It would be easy to hide under the thousands of branches, but I would get squashed.

The whoosh of wings reached me. Their deep boom vibrated my entire body. I was out of time. When I knew I was far enough off the ground that I wouldn't send any of the sticks rolling and give evidence to my presence, I lifted inches into the air. Dodging wood sticking out in every direction, flew as low and fast as I could. I'd never make it out in time. Where could I go? About halfway up, a narrow gap revealed itself. It would have to do. Alighting next to it, I crawled into it and wriggled my feet down to create a deeper crevice. It was just enough where my feet could fit. I felt like a kid in the sand playing the most dangerous game of hide and seek ever, but it would work. I'd just reached out and pulled the sticks over my head when a shadow fell over the nest. Squeezing my eyes shut, I prayed.

The temperature dropped as all of the sun's warmth disappeared. The sudden absence made my eyes fly open. Without warning, a giant head dipped in. The dim light played off its scales. If they had been eye-catchingly scattered in the nest, they looked mesmerizing on her regal brow. They highlighted the narrow bridge of her nose and rose to the fireball of black and dark violet that were her wide eyes. The only thing that broke their hypnotic spell was two long horns born from the arches of her brow. They reached up to the heavens like dark gray arrows.

She was a beautiful nightmare.

Her nostrils flared as she passed my hiding spot. Then she stopped. A chill ran down my spine as her eyes scanned the nest. I held my breath. It was stupid because it's not like it could have heard me breathing. Right? I kept it held.

I don't know if it was my strategy or dumb luck, but she kept moving to where her egg lay. I followed her with my eyes, not daring to move my head. With her muzzle, she nudged the branches out of the way. In no time, the egg was uncovered again. Since I hadn't taken my time covering it back up, I was just grateful she didn't find anything about the heap that caught her attention.

The two tones in her violet eyes searched the otherworldly surface as she moved from one side and then the other. When she was assured the egg wasn't harmed, she laid her muzzle against the opaline shell. Her dark grey lids fell closed. After a brief moment, her eyes came back open, and her long neck pulled out of the nest. Her wings reached wide, the deep blue veins stretching over the leather hide as she pushed her wings down. The nest bowed under her feet, pressing the logs uncomfortably into my sides as she pushed off.

My breath released in a whoosh, and I collapsed in my makeshift hideaway. I placed my hand on my chest as I watched as the majestic guardian beat her powerful wings on the air. Her graceful outline shot upwards. Thank, Danu. Without warning, her body twisted mid-air, and she fell back towards the nest like a bullet. Shock stole my breath.

Thirty feet away, she started to spiral. Rainbows sprayed from her iridescent body as the sun struck her hulking mass. A mass that turned faster and faster like a winding top. Then the craziest thing happened as she reached the top of the nest.

The blinding spin took on an almost liquid property, and she shifted. Giant masses of shimmering cloth flew everywhere, whipping with the velocity that it fell. As the spectacle reached the nest, it slowed. The force of the stop blew back the cloth to reveal a beautiful woman.

She dropped down onto the sticks and logs without one becoming unsettled. The cloth had become her dress, and its giant train fell in a whisper of blue velvet fabric behind her as she touched down.

Slippered feet moved with a grace I could never match as the fabric flowed over the uneven terrain. Seemingly without direction, she moved around the nest.

Then she spoke, and it froze dread into my bones.

"I can smell you." She said, her voice deeper than I would have imagined as she swung around. "Your rotten stench covers my nest."

Rotten?

There was no doubt she was looking for me. She glided

over to the spot I'd fallen earlier. Reaching into the pile of branches and logs, she tossed a dozen of them to the side. Her silky, dark gray hair swung wildly as the branches, each easily the size of my leg, flew to the side with ease. In a wave, they crashed back down, five feet away. Tumbling branches smashed into each other in a crashing thunder as they came rolling to a stop a few feet away. I flinched. Her muscles hadn't even bulged.

"You really should come out. There is no sense in playing these games. I will find you." The calmness of her face belied the rage I could hear simmering her words.

She moved towards my hiding spot with the weight of a beast but the elegance of a queen. "You are testing my patience. Reveal yourself before I find you. Maybe I won't crush your bones."

Maybe, it wasn't what I'd call an inspirational speech. Still, the dragon came closer. Her face stopped a mere foot away from where I hid. I prayed she couldn't hear my heart slamming against my rib cage. I don't know how she couldn't, though. From where I sat, it sounded like a million base drums.

Then she passed me. Her train tugged behind her. It had a scale pattern identical to what her body had been just minutes before. It even had the same iridescent undertones. I didn't have long to think about that, though, because it moved one of the sticks from my hideout, uncovering my left hand's fingers. My nostrils flared. I bit back a whimper. Her face moved back into view with a quickness that made my heart stop. She was so close. Did she know she could be looking into my eyes? How was I going to get out of this? She leaned closer to the sticks. Glitter hissed onto the branches underneath me as I clenched my jaw. Was this how it ended?

I closed my eyes in defeat.

A crash behind her made her swing around with jerky

movements that were more lizard than human. Then she was off running and leaping across the nest, getting more air than should have been possible. When she jumped into the air, I could see what had made all the noise.

Anthony stood there in all his golden glory, holding a log high in the air.

"Uh, oh. You better get this one!" He said, the crack in his voice evident even across the expanse of the nest.

I about fainted as he threw it right at the egg. Was he crazy?

The mama dragon dove to intercept the log. Her body wrapped around it as she tumbled across the nest. When she was clear of the egg, her body uncoiled like a cobra. Fire blazed in her eyes. She opened her mouth and let out a roar that grew deeper. It wasn't until then that I realized she really was growing.

"Now!" Anthony shouted as he turned and flew off the edge of the nest.

She was off running full tilt towards him. With my heart in my throat, I pushed the branches off. The shifting nest and trapped me beneath their weight. Panic clawed at my throat as I struggled to free myself. It took a few tries, but I finally was free.

I leaped into the air. Oh, right. The scale. Reaching down, I trailed my hand through the thick blanket of them lining the nest. They shimmered and danced away, slippery as I grabbed at them. After I figured out how to catch them, I stuffed handful after handful into my pockets until I crested the edge of the nest.

Landing onto the edge, I scanned the skies above and below me. All I saw was blue above and the trees far below from my high perch. The boughs swayed in the wind. That was the only motion anywhere, though. Where were they? Had she caught him and was now eating him? My limbs trembled. No way. He was fine. Fine, you hear? Then I saw them streak into view below me. My legs felt weak. Thank the Gods.

They flew around the nest, circling the stone perch the mama dragon had built her nest on. Her huge bulk made it hard for her to make the turns, so Anthony stayed ahead of her. A slow smile spread across my face. He was brilliant. My smile was wiped away as a reddish-orange sent the dragon's veins glowing. A heartbeat later, her giant maw yawned wide, and fire bellowed out in an explosion of terror. My heart stopped. The fire just skimmed the tips of Anthony's feet.

Relief made my knees weak. Thank Danu, he was safe. For now. I had to get him out of there. There was no telling when that flying blowtorch hit her mark and successfully made an Anthony-kabob. I bit the inside of my cheek. But how did I get him out of there?

Maybe it would help if I got a better view. The branches groaned underfoot as I pushed off. The key would be to stay out of sight. Since I was a bounty hunter, I was good at hiding. The best place to hide was in plain sight.

When I was up high enough to be in what I guesstimated was their blind spot, I beat my wings slower. The idea was to sort of tread air like treading water. I didn't quite have the hang of it, though, because I kept dipping and rising. But it would do. Most importantly, it let me do what I needed to: focus on the action below.

Anthony stayed just ahead of the dragon. Did he do that on purpose, or was it really as fast as he could go? That wasn't a comforting thought. The angry mama opened her mouth again. My whole body tensed, and I dropped a couple feet as my wings stopped moving transfixed on the action below. A river of fire shot out. Anthony skirted the turn just in time. The blast went wide. My wings picked back up, and I stopped my descent.

Gods, I couldn't watch it. I looked towards the heavens. My nails dug into my palms, and my feet flicked nervously. No, I had to watch. It was the only way I was going to be able to do something. I looked down again.

A shimmer caught my eye. As I fixated on the nebulous image, it sharpened. I groaned.

Scales sparkled in the sunlight as they floated down with the laziness of crepe paper. They were coming from me. I'd stuffed my pockets to make sure at least one of the thin, slippery things got back with me. Now, they were a blazing breadcrumb trail. So much for hiding. Shit. On so many levels, shit.

Anthony and the dragon weren't around the corner yet. Maybe, they hadn't noticed. Ripping off the hem of my shirt, I tore the fabric in two and stuffed the pieces in my pockets to stop the tide of runaways. It worked. The scales stopped, the last of the trail winked down like disappearing stars. Anthony flew around the corner while the last of my precious treasures floated down. It must have drawn his eye because his head cocked to the side and then looked up. My stomach twisted when I saw a smile blossom on his face. He gave me a little salute and kept flying. The dragon came around the bend as he rounded the next corner.

Excitement and eagerness collided inside me. We might just be able to do this. But what now?

Thankfully, I didn't have long to wait before my question was answered. Anthony came around the corner of the nest again, this time faster than before. I expected him to go right around the next corner as well. My eyebrows rose as he ducked between some rocks on the stone formation that held up the mammoth nest.

Was he going to hide? He couldn't. She would see him in a

heartbeat. My heart crawled into my throat as he flattened himself further into the shallow cranny. No way was she going to fall for that. I looked around wildly. There had to be something I could do to help him. I'd have to get her attention like Anthony had done for me. Fear sent my heartbeat galloping like a thousand horses as I pulled off my shoe. This should get her attention.

Her hulking mass careened around the corner. Terror gripped me as she drew closer and closer to Anthony's hiding spot. My arm shook as I pulled it back to whip my shoe at her. To my shock, she sailed past Anthony's hiding spot and rounded the corner. My mouth dropped open. Shaking my head, I stuffed my shoe back on. He had to be the luckiest fae I had ever met.

Anthony crept out of his hiding place. He was flying towards me. I couldn't believe he was still alive. My wings beat faster than I'd ever beat them before as I rushed to meet him. Tears leaked out of my eyes.

Before a dozen seconds had passed, we met each other in the air. Anthony's arms came around my midsection to catch me. The momentum spun us in the air.

My arms came around him, and he folded me into a hug. Gratitude surged through me as I hugged him back.

"You idiot," I whispered into his neck.

He laughed and dropped a kiss on my shoulder. "You can thank me when we get-"

But he never got to finish his sentence. He was cut off by a roar that split the air. This was it. My eyes dropped before I could stop them. I knew what I'd see before I saw it: the dragon coming straight for us.

Anthony and my eyes collided. We disengaged our twined bodies like we'd been burned.

"Follow me," he said, grabbing my hand and flying up into the sky.

I beat my wings, rocketing after him. Or I imagined I was. In reality, he was flying much faster than I was. And no matter how fast I beat my wings, I couldn't match his pace. I could feel glitter flow out of my pant leg. If there was no way I could keep up with Anthony, there was no way I could outfly the dragon. My stomach sank. We were going to die.

After a few more vain seconds, I finally said what we both had to be thinking, "Anthony, you have to get out of here. I'm going to get you killed."

Anthony's jaw ticked in the setting sun. "Just stop-"

"No, listen to me. For once." I put on the bravest face I had. At least I tried to. I felt it slip but continued on anyway. "The dragon is gaining on us faster, and it's because of me. I can't fly fast enough."

He looked down. From the anguish that spread over his features, I could tell he knew I spoke the truth.

"Look, I'll meet up with you somewhere. I'll figure a way out of this like I always do." I knew it was a lie even as I said it, but I gave him a smile to show him it was ok.

Topaz eyes searched mine even as we continued our ascent. He knew it was a lie too. His Adam's apple worked in his slender throat.

When he spoke, his words were angry as he forced them out, "I'd rather die first."

I didn't blame him for being angry. These moments weren't full of pretty poetry of acceptance, like the movies made you believe. They were rank with anger and overflowing with unfairness.

As if to put weight to his words, he pulled me back in for a hug.

"What are you doing? Now's not the time." I shouted, pushing away.

"Just hold on. I think we're high enough up," Anthony

said, then he wrapped his arms around me. "Stop beating your wings."

I looked at him, fear and doubt mixing up my insides.

He looked me in the eyes, love, and sincerity shining bright. "Trust me."

Did I trust him? I did. Finally, after all these years, I trusted him. Funny how it took death to make you realize something like that.

Even still, I couldn't let him see into my heart, so I said, "Trust you to get us killed. But ok."

And then I stopped beating my wings.

He wrapped his wings around me, and then we dropped like a sack of rocks. Wind rushed around us, snatching my hair and hair in its reedy fingers. Around and between us, it whistled. I don't know what was more terrifying, that or the dragon below.

As if it knew I was thinking about it, the dragon roared. It was so close I could feel the reverberations in my bones. Its roar got louder and louder as we dropped, and I realized it wasn't the dragon getting louder but our proximity to it. I wedged my fingers into my pants' pocket and fingered the scales as I prayed that we would make it out of here alive. As if to mock me, the roar rose to deafening levels. The sadness of defeat tore through me as I felt heat on my heels. The roar grew to a decibel that rang my ears.

And then there was nothing.

CHAPTER 24

*W*ere we actually alive? Stiffness screamed from my joints as I rolled my shoulders. Yeah, we had to be alive. I was in too much pain to be dead.

Turns out, we were back on my living room floor.

Anthony's arms reflexively pulled me closer as he groaned between his gasps for breath. It was a groan of pain, but the press of his front against mine had me thinking of how all man he was.

His teeth ground against the pain. Then he laughed and said, "What would you do without me?"

"I could only imagine the things." I teased back, smacking his solid chest.

He pulled my head into his chest. "That should have been a lot easier than it was."

Hints of sandalwood tickled my nose. I breathed it in deep; it was a scent that was all Anthony.

"I think you like this life-or-death stuff." I teased, my breath hot against his chiseled chest.

"Can you blame me? It *does* get me naked with you." He teased back as he trailed his fingers up my arm.

Goosebumps of anticipation broke out along my arms. I wanted him to touch me. I wanted it with a gut-clenching need. I didn't know if it was because of what we had just gone through or if it was because of how I felt about him.

"Well, we only have one more ingredient left, so I'm afraid your chances are running out." I meant it to be teasing, but there was too much truth about us in there.

Our chances *were* running out. We had become just as close in our little adventures as we had been before when we were best friends. The fun. The trust. It was all there.

But it was different this time.

He loved me. I could feel it in the way he spoke to me. I could feel it in the way he watched over me. I could feel it in the way he was holding me now.

From the way his body stilled, I could tell he knew what I was thinking.

There was no quick joke or witty retort. Anthony seemed at a loss for words as he tilted my head up. His eyes searched mine, questioning. I didn't know how to answer the questions there. Did I love him? Yes, but was it like that? From the excitement that zinged through my veins, I was attracted to him. There was no question there. Then I was out of time. He closed the distance between us. He kissed me.

The way his lips touched on mine almost broke my heart. I could feel his ache. It was the ache of decades of pent-up, unmet desires. His plump lips trembled as they touched mine, soft and seeking. His grip was like a vise on my bicep was a contradiction. There was tentativeness to it like he didn't know if I would return his kiss. He might as well have torn out my heart and stomped on it.

Then he deepened the kiss. It tasted of loss and pulled at the strings of my heart. He kissed me like he was losing me.

With everything that had happened, with everything that was coming, I didn't know if I should want this. However, I knew one thing without a doubt: I wouldn't turn Anthony away this time. I needed to make the pain go away.

His pain from my loss. My pain from the choice I had to make. All of it. We were both hurting. If I could make it go away, how could that be bad?

So I stopped thinking and kissed him back.

That was all the encouragement he needed. He reached his hands up to cradle my head as his lips slanted over mine. My hands started to shake as they found the way to his face. Was this really happening? After all these years?

His hands trailed down my body. My breath hitched against his lips.

I whimpered against his lips when his palms covered my hard nipples.

Frissons of excitement shot through me. Then a knock sounded. It was coming from the front door, ten feet away.

Anthony heard the knock, too, because, between kisses, he said, "No."

It was hard to argue with his hands memorizing the curves of my body. His wings came around me. Their whisper warned me of their presence long before they tickled my back.

I didn't have time to think beyond that because every nerve held my attention as he made his way down my chest. When his lips clamped around my nipple, I closed my eyes in bliss.

Soft air teased the back of my neck seconds before I felt the caress of sand on my legs. Its cushiony softness moved under my wings that were trapped underneath us like the world's softest bed. Then the gentle crashing of waves tickled my toes.

The unmistakable call of a seagull above made me smile against his lips. "You didn't."

Breaking the seal of our lips, he looked down into my

eyes. There was an intensity there I didn't often see in Anthony's face.

His trailed tender fingers down my body. "Cy, never in my wildest dreams did I imagine you would actually be in my arms. I'm not letting anything ruin this moment."

"But *this* isn't what you want," I said, trying to warn him that I couldn't give him everything he needed as my focus warred with his hand making its way down my body.

He wanted more than a fling. A commitment was what he wanted. I knew it as surely as if he'd told me a hundred times, and in some ways, he had. But I couldn't give that to him. There was no future for us. How could there be when I was leaving?

Emotions chased themselves across his face before the stubborn set of his chin lifted. "Stop fighting, and just feel. Understand how I feel about you."

The intensity in his voice carried a heat that far surpassed the sun above.

There were so many reasons this shouldn't happen. "But-"

My words stopped when his hand moved lower. He cupped me. I couldn't stop writhing my hips against the warmth of it. Sweet Danu, did I want this. I needed it.

"Shhhh…just feel…" he said.

And then he slipped his finger inside me—forbidden perfection.

Sensations danced through my body. "Anthony?"

He shouldn't continue, but I didn't want him to not. And I was beginning to forget why. He didn't stop his sweet assault, but he moved up to answer my unspoken question with his lips. And I let him. I let him show me. Show me the wonder only he could show me.

His lips left mine, and he kissed his way down my body.

My back arched at the attention he gave my breasts. I murmured my approval as he teased and caressed them.

When he moved lower, though, anticipation shot through me. He left my body, and I raised my head. I wanted to see what he was doing. When he slipped his arms under my legs and lifted them, my eyes went wide. Was he really going to?

I ground my teeth into my bottom lips as he positioned his face below me. With a dark look in his eyes, his lips were on me. I dropped back with a guttural moan. Sparks danced up my body as his mouth devoured me. Goosebumps flared across my body in a wave of pleasure.

His fingers replaced his tongue, and he brought that incredible tongue up to swirl around the peak of my intensity. I cried out. He curled his fingers inside me as he went in and out. It was like a million wishes that I'd never know I'd had being granted at once.

My eyes fluttered, strobing the blue of the sky with the blackness that threatened to consume me. It was too much. I brought my hands down to pull him up. A long flick of his tongue sent them into his hair instead. More of those same licks had me pushing him into me. I was so close. So...

And then the world exploded in a spin of stars and relief that shook my body.

Glitter pooled under us at my release. I knew it did because he was covered in glitter when he came back up to me. The blue glitter mixed in with the purple showed me just how much this meant to him. My heart swelled in my chest as I admired it gleaming and winking on his shoulders like diamonds in the sunlight.

"I'm a big boy, Cy. I know what's at risk." He came between me and said, "You just don't realize I'd risk it all for you. I was stupid enough not to do it before. I won't make the same mistake again. There is no other person in the world like you."

His words touched my heart. They were beautiful. He leaned over me to cradle my head, the smooth muscles of his abs pressing into my stomach.

His lips pursed as his eyes seared me with their intensity, "Listen, if you say we can't be together, I promise I won't ask again. But don't say it now...I have to have you right now. I need you."

I stared into the seriousness of his expression. He meant what he said. If I wanted, he would just leave. He would let me break his heart. But did I break it now or later? The sun haloed around him. Was I going to break his heart? I didn't know. I felt like I should say something to tell him what was in my heart, but he already knew. If he hadn't, he'd have never said what he did. So I didn't know what to say. I settled on saying nothing, just stared at him, knowing full well the desire to share this moment with him was clear in my eyes.

And then there was nothing to say as he pushed into me. It was a slide of heat that built a fire inside me. Our bodies fit together like they were made to be there as we spoke all the words of love that never left our lips. Tears of overwhelmed gratitude pricked my eyes when he picked up the pace. I laced my hands around his neck and held tight as he rode me into the stars.

CHAPTER 25

The smell of fresh baked bread floated to where I walked a path in the Courtyard. Unable to keep still, I had come down here to think. Others were just as occupied, but I was willing to bet they weren't thinking of the fact that they'd slept with their best friend. Ok, former best friend, if I was being honest. No, the Feast of Midsummer Night was on their minds. It was just a few hours away. And the excitement zipped through the air. Everyone was running around making final preparations. I couldn't be at my apartment, though. It reminded me too much of Anthony. And I needed my head free to think, so here I paced, weaving in and out of the chaos. It was appropriate, considering how I felt at the moment. My head was pinging between two thoughts. The first one being that I had only one more ingredient to get before it was go-time on one of the biggest risks I'd ever taken. The second being that I'd slept with Anthony. It had been beyond my wildest dreams. Even now, I could feel his mouth devouring me. Hell, just thinking about it made me squirm. I kicked a rock out of my path. It skipped through the grass like a bounding puppy. I wish I could feel that way.

Who was I to sleep with Anthony like that? Granted, I wasn't with Sven anymore. Not that it meant anything where he was concerned, I couldn't be with him. Thinking of him, my heart squeezed like it was held tight in a fist. I shifted my shoulders to make the feeling go away and ignored it. It was no small feat. I had to do it, though. He was out of the picture at this point. No sense reliving the pain. Now, if I could just convince that stubborn thing in my chest.

At the thought of Sven, I felt him next to me. It was beginning to be such a frequent episode that it didn't come as a surprise this time. It was different this time when he felt my thoughts. His anger flared. Oh shit. The last thing I needed when sorting through my own feelings was to work through his too. I gave him a metaphysical push. It took a second, but I felt him leave. The pounding of my heartbeat said that wouldn't be the last time I heard from him. After my heart quieted, it dawned on me that it hadn't been as hard to do this time. Maybe, this was getting easier. Easier. That was rich.

Anthony was an entirely different story. Despite our incredible time together, I didn't think I loved him. But he was very much in my life. Not to mention he was vibrant, kind, courageous…hell, I could give him a dozen adjectives. Add in Avalynn, and even, I hated to admit it Iris, and I was starting to wonder if leaving was worth the risk of leaving. Especially when you considered that my people were going to need someone to look to if vampires ever showed up.

But what about the threat to the lives of the people I loved? Could I just ignore that? No, I couldn't. It was my loved one's lives we were talking about. I couldn't let my life be dictated for me, though. I'd have to find whoever was behind the threats if I stayed. If I stayed. Was I really considering living in Knockaine? In the very place that ridiculed everything, I stood for?

My steps lengthened as I took another turn around the Courtyard. I'm sure people were going to start wondering why I was pacing, but I couldn't bring myself to care. I needed to figure this out. I was running out of time. By Mother's celebration tonight, I needed to either step up or step away.

Could I leave? After all, Anthony and I had gone through to get the ingredients, how could I not? We'd risked our lives. And for what? Because I needed to leave with a fevered intensity that I felt in every bone, every second I was here? Yes, there was that. But if Anthony was willing to risk it all for me to be happy, shouldn't I be willing to do the same for him?

If that meant staying here, I just didn't know the answer to that. A line of children parading decorations across the grassy expanse rerouted my path sooner than I'd expected.

I turned just in time to see Harmon. His beefy shoulders strode from between the broad steps of The Tearmann and squat round building next to it, the Panem Coquere. He looked around. That wasn't suspicious at all. When his gaze fell on me, his expression grew heavy with hatred. Clearly, he'd not gotten over our little bout in the combat circle. I bounced on my toes. I suppose if we were going to have it out now, this was a good time to do it. There was nothing like your fist against someone else's flesh to let out some aggression. And I had plenty of that borne of frustration.

But he did something that surprised me. He turned and walked away. I watched him pass a young fae woman who stood just inside the open-air entry, shoving fresh loaves of bread as big as my forearm into baskets. She didn't spare him a glance, and neither did he as he rounded the corner and went...the gods only knew where.

Ok. That was odd. My gaze swung back to where Harmon had come from. The narrow passage was used for trash. He didn't work at the Panem Coquere, did he?

What had he been doing between those buildings? People didn't just hang out in what amounted to an alley. I went to look in there when four men carrying a giant ornament passed in front of me. They were shouting instructions at each other while sweat tracked down their faces.

I wanted to see what was in the alley before Harmon got too far away. Standing on my tiptoes, I tried to put my eyes on him. The monstrosity of a decoration blocked my path, though. I even tried to the left and right to look around it, but still nothing. When the ornament slipped out of one of the handler's grasp, I could feel my patience snap like a rubber band. It shook the ground as it fell amid curses and shouts.

I stormed around them only to be met by that same line of children. They danced the same decorations around and above their heads. Of course, that was the kind of help you typically got from young kids. They started helping, but eventually, everything dissolved into a mini-riot.

When I'd finally made my way through them, I strode over to the young aid, still shoving bread into an impressive number of growing baskets. Only when I was almost standing on her toes did her arms stop their work. With a heavy sigh, she didn't look up.

Instead, she said by way of greeting, "I am very busy."

She was a charmer, wasn't she? I gave her purple hair, so similar to my own, jutting out of her spotless, slouched white hat a once over.

I kept my eyes on the alley as I said with as much regalness as I could conjure up. "I'm sorry to bother you. I'm Princess Cy."

The act reminded me of the years I'd been forced to be

something I wasn't, and I itched to drop the charade. I needed answers, though, and she was clearly serious about her job. Considering the Grand Panetier had power envy over the Royal Chef, I knew titles would mean something to her.

It worked because her hand stopped in mid-stuff. "Your Majesty. We all look forward to honoring you at tonight's celebration."

"I'm merely a token mention in my Mother's Party." The idea sat like rotten fish in my gut, and I wanted to move past it as quickly as possible. "What's your name?"

"Tessa," said with a curtsy then added, "You're not a token. You're the Princess."

It was a proper curtsy, and the sick feeling in my gut intensified, sending my insides roiling.

"Tessa, it's a pleasure to meet you. The man with the navy hair and…" cattlelike, barbaric, unnatural "large shoulders that walked through here just a moment ago, do you know him?"

Her ears tipped pink. "I am sorry, your Majesty. He doesn't sound familiar, but I didn't see him."

I nodded. Something told me even if she had seen him, she wouldn't know who he was.

"That's ok. Thank you for your time." I said, turning to leave.

"Is the Heir Anointed as happy to see you as the rest of us are?" She asked, a sly look coming across her face.

Who in the hell was that? I stopped and turned.

"Excuse me? Who?" I asked, not wanting to waste precious time, but unable to help myself.

"You know, the Heir Anointed?" When it was clear I didn't know what she was talking about, her face flamed. "You know, the girl who the Queen selected to take your place when you left the Mound."

Shock froze me. "My...my mother was going to have someone take my place?"

I almost couldn't get the words out, they hurt so badly. Sure, I'd told Mother when I left that I was never coming back. That had been spoken out of anger more than anything, though."

"I'm sorry, Princess. I thought you knew. I never would have been as insensitive..." her words rattled on, but I'd stopped listening

My attention, torn as a round, fae with threadbare, windswept hair stopped at the mouth of the alley.

He stooped over his large belly to pick up a shiny, silver piece. With a frown, he held it up to the light and turned it over in hand. Was it something Harmon had dropped?

"...sometimes my mouth runs away with me. My grandmama always said..."

The man deposited the piece in the pocket of his coat and patted it. On unsteady feet, he toddled into the crowded Courtyard. Oh, no. I wasn't going to lose another clue.

"It's fine. Really." I said. So Mother cared so little for me that she wanted to replace me. Of course it was fine. Since when did I have control of my own future anyway? Keeping my thoughts to myself, I added. "Please excuse me."

With a wide step to dash out, my foot connected with a basket of bread sending loaves sailing into the air. For the love of the gods, could anything go right? Picking up my pace, I sprinted to the man who was fast getting away. I grabbed the tweed of his jacket. Surprise widened his eyes as he turned around.

"Pardon me, but I believe you picked up something of mine. I'm going to need that back." The lie escaped my lips with more ease than made me comfortable.

He hesitated at my words and then gave a tight smile. "Of course, Princess." He fished into his pocket then placed the object into my outstretched hand. "My apologies. If I would have known it was yours, I would never have taken it."

Eagerly, I looked at what he'd given to me. Sunlight glinted off the small silver and diamond stud earring.

"Think nothing of it." I said, hiding my disappointment as I bid him good day.

Could it be a more generic earring? Maybe there was something else that would help in the alley. When I got 15 steps into the passageway, my mouth went dry, and what I saw made me run. I ran between the buildings as fast as my legs could carry me, ice in my veins.

Anthony was slumped over, next to some garbage cans. Danu, please let him be alive. Hands trembling, I threw my hand in front of his lips. Hot breath hit the back of my hand. Thank Danu, he was alive.

"Anthony?" I slapped his face with little pats. They became increasingly harder when he didn't respond. "Anthony, answer me!"

I think I must have slapped too hard on that last tap because his lids fluttered. He moaned. I choked back a sob of gratitude and wrapped my arms around him, ducking my head against his cheek. I don't think I was ever so grateful to hear a moan of pain in my life.

When I didn't let go of him after a second, he lifted his hand and wrapped it around my bicep. He gave it a little pat. The weakness of the pat made me raise my head.

"Where are you hurt?" I asked, running my hands up and down him.

He shook his head and then grimaced. "My head."

"Tor Mór," I moved my fingers across his skull. Sure enough, a bump was starting to form at the back of his head. "We need to get you to a healer."

I started to help him up. He shook his head.

Pushing at my arm, he said, "No, it's going to hit Cecht's radar."

Why did that even have to be a thought? Was I selfish enough to put my friend's life in jeopardy just because I might get in trouble? I gritted my teeth. No, I wasn't.

"I don't give a damn about that. I care about you," I said. Anger roiled in my gut. I had to do something.

"Look, this is my decision. Not yours. And don't even think about trying to guilt me into going to the Department of Truth. They'd require a visit to the healers. I refuse to stop when we are so close and have all of our work for nothing."

Of course, he was right. As the Royal Physician, the Grand Duke was informed of all healer activities that seemed out of normal. Since we'd already been to the healers, I didn't want to chance this being flagged as one of those incidents. One visit we could explain away, two we could not. My stomach roiled. I clenched and unclenched my fists. I felt so useless.

He must have sensed my frustration because he ground out, "I'll live, but I won't guarantee the same thing for whoever did this to me if I find them."

The look was so at odds on his usually easy-going features that I had to blink twice just to process it. A shiver danced down my spine at his intensity. I couldn't say I blamed him. It wasn't every day someone tried to kill you. And judging from the size of the knot on his head, his attacker's intent was clear.

"Let me guess, you didn't see who attacked you either?" I asked, bitterness riling like bile in my throat.

"No, I was passing by when I heard my name, so I went to check it out...I don't think I'll be making that mistake again." He said, rubbing the knot.

"I think it was Harmon." The words came out of my mouth in a tumble.

I didn't like to point fingers without having all of the facts, but I couldn't stop myself.

He lowered his hand, slowly; his eyes never left my face. "The Muay Thai champion? Why would he attack me?"

"Because he can't stand that I made a fool of him, and he wants me gone." My fingers ached like my heart when I spread them wide to get him to see my point.

I was sick of seeing my friends get hurt. I'd never felt so powerless.

"You did trounce him pretty bad," he admitted with a sigh.

"Exactly." My mouth fell into a grim line.

"Still, the voice...was it him?" He chewed on his cheek, deep in thought, and shook a dazed expression from his eyes. "Yeah, I guess it could have been."

I exhaled, the sound loud in the small space. "Well... regardless, I guess it's just as well that I'm leaving. I can't stand to see you hurt."

I could tell the thought of me going didn't bring him any peace. Honestly, it didn't comfort me either. I didn't like the idea of leaving him here by himself. And it was coming quicker than I could put into words. Because we only had one ingredient left. And demons were just as likely to kill you like a vengeful faerie.

CHAPTER 26

I was in Hell.

No, literally.

I'd never been here, and frankly, it was as bad as they said it was.

"Don't you dare open that door," I said, pointing to the rusted knob Anthony currently had his hand on.

The knob's aged crevices reached to me. Beckoning, crying of the dark horrors inside.

Anthony sighed.

"This is such a bad idea," I said.

I said it to underscore my point, but I had the feeling it came out in more of a scared-Kindergartener voice.

Anthony dropped his head. "Look. Do you want to leave or not? Because we're never going to get a demon hoof if we don't look for a demon."

I wanted to be grateful things hadn't become weird between us since what had happened, but I was too busy trying to keep my stomach from doing a jig. One did not stroll calmly around Hell and not think of all of the soul-damning things we were possibly subjecting ourselves to. I was torn. On the one hand, I wanted to get the hoof. On the other hand, I didn't want to move from this spot. To Anthony's point: a Demon foot wasn't going to be just lying around. They didn't shed like scales.

"I can't believe you are crazy enough to do this," I said to him as I stared dejectedly at the door.

"I can't believe you were crazy enough to want to do this *alone*," he said with a flat look.

I pressed my mouth together. I had to. Otherwise, the words I'd said a dozen times already would come out- again: At least I'd be only about to condemn myself to an eternity of hellfire, not anyone else.

Instead, I pointed at the door in question, "Ok, ok. Just not…that one."

Granted, it looked like all of the others in the infinite hall we stood in. I couldn't put my finger on it, but every hair on my skin crawled when I thought of going through that door. I didn't care if it was unreasonable.

A rueful smile crooked his mouth as he shook his head. No doubt, he thought we wouldn't find anything less soul-ripping in the next room. He was probably right, but to my relief, he let go of the handle.

He crossed the hall. His palm reflected on the shiny gold handle just before he swung it open. I closed my eyes against what was inside. For a few heartbeats, I listened. No screaming of tortured souls. No rattling of chains. No calling for my blood. I peeled each eyelid open one at a time. A huge room, as long as it was tall, stood empty before us.

"See? Not too bad." Anthony's voice held a note of relieved laughter.

Fear beat my heart in a staccato. For now, it wasn't too bad. I'm sure rooms in Hell didn't stay empty long. Just how long before something came after us? My boot crossed the threshold of the room. I stopped. Nothing. Taking two more steps in, I turned. The room was sheer walls of stone. It had all the charm of a 500-year-old crypt. I'll give it to him, though. It seemed oddly empty.

I turned back to him and shrugged. "I guess, you're-"

That's all I got out, though, because, in the next instant, I was lifted into the air by a steel grip.

"Cy!" Anthony screamed from the door.

His feet pounded on the cement. He was still too far away to help me, though.

I swallowed the lump in my throat. It was go-time. Careening my head, I managed to snag a look at his legs. Thick soled, black boots adorned his feet. Dagda be damned, it wasn't a demon. It looked like my new plan was to get out of here as fast as humanly possible. Preferably before I died, for real. Flexing my stomach muscles, I swung my legs up. It wasn't enough. All I succeeded in doing was catching a glimpse of an obviously male body, encased in black and the muscular arms they were attached to. Again I swung my lower body. This time a jaw-jarring thud didn't phase him.

We dipped lower, and when we reached the corner, he let me go. Panic clawed at my throat. What was he doing? My feet hit the cement, but it was from too high. I dropped. Somehow, I managed to tuck my shoulder and roll. My shoulder hit the dirty concrete. Hard. The world wheeled as I rolled. Momentum spun me with such force that I only stopped when I hit the wall with a painful crack.

My body screamed in pain. Get up. Not knowing what was coming next, I pushed myself to my throbbed. I gritted past the throbbing pain and turned away from the wall, seeking out Anthony. He was running towards me. What was he doing? We needed to get out of here. There weren't any demons.

I started to run towards him. "Get-"

My attention was taken away as I saw a dark shape come

from above. I ducked but not in time. Rough hands grabbed me. My shirt came up to cut off my air, my own shirt becoming my death. I clawed at it, desperate to get air. This time he didn't throw me, but came with me, flattening against the wall.

The man plucked my wrists with ease. Giant black wings like an angel came up as he wedged himself onto me. Not man, angel. Was he a fallen angel? Considering how he was wedged against me, I couldn't care if he was a fallen angel or Godzilla. I wasn't about to go down like this.

I twisted and bucked against his hold. He didn't release me, but the struggles did make him tip his head down to really look at me. I'd clearly struck his curiosity. From the centuries that oozed from him, I'm sure it wasn't an occurrence that happened often. He clearly didn't expect a faerie to be so strong. A fat lot of good, my enhanced strength was doing.

Where was Anthony anyway?

His body pressed against mine to hold me down. A viselike grip let up on my one wrists in an attempt to secure the other to a set of cuffs rusted to the wall. Now, it was my chance. I wrenched my hand free and slammed my fist into all of the tender parts I could find while jerking forward. I could free myself.

All that succeeded in doing was bruising my ribs. The cold metal inevitably latched down onto my wrists. I heard scuffling behind me as the angel made quick work of my other wrist. That didn't stop me from arching my back to kick at him.

His lips cocked in a smirk. He was laughing. At me. At my helplessness. Fury boiled my blood. I'd die before I sit by and let that happen.

I heaved myself forward. The restraints jerked me back. Bracing my arms and shoulders against the wall, I lashed out at the angel with my foot. He backed away, laughter rocking his shoulders. What I wouldn't give for just one of those kicks to knock some of the cockiness off his face.

That was as far as the thought got though, because he backed out of the way, opening up my line of sight. What I saw shot fear into my toes. Half a dozen vampires had lined up. Their backs faced me because their attention was on something in front of them.

Anthony, barely visible from between their tight-knit bodies, paced. His mouth an uncompromising line as he pushed into the air, his wings beating. Elation rose in my chest. He was going to fly over them.

But then a dark figure dropped down from the ceiling. Wings, as black as night, were raised up so he could drop cleanly. His feet connected with Anthony, and Anthony dropped.

"Leave him alone!" I screamed, flexing against the bonds.

It echoed in the chamber. The dark head came up to regard me. Then, in a miracle, he flew away.

"No way, little fae. This is between you and us. You can't just fly away. You have to stay and play." One of the vampires taunted, turning her bronze head at a queer angle.

Power corded Anthony's thighs as he stood up. "This isn't a game. Cy is mine."

The tall vampire in the center, cloaked in a black trench coat, stepped forward, his voice shrill as he said in a mocking voice, "Oh, I think it is. And we very much want to play. Winner keeps her."

I dropped my head to my chest. No longer was I worried for me. In every room, we'd noticed that one of our deepest fears had manifested. The fact that they weren't talking to me said it wasn't mine. Apparently, this one was Anthony's. If anything they were saying was to go by, it had to do with his fear of not being able to save me. Particularly from vampires. Just great.

The realization pulled at my heart because of the whole thing with Sven. How hard it must be for Anthony that I had gotten mixed up with Sven. I was pulled out of the bog of my guilt by Anthony's growl.

"Like hell, is she staying here with you bloodsuckers." He spat.

I could practically hear the lead vampire smile. "Precisely."

There was a deadly look in Anthony's eyes. When he wrapped his wings around himself, it was my turn to smile. I deserved whatever happened to me, but him... I just wanted him safe.

Dust from the floor spun in the air, and then he disappeared in a pop of blue sparkles. Their glorious shimmer looked out of place in the aged room, very Miss. Havisham.

The vampires looked around, confusion etched on their faces. An ache started in my chest. Anthony was safe. What now?

I didn't have to wait long for the answer. Seconds later, he popped in front of me. Joy burst in my heart at seeing every detail of his beautiful, tanned face.

It was sobering when he eyed my restraint, though. Seconds later, we weren't alone.

The head vampire snatched Anthony's elbows and ratcheted them up behind him. Gritting his teeth, he screamed. That scream echoed inside me as the black vampire came up and bent over my neck.

Her breath was hot against my nape. The short hairs there stood on end.

"Mmmmm...it's been a long time since I've had a faerie. I wonder what power I'll have after I drain all of that delicious blood. Fist of fire? Spears of Ice?" She inhaled deep and gave a lustful sigh. "I've been waiting for this for a century."

She craned her neck over mine. The long points of her fangs pricked my skin.

I did the only thing I could think of, I closed my eyes and prayed. Danu, please save us. Free us from this Hell. Please. Help us. We need you.

And then the pricks were gone. Soon after, the pressure that pushed at my wrists was gone. Confused, I flexed my hands, testing. Nothing held them. I opened my eyes in disbelief.

Anthony's eyes, wide with disbelief, looked around. I did the same. Shock rippled through my body when I saw we were utterly alone. Had my prayer done that? Could prayers work in Hell?

Anthony's lips worked like he didn't want to ask the question, but he finally did. "Where did they go?"

The deep base of a roar echoed across the stone.

Then the walls started to crumble in on themselves.

I leapt to my feet. Grabbing Anthony's hand, I ran to the door. I half drug him with me for a few steps, but then he was on his feet, running with me, which was helpful because the floor started to fall away. I screamed through my teeth. In panic, fear, determination. A burst of energy coursed through my body.

I ran even faster, Anthony at my heels. The ground from the backs of our feet came loose. I could feel it fall away as I took my last leap.

CHAPTER 27

*A*nthony and I rolled through the door in a synchronized dance as the rest of the ground crumbled away. I swallowed a hysterical laugh. If I hadn't been so frazzled, I would have stood up and done a gymnast pose.

I pressed my eyes closed, my breath coming in burning gasps.

When I felt less like a steam engine, I rolled onto my stomach and stared into the pit that was now the room. Black nothingness went on as far as I could see. I sent another prayer of thanks to Danu. Anthony put a hand down to help me up. Saying a quick amen, I took it.

When I was standing, he pulled me in for a bear hug. "Gods, Cy. Are you ok?"

I laughed, the burst of air blowing my hair out of my face. "I could ask you the same thing."

A hard squeeze was his response. I squeezed him back, feeling his sinewy muscles under my palms.

He pulled away to look at me. "We don't have to do this."

As much as I hated to admit it, he was right. We didn't

have to do this. I could call the whole thing off, and we could be back at Knockaine in the blink of an eye.

If I did that, though, I'd be right back under Mother's increasingly insane thumb. Right back to not fitting in. Right back to not belonging.

My heart squeezed. I couldn't go back to that life; I had to follow my own path. I would just as soon lose my mind in Hell right now rather than live a lifetime in another hell.

It didn't make sense to have Anthony go through this with me, though. This was my journey.

I pulled out of his grasp and said, "I want to keep going."

He thinned his lips in hesitant understanding before he started to nod.

I interrupted him with a hand on his chest. "It isn't fair to ask you to do this with me, though. I want you to stay in the hall for the next one. If I'm not out in a reasonable time,…" I swallowed, not wanting to think about it, and said, "Just go home."

Hurt and anger warred with each other on his face. "Not a chance. I'm going with you."

"No, it isn't fair to you. Besides, I think my praying is what saved us. I'll do that again. The Gods are with me. I'll be fine." I tried to make it sound convincing even though I wasn't entirely sure that was what just had happened.

"I'm not doing it." He said, his eyes narrowing in anger.

"Listen, I'm serious-"

His fist slammed into the wall.

A hollow echo pulsed down the corridor as he said, "Just drop it, ok? I'm not letting you down. Not again."

Again? That made me stop. He was talking about his betrayal. Inside I turned into a bowl of sticky, peanut-buttery goo. What made it worse was I didn't feel any of the anger I had before. Our time together had made me realize there was more to life than past mistakes. It seemed like he would live with regret forever, though.

How did I explain he didn't have to. "Listen, Anthony. It wasn't your fault. It wasn't fair of me to-"

He held up a hand, and I trailed off. I bit my lip. Maybe, I'd never understood. If I was honest with myself, it wasn't my decision how he moved forward. All I knew was that if I could do anything to make that easier, I would. So I nodded my acceptance. Of where we were. Of who he was.

What I didn't anticipate was his reaction to it. His lips were on mine in a heartbeat. I closed my eyes, reveling in the warmth of his kiss. It swirled memories through my body as his lips slipped over mine. It wasn't a happy kiss. The way his lips tightened at the end spoke of sadness and pride. I understood the sadness. The sad finality of what it would mean after I took the potion. The sadness of leaving.

His eyes searched mine, saying so much. But none of it passed his lips. Did it matter if he spoke the words out loud, though? I already knew what they were.

Instead of saying what I knew he wanted to, he held his arms wide and said instead, "Ok, which one?"

I didn't know whether to be proud or heartbroken for him at his ability to move on.

I picked up his cue and moved on too. Well, I tried to.

I searched the identical doors in front of us. Nothing. I don't know what I was waiting for. Maybe unicorns and rainbows to spray out one of the doors? That was pretty unlikely unless they were demonic unicorns with rainbow laser beams. I could tell Anthony sensed my hesitancy.

"We have to keep going. A demon isn't just going to fall into your arms." He prodded with a smile that didn't reach his eyes.

The air changed above me. A black hole yawned open in

the ceiling. My heart dropped. Swirling black clouds made it impossible to see through.

This couldn't be good.

Was there a speck of gold in the swirling blackness? I tilted my head to get a better look. No, my mind wasn't messing me. It was. And it was growing. I gaped in shock as it became...of all things, a demon. Without a sound, it fell from the hole. Surprise jerked my arms up.

The demon landed in them with the force of a small linebacker. The weight wrenched a groan from me. The impact shot spikes of pain through my arms.

She smiled at me in her little bikini that screamed Princess Leia. All I could do was stand in shock and blink at her. The smoothness of her skin ended at the fur on her knees. Knees that I cradled. My eyes shot down the length of her body. Dainty, cloven feet kicked merrily in the air. I reached out to them, uncertain I was seeing them right. A shift of her shoulders brought my eyes back. The black of her eyes smiled up at me in a face of pure gold. Pure, flawless gold. It seemed to glow from her, around her. I'd never seen a demon in person before, just in pictures. She was mesmerizing.

Wait, were we sinking? It took me a second to realize it wasn't just vertigo messing with my head as I looked around. We were currently about halfway through the floorboards.

I dropped her. She fell with a little eeep, followed by an echoey laugh.

"Hey, what the hell?" I said as I looked around.

There was a golden circle around us that flared up to form a barrier of shimmering, pulsing light. Through the undulating strains of light, I could just make out Anthony. Shock dropped my stomach. Another demon had Anthony's face pressed to the ground, his goat-foot rooted into his upper back.

"Anthony!" I screamed as I clawed at the now shoulder-high floor in an attempt to pull myself up.

But I was sinking too fast; my fingertips could barely touch the top of the floor anymore.

And then they were gone.

The sensation of sinking continued as tears streamed down my face. I sank to my knees. My fault. This was all my fault.

I dropped my head into my hands. Silent sobs wracked my body, burning tears down my cheeks. The tears wound around my wrists as they continued to fall.

"Such a beautiful sight," said a dark voice that seemed to fill the room.

As soon as I heard the voice, I felt a tug. The tug came from inside me, but it was a physical thing, so powerful. My tears dried in an instant. Already knowing who I was going to see, but not knowing how I knew.

I looked up.

The Devil. He was simultaneously what I thought he would be and not what I thought he would be at the same time. His red skin, viewable through his open dress shirt, looked like leather. His black hair was the very definition of bed head. In fact, from his casually disheveled appearance to the amused look on his face, you could have mistaken him for a playboy. If it weren't for two massive horns jutting from his temples anyway.

He sat on a high wingback chair. His foot rested casually on the knee of his black trousers. His fingertips idly caressed a skull he held in his lap. Even though he lounged in the chair, it was deceptive. I could tell he was anything but laid back. There was an intensity that radiated from him that made me want to run screaming.

"Your sorrow touches me. Sadness. Fear. It's the soul's

way of reaching out. I feel your sweet soul calling for me." His eyes closed.

From the expression on his face, I could almost see him tasting my soul and rolling it around in his mouth like a fine wine. It was erotic, intoxicating.

I wanted to shut my eyes, cover my ears, and scream for him to stop. Why? Not because he was alluring, beckoning me. Mostly because he was right. What was he right about? Everything. I'd spent a lifetime pretending to be someone I wasn't. I didn't fit in at the Court. It was as obvious as a full moon on a clear summer night. And now, I was scared out of my wits because Danu wanted me to lead the fae. How could I lead a people I didn't even belong with?

He picked up a strand of my hair and flipped it over his fingers. The firelight from the torches lining the wall danced off the purple strands.

"But I can make you feel better, little faerie. Can't I, my pets?" He threw the question over his shoulder.

That's when I noticed we weren't alone. Men and women alike were draped and perched on couches placed at odd angles in the room. Their occupants made the Devil appear almost tame. A man without a shirt on who made up for it by adorning miles of shiny leather that inexplicably made up his pants had a full mane that sprouted like a horse's tail down his head. His face had a horse's head blackened over the bridge of his nose and flared up to his eyes. Not to be outdone, another woman had a full model replica of a pirate ship woven into the waves of her piled hair. There was a woman with knives sticking out of her hair like a peacock's plume to his left. The trio shocked me considerably less than the giant skeleton crouched in the corner. It hunched in the corner, it's back reaching the 15-foot ceiling. Indescribably, the monster's frame was made up of dozens of skeletons, piled atop each other to form legs, torso, arms, and fists. A moan pulled itself from the tortured horrorshow.

The group twittered as if he had said something incomparably funny. I'd almost forgotten the Devil thought he'd made a joke. Too bad, he wasn't funny. I was less worried about his lack of humor, though, and more concerned with his propositioning me to join him and his crazy train pals.

But what did you say to the Devil when he wanted you?

I settled on keeping it simple. "Fuck you."

A slow smile spread over his face before his head fell back, and a dark laugh rolled out.

"Oh, yes. You would fit here nicely." His eyes found me again, assessing. "Though I can't say I've ever had a faerie in the center of hell. You would be a new toy."

His power breathed over me, raising goosebumps of awareness over my body. "Do you want that, little fairie? For me to give you everything you've been missing in your empty shell of a life?"

Fear clenched my heart. Could he do that? I didn't want to think about that. Staying wasn't even an option. I opened my mouth, but he cut me off.

"Your lips say no, but your heart says yes." He tsked his tongue against the roof of his mouth and then shook his head. "You want to let it go, though. You want to give yourself over to me. Let me make it all go away. I can do that, you know."

He breathed his words, a silken caress in my ear. I turned into the sensation, heat washed over me. My body tingled, alive with possibilities. What I wouldn't give to stop the madness. Kill the cycle of pain. I shook my head. No, life was worth living—pain in the ass and all. I shook my head to clear the cloying seduction from my head.

The Devil acknowledged my break of his spell with a nod,

his black mass of hair falling over his shoulder. "But you aren't here to join my nest, are you? In fact, you aren't even supposed to be here. I can taste the life clinging to your essence still."

He rose from the chair, his shirt falling off his shoulder, exposing his bare shoulder. The dip of his collar bone made me want to dip my tongue into it. I shook my head. I had to separate the real him from the power of his seduction. When I cleared my head, if it was at all possible, he was even scarier. His features twisted and then smoothed back out. The Devil's stride was predatory, otherworldly as he slid over to me.

All of the hairs on my body stood, instinctively on edge. I rose to a standing position myself, my eyes never leaving him. If I was going to die, I'd be damned if I died without defending myself.

"I'm not going to ask how you came to be here. I don't care about something so trivial." His long legs brought him inches from me quicker than I was ready for.

He must have been seven feet tall. I forced myself to breathe evenly. He leaned towards me, his long black hair spilling over his chest like black satin sheets.

His coal eyes roved over my face, violating every inch of me as he said, "What would make you brave the fires of Hell? I've seen you in the rooms. While it was vastly entertaining, I must admit I couldn't help myself any longer. I had to bring you here. As you can imagine, I'm not used to denying myself."

"I find myself wondering, little faerie," he leaned over me, his hair teasing my neck and whispered in my ear, "What are you searching for?"

He breathed his inquiry, hot on my face. My lips ached. I pressed them together, hard. I'd die before I told him anything because the more secrets he knew, the more

Anthony and my chances of getting out of this hole alive dwindled. Nobody had to explain to me the Devil knew knowledge was power; he'd been playing this game for thousands of years. He was bound to have tricks up his sleeve.

He leaned back to look at me. I glared back at him. Not a chance in hell was I going to tell him anything. A smile curved his lips. He closed his eyes, and energy surged from him.

Suddenly, I wanted to tell him everything. I yearned to expose secrets I'd never spoken before- only things I'd felt in my heart's deepest, darkest parts.

His pupils, now so much like a cat's eyes, flared. And I was falling. It was like slipping down an oil-slicked slide. I couldn't stop myself from staring, falling.

Gone was the easy-going playboy. In his place was an intense monster.

"What is it, my little faerie?" He spoke the words to my being.

I felt calm like a summer day. Calm like I'd downed Iris' sleeping potion. Deep inside, all of the bells were going off. But I couldn't figure out why.

"A demon's hoof," I answered the words pulled from my vocal cords.

He blinked, and the world came back into focus like a movie being pulled out of slow potion. "What?" he asked like he hadn't heard me right.

Well, shit. This wasn't going like I'd planned. I guess since I'd already opened my big, fat mouth, there was no reason to stop now.

I tried to put an expression on my face that said I'd told him of my own free will as I said, "I'm looking for a demon's hoof. You know, like the one that was pressed against Anthony's back?"

I bit the last sentence out. What was happening to Anthony right now? Were they torturing him? Bringing him through his own personal Hell? Was he...alive? Bile rose in my throat.

A smile lit up his face at the memory. Hatred boiled in my veins.

"Ah, yes. Your partner." Apparently, he'd brought the skull with him because he started tossing it into the air. He stopped. A small frown pulled at the corners of his mouth. "He's not as fun as you are. He's too predictable, by far."

Now, I liked being told I was fun just as much as the next person. But there was something about the Devil calling you a good time that put a black hole of uncertainty to it.

He started tossing the skull again, with an air of aloofness. "As much as I like you, though, I can't just hand you a demon's foot. I am fond of my servants." He caught the skull in one hand and turned with a crooked smile. "Unless you want to cut it off yourself?"

From the smug look on his face, he knew how much the idea repulsed me. He started tossing the skull again, a chuckle rumbling in his chest.

Dread squeezed my gut. This whole scavenger hunt had seemed so much more innocent when it was a dragon scale or a bone I could pick up along the way. I guess, on some level, I'd just thought I could do the same thing here. I mean, let's be real. Hell was nothing but death. I was way in over my head, though. It was time to change tactics. I had to get Anthony and get out of here. Leaving in one piece would be a bonus at this point.

"I can see you are. It was wrong of us to come here. I'll just get Anthony, and we'll be out of your hair." I said, moving to pass him.

He stopped tossing the skull. Panic jumped in my chest, and I stopped too, afraid any movement would goad him into action. Silence ate the space between us. My skin crawled at the way his head tilted as he assessed me. It said he knew he had me.

"No, no. You went through a lot of effort to come all the way here for a demon's hoof and a demon's hoof you will get," he said, snapping his fingers.

A giant of a demon stepped forward. He walked with his chest stuck out like he'd eaten a barrel. In any other situation, I would have wanted to thump it. In this situation, I was rethinking all of my recent life choices.

His gold skin glowed in the muted light. His hooves clomped across the gleaming cement floor.

There was a delighted gleam in the Devil's eyes as he leaned down to whisper in my ear. "What's the matter, little faerie? Does he scare you?"

An angry retort stuck in my chest. There was so much I wanted to say, so much I wanted to do, but you didn't play with the Devil unless you were willing to accept the consequences. He sneered at me and then laughed. I winced as the bark grated my ears.

The monster of a demon made one thing perfectly clear: we'd snuck into the Devil's domain, and we would pay for trespassing. My legs froze. I stomped feeling back into them. Now was not the time to panic. I could hate myself later for getting Anthony into this. Now was the time for a miracle.

I steeled myself against the uncertainty riling in my gut and said, "I'll fight your...monster. But when I beat him, Anthony and I leave, unharmed."

"How cute is that? You're scared. He's just a demon, little faerie. Not a monster." He tapped his chin. "Now, I could show you monsters. Ones that would guarantee you never slept again."

I could tell from the way he paused that he was waiting for me to say something. There was no way I was going to give him a reason to bring out something else horrific. I stared into the distance, unseeing.

When it was clear I wasn't going to rise to his bait, he said, "Fine. I'll agree to your game. But only because I love games. Not to mention, it will be that much more enjoyable to see your death on the face of your lover."

With a snap of his fingers, Anthony appeared. He was in a chair made of bones. The bones had wrapped around him to hold him down; Anthony strained against them when he saw me. A demon moved behind him. She made a show of running her hand down his chest, her fingertips splayed wide across his tanned flesh. I wanted to punch her.

Upon seeing me with the Devil, the look on his face changed from rage to terror. He struggled harder against the bones. From the way his face moved, it was clear he was trying to open his mouth to say something but couldn't. His struggle made everyone in the room smile. Except me. I wasn't smiling. My mouth was pressed into a line of fury.

The Devil trailed his finger around my shoulder as he walked around me. My skin crawled at his touch. I wanted nothing more than to throw his hand off me.

"If you didn't want to play with the big bad things in the world, you should have stayed up in your fairytale world. It's a shame you have to die. I like your spirit." He nodded to the demon giant as he left my side to reclaim his chair across the room.

The giant grinned at me from ear to ear as he came toward me. My heart slammed against my rib cage in an attempt to flee.

Gritting my teeth, I pulled Kundalini energy up from my spine. It flowed until my body was full, pulsing in time to the adrenaline surging through me. I could do this. The only thing between us and our deaths was this giant. And I'd be damned if Anthony died because of me.

With that grim thought, I shot lightning forward. Shock registered on the demon's face. He did something I didn't expect too. He shifted out of its path. Shifted as in his body slid to the side in a gold-haloed outline. It looked like a blurred stop-animation.

Raw fear froze my brain. If I thought the beast had looked scary before, he'd just leaped to the stuff of nightmares. He knew it too. A grin twisted his beefy face.

There was a whole new level of fear that burned through my veins when he came at me this time. Just how was I supposed to beat this behemoth? By the time he reached me, I still didn't have a clue, so when he swung a fist at me, I dropped to the floor. I fell back on my years of Muay Thai, and I leg-swept at those small cows he called legs.

To my amazement, he fell. For the first time since I was bitten, I was grateful for my heightened abilities. There was no way I'd have been able to do that before.

I wasn't the only one who was surprised. After I'd somersaulted out of the way, I came up to see the Devil's eyebrow raised. I didn't have time to glorify in it, though.

A hoof smashed into me, lifting my body off the ground a few inches before sending me face-first into the concrete.

Pain was my world, exploding in my ribs. It burned where my face had planted. I moaned. There was no way I could take many more of those and live to tell about it.

His hooves scraped along the floor with the barest of noises. Gut instinct screamed "move," so I wrapped my wings around myself and rolled.

A hoof smashed next to me, just where my face had been seconds before. My stomach climbed into my throat as I kept rolling. Earth-shaking smashes followed shortly after. The ground shook as his foot came down one after another, getting closer and closer. Panic lodged in my throat. How could I beat a supernatural beast like this?

I don't know if it was the spinning world that scrambled my brain, but it dawned on me his feet hadn't been blurred or haloed in gold as he'd smashed down. He didn't give me time to think as he crashed his feet down over and over again. After a few crashes, the glow came back, shining through my wings' thin membrane as I spun. Odd. I didn't have much time to think about the light, though, because seconds later, it flared. He was phasing. Shit. I threw out my arm, stopping my spinning. My arm stretched in my socket with the momentum. Screaming in pain, I never took my eyes off him. I got to see him as he phased this time.

He didn't move as he faded to the left in his gold blur. It was almost like he was frozen for the space of time he was shifting. Like he was suspended in time. I'd jumped to my feet by the time he'd stopped phasing. Rage bent his features. I winked at him. Talk about showing promise. Now, how could I use that momentary paralysis to my advantage?

He must have known I was up to something because he charged at me instead of phasing. Adrenaline ran down my spine. I dove out of the way, right into a woman in the crowd. Her skirt made of bones clacked as she pulled them out of the way with a swish. I narrowly missed her and fell just inside the carpeted spectator's circle. My eyes connected with the peacock-knife girl. The knives' razor edges plumed in her hair glinted in the soft light, catching my attention. That was it. A flutter flitted through my chest.

Footfalls rocked the ground in booms of foreboding. Dragging in some Kundalini energy, I twisted. It wasn't a full charge, but it was enough. Lightning cracked towards him in a deadly spike. Immediately, I pulled more energy in. He crouched to move out of the bolt's path. Perfect.

While his focus was on the deadly strike, I somersaulted to the girl. In one fluid movement, I came to my feet and shot a charge of lightning into her. It wasn't enough to kill her. I hoped. Hell, or not, I wasn't that cruel.

Surprise parted her pale lips and widened her red eyes right before they slumped closed. There wasn't any time to waste. The demon no doubt knew what I was going to do now. I rushed my intended victim. The air sucked out of the small sitting area as the rest of the lounging spectators watched me advance. In any other place, I would imagine they'd be up in arms, but in Hell, nobody moved as I slid two of the knives out of the knife-weave of her hair. The blades made the unmistakable scrape of metal sliding against metal. There was no doubting my intent. Fear stretched my gut. My teeth ground against each other as I acknowledged what I was about to do: I was going to that demon.

Turning back to the fight, shock mixed into the adrenaline cocktail mixing into my blood. I'd known he was near, but he seemed much closer than he should have been. Rapidly, he closed the last few feet between us.

With a war-cry, I slashed one of the knives at his abdomen. Given his towering height, it was the closest thing to my hand. His beef stick of an arm came up to block it, knocking the knife out of my hand. It skittered across the floor, almost lost against the glossy surface. Almost, but not entirely.

The sliver of silver imprinted itself in my memory as I was brought back to the fight by a fist yanking my hair. Pain pricked all over my head as hairs pulled out when the behemoth lifted me off the ground by my ponytail. Glitter hissed to the ground beneath me as I struggled against his grip.

I curled the knife-free hand around his bicep to take some of the weight off the tension straining to break my neck. I felt not unlike a monkey as I held onto it. Stubbornly, I clung to the other knife in my left hand. It wouldn't buy me much time, either my grip or my hair would give out. I slashed wildly with the knife in my left hand at the hand that gripped my hair.

Could I electrocute him with my hand already on him? It was worth a shot. Magic coiled in my spine. He must have felt it because his shoulders twisted. Since he wasn't doing anything but treating me like a rag doll, it had to be his other hand. A chill washed over me. It wasn't enough time to ready my lightning. Thinking fast, I swung the knife around and stuck it into his arm that came at me like a freight train. A scream so loud I felt it in my bones shook me. I struggled to keep my eyes open, wincing against the deafening sound.

Black blood spurted out around the knife's handle as he dropped my hair. I came down onto the balls of my feet. Not stopping to think, I darted to the knife on the floor. I heard the other blade clatter wetly behind me just as I snatched the other one into my sweat-slicked palm.

This time I was ready. I turned as the ground below my hand shook. Blood dripped down his arm in a trail of pain that dripped off his fingertips. Pushing myself off the floor, I stood straight. I stuffed the fear clawing up my throat back down and shot lightning at him. He blurred out of its path. That was fine. I already knew by now I wasn't going to beat him with my powers. I just needed to buy time to think. I needed to get close enough to him without him getting those meaty claws on me. Another shot of lightning ensured I had a couple more seconds. Then an idea zapped me. It would either work or get me killed. I prayed it would work.

With quick steps, I backed up. I let the fear racing through my veins show on my face as I shot another bolt at him. I followed another quickly after as I backed up faster and faster. Sure enough, he dodged every one.

I gripped the knife, feeling the coolness of the blade as I shuffled backward. Faster and faster, I went. It wasn't easy, and by the smile that twisted the demon's face, I knew he could tell I was struggling. Finally, I let my feet do what they were inevitably going to do anyway. Crash into each other.

Purposely aiming a shot towards the ceiling to make it look believable, I fell backward. I could hear the shift of his blurring seconds before the bolt I'd sent high.

Sparks fell around me as I whipped the knife around. I grasped the handle and beat my wings so I wouldn't fall to the floor. The demon was still coming though, in a blur of golden regret. His path's end was clearly where he thought I'd fall.

I angled the knife into his path. Using his forward momentum, I drove the point through his chest. I couldn't feel it pierce his heart, but I knew the moment it did because his black eyes speared me. Then his blood was everywhere, covering my hands, drenching my clothes. I didn't let up. Stopping now would be a death sentence. I screamed as I twisted it deeper into the meaty flesh. Then slowly, his golden glow drained from his body along with the life in his eyes.

His body fell to the floor with a heavy thud. I'd never heard a dead person hit the floor before. It would haunt my dreams. I didn't need a seer to tell me that. I could tell by the way my whole body felt heavy afterward. My eyes sought out his limp body. Whether it was to make sure he was really dead or try to make sense of what had just happened, I wasn't sure.

Sure enough, there he lay, the knife still stuck in his chest. His gaze staring, unseeing into the ceiling.

Staring at him, the reality of what I had done sped into my chest. Guilt seeped in, close behind it. What had I done? I had killed someone for my own selfish gain. That made me as bad as the Devil himself.

A slow clap echoed through the vaulted room. My head

snapped up. In my exhaustion, I'd almost forgot the only real rule that applied here: One didn't rest in the Devil's Den. The Devil, back in his leather chair, let his claps fade away. A smile teased the corner of his mouth.

He leaned forward, the smile never leaving his face. "Now, you, little faerie, are full of surprises. The way you used my people, innocent people, for your own gain, was truly a thing of beauty. Truly malicious. You could have killed her for all you knew." He threw a hand to my unintended victim. Her posture was stiff, her shoulders squared off. She'd pulled a knife out of her hair and was twirling it between her fingers. "Don't think for a moment that I'm not furious that you took out my number 2, but what a show. You know? I think I'd like to keep you, after all."

Fear iced my veins. I struggled to keep my voice steady as I said, "I've done what you asked. Now, let Anthony and I go."

The room stilled. The air became hard enough that you could've almost bounced a ball off of it. You didn't go against the word of the Devil.

"You gave your word," I said it less to remind him and more to remind the simmering would-be lynchers on either side of him.

He spread his arms wide, his suit parting to bathe both of his pecs in light. "The word of the Devil. What a naive world you live in if you think that means anything."

Tingling numbed my limbs at his admission. We were going to die here. Everything that I could have been, should have been, pulled at me. I wasn't going out without taking some of these mother-fuckers with me, though. My breath came out in a shaky exhale.

The lines of laughter left his face. His eyes stared at me, draining of warmth. "Little faerie, you and your worthless companion can leave."

Tears pricked my eyes. We were getting out of here, thank

the Gods. But the Devil's next words dried any tears of gratitude from my eyes. "But you will come back here one day. And on that day, you will stay. On *that*, you have my word. I have spoken."

At his words, the bone chair spit out Anthony in a throaty chuck. He dumped out onto the shiny cement, his body a limp pool. My feet were silent as I rushed over to him. I wanted to wrap him in an enormous bear hug, but I kept my head as I held out a hand. I had to keep my wits about me in case the Devil changed his mind. My throat was thick as I strong-armed him into a standing position. With trembling hands, he squeezed my arm. His gratitude was palpable. I was saving relief for later. Relief and a good cry.

"Let's get out of here," I said, my voice cracking.

His hand came up to stop me. He gave a long look to the demon, dead at our feet, "Do you want me to do it?"

The hoof. Anthony knew me too well. I didn't want to have to sever that from the demon's leg. It was bad enough that I'd had to kill him. As it was, I didn't think I was going to get over that.

It may have been cowardly, but I nodded. I was grateful that Anthony didn't say a word as he knelt down. The slurp of the knife being brought out of the demon's chest made me want to cover my ears. If he was going to be strong enough to do it though, I could at least be strong enough to hear it.

There was a soft swish-swish as the knife cut through his flesh, and then the leg's heavy thump hitting the floor. When Anthony came back up, his arms were covered in sticky, black blood. I averted my gaze before what was in his hands reached my scope of vision.

My gaze met the Devil's. His horns shone in the dim light as he turned his head to regard me. A smile hooked his lips.

Nausea roiled my stomach. I couldn't tear my eyes from the Devil and his knowing smile as Anthony wrapped his wings around us. His words echoed in my head: you will come back here one day. And on that day, you will stay.

Fear and hatred fought inside me. I didn't want to believe he'd put us into this position. Didn't want to think about everything he had just made us go through, like puppets on a stage. He toyed with us and our lives the same way, pulling our strings and making us dance. It was so unfair.

It was so much easier to blame him for what had happened. I didn't want to admit the real reason for all of these horrors was myself.

CHAPTER 28

*A*nthony clasped me to him; I clutched him just as tightly back. He'd bent the Spaces Between quickly to leave Hell, so we were naked. Again. Anthony's body heaved at the exertion, pressing against mine as he struggled to reclaim his breath. Any modesty I had started with was fast disappearing with all of this constantly-naked business. That had to be why instead of running to find clothes, I found myself going over what had happened even though my body was growing cold against the wood floor.

It was a good thing that was the last ingredient because I don't think I could have done any more. Anthony interrupted my thoughts.

"I can't believe I almost lost you." He said, his voice thick.

I could feel his relief. I wished I could feel it too- I ached to- but that wasn't what my mind kept replaying. It was going over and over again, shoving the dagger into the demon.

"I can't believe I killed someone." Hollowness yawned inside me as I said it.

"A demon, Cy. You killed a demon." Anthony said. When it was clear, his words were giving only the barest of condolences. He ran his hands down my arms. "Besides, at least you're alive. He would have killed you without even a second thought."

Would it have been? Yes, of course, he was right. And we were here, alive no less. If it had to be us or the demon, I was glad it was us. After a few breaths, I worked to let go of the death I'd caused. With a hand caressing my cheek, he searched my eyes. We shared the warmth of the moment. His eyes turned serious as they moved over my face. The setting sun trailed in to tease at his blond hair. Finally, his eyes found mine, and I knew what he was going to say even before he said it.

"I love you, Cy." The words seemed to come out in slow motion.

Even though I knew what was coming, the force of his words hit me. I looked at him and then looked away. What did you say when your best friend said they loved you? Did I love him? Of course. But did I love him like that? No. I thought I'd loved Sven. Maybe I did love him. But it hurt that he could treat me like that. If I was honest, what hurt most was that he wasn't the man I thought he was. But here was Anthony. He was everything I wanted in a lover. Being fae, he could give me everything I'd ever wanted. And he was my best friend. That was enough. Wasn't it?

Gazing into his familiar eyes, I could see myself spending my whole life with him. I could imagine every second as vividly as if it were a memory. And it was perfect. But was it perfect for me? The other thing that wasn't perfect was that I was taking far too long to respond. From the way the corners of his eyes started to drop, I could tell it was. I would give anything to see him stop hurting- anything but myself. From the way his expression twisted, he knew what I was going to say. If only that made it easier.

I laid my hand on his heart. "Anthony, I-"

A pounding at the door cut my words off. My face fell as I searched for any sign that he was going to be ok. Bitterness scrunched his eyes and forehead, it curled his lips. I could see him struggling with wetness in his eyes as he pressed his lips together, shrugged, and nodded towards the door. Like the coward I was, I took the permission he gave.

Scrambling to grab a royal blue halter dress, I threw it on as I sailed to the door. Short on breath, I threw it open. Avalynn stood at the door, resplendent in a shimmery pink gown. The fading sun gave her an otherworldly glow.

"Hey," she said, with a peppy wave. "I came by earlier, but you didn't answer. I think you were out…"

She trailed off, her gaze blanking as her eyes sought into the dim interior. I threw a look over my shoulder to see what held her attention. Inside, Anthony leaned his muscular frame against the door jamb of my bedroom. The French doors didn't hide the fact that he was utterly naked.

Her face flamed. Then a realization widened her eyes. "Bless Danu, you're trying already. That's so great!"

Regret twisted my gut. I should never have told Avalynn about Mother's edict. At the time, I hadn't known what else to do. She'd caught me right after my meeting with Mother, and I hadn't been able to hide how upset had been. So I told her about the ridiculous demand. She'd known I wanted nothing to do with it, but apparently, she thought I'd changed my mind. With our current state of dress and undress as far as Anthony was concerned, it wasn't hard to see why.

Avalynn's wide grin drew Anthony farther into the room.

"Trying what?" he asked, confusion knotting a frown on his forehead.

No, please. For the love of Dagda, please let this not be happening.

"For a baby, silly." She said with a giggle.

"A...baby?" He rocked back on his feet and looked between the two of us, finally settling on me. "Cy, what is she talking about?"

His tone smacked of foreboding. I flinched.

"Let's talk about this later," I said, anger spiking inside me.

After all, we'd been through, this was not the time- and there was the little fact that he was naked to consider.

He crossed the room, his movements slow, his expression grave. "No, we'll talk about this now."

Red mottled Avalynn's cheeks, and with an unsteady hand, she tucked her hair behind her ear, "Should I not have said anything?"

"No, no, you most definitely should have said something," Anthony said, with a grim twist of his mouth. "In fact, it shouldn't have been you saying something."

Grimacing, my chin dropped to my chest. Could I mess things up any more? I wish I would have told him to begin with. Then this whole ugly mess could have been avoided. I guess I could try to do that now. But how could I explain this in a way he would understand and not give him hope? Lost in thought, I pinched my bottom lip. He gave me all the time in the world as he sat there boring holes in me with his eyes.

When I couldn't take it anymore, I said, "You know, Mother and her crazy edicts. And can I say they are getting crazier and crazier? I really think she is on the verge of snapping-"

"Cy, stop. Stop!" he shouted when I tried to talk over him. Then he continued on with a heart-wrenching quietness, his face carefully blank, "Did your mom say something about us having a...baby together?"

I grabbed fistfuls of my hair. Why did things have to be so fucked? There was no way to make it unfuck it now.

I threw my hands in the air, "Yes, ok? Yes. She said that since we were the only ones with wings in this generation that we were required to produce an offspring to increase the odds of having a child with wings."

After my rushed declaration, he just stared at me. I saw all of his emotions running across his face. Disbelief. Frustration. Anger. Sadness. Betrayal.

The last skewered me. Anthony stood there, and a small shake started to tick his head. It wasn't long until he was full-blown, shaking his head.

"Is that why you and I...why we..." His sentence choked off.

I knew what he was asking. Is that why we'd had sex? It wasn't. But what was better? That it had been in the heat of the moment? That I'd wanted to make, him feel good, if just for a minute? That I wanted to feel accepted? The why's seemed pale in the light of the day with Avalynn standing two feet away, and Anthony's hurt eating me like acid. I struggled to catch my breath.

Guilt squirmed in my stomach as I said, "Of course not."

Why was I feeling guilty? It's not like that's what had happened. Nevertheless, the emotion was there, raw and real, making me sick.

His torso bowed like I'd punched him in the gut. From the way he looked at me, I knew he could tell how I felt. And in his mind, that made me guilty as hell.

"How could you? You know damn well how I feel. You *know.*" He shook his head as he broke my heart. "Yet, you let me go on like a fool. All the while, you were just following your mother's damn edict."

I wanted to scream that it wasn't true. It wasn't right. I loved him. *Him.* For who he was, for how he was- even in the darkest moments. Like right now. I loved him for not raving on like a madman. But that wasn't enough; he didn't want the love of a friend. He wanted the love of a partner. How could I make him see?

"No, it's not like that-" I said.

He cut me off and scoffed at himself. "Hell, I am a fool. You don't want me. You want some vampire."

He said the last as if the word would cut open the earth and hot lava would flow out.

Everything in me pleaded to tell him he was wrong. That I wanted him. But it wasn't true. I wrung my hands.

"I'm so sorry. You obviously need to talk." Avalynn's steps shadowed backward with uncertainty.

"No, you stay." Anthony brushed a hard shoulder past her. "I'm going."

No, not like this. He couldn't go filled with hate and anger.

"Anthony." I went to go after him.

He leveled a glare at me, his chest heaving. "Just go to him. That's who you want anyway."

They said love could turn to hate in a heartbeat. This had to be what they were talking about. Because there was no doubt in my mind that he hated me at that moment.

Coal lumped in my gut. Avalynn stumbled backward in an attempt to get out of his way.

As I watched him walk down the glowing steps and across the bridge, a piece of my heart broke.

"I'm so sorry, Cy. Since I heard the two of you in here earlier, doing...ummm...intimate things, I thought he knew." Avalynn said over my shoulder.

So it had been her at the door. At least it wasn't someone who would think I was a mammoth whore.

My eyes stayed on him, long after he'd disappeared through

the door to the main building. Nothing I could say would begin to cover the ache in my heart, so I didn't even try. What could I say? She didn't know I hadn't told him. How could she? It really wasn't her fault. It was mine for not being open with Anthony.

I turned, not quite sure what I was turning to. Avalynn followed me inside. I closed the door behind us, mostly because I was trying to find a way to occupy my time with something. The place felt empty. I couldn't bring myself to look at Avalynn. My heart was too close to the edge. The smallest thing could push it off and shatter it.

"What now?" She asked.

Her voice was quiet like she was almost afraid to ask. Afraid to make me think about it. She was right. I was afraid. Afraid of the future, afraid of the past. But it was better to look forward than back.

The silence must have made her uncomfortable, though, because she rambled on. "I'm sorry you won't be able to get those ingredients anymore. I know how much they meant to you."

I just shook my head, suddenly tired. Flopping onto the couch, I closed my eyes. The cushions were too comfortable. My eyes stung with unshed tears.

When I didn't answer her, she asked. "What?"

"I have all the ingredients already," I answered back in a whisper.

"How fantastic is that?" I could hear the smile in her voice. When I didn't respond, she said, "At least you can get what you wanted, right?"

My mind was numb as I thought about what she said. She was right. Now was my chance to leave. Maybe it was for the best that this happened. I wasn't going to stay here anyway. It could be a clean break this way.

She let the silence fill in the space until it stretched

painfully, and then she said, "Unless...you don't want that anymore?"

"No, I definitely do. I'm not meant to stay here," I said, wiping the moisture from the corner of my eyes.

And remembering the look on Anthony's face as he left, I couldn't help but think that was never truer than right now.

CHAPTER 29

The quilted bag sat on the floor, empty at my feet. I kicked it.

For what had to be the hundredth time since Iris had disappeared behind the suffocating black curtain with the ingredients I'd toted in, I wondered if I was doing the right thing.

My uncertainty was cut off, though, as the heavy curtain was thrown back. I almost bolted at the suddenness of it. It was only with a monumental effort that I remained in the same spot.

I rolled my eyes at myself. Talk about jumpy. But then again, I had good reason to be. And that even wasn't considering all of the stuff I'd been through to get the ingredients.

In this case, what was making me, the jumpiest was the long-necked bottle clutched in her black-gloved fingers. She waved it in the air. The glowing liquid sloshed around inside.

"Here it is," She shouted triumphantly.

I cringed at the way it danced over her head. With quick steps, I tiptoed over to her.

"Ok, ok." I snatched the bottle out of her hands.

Exhaling a breath I didn't know I was holding, I clutched the warm bottle close to my chest.

I knew I was holding it like it was a bomb, but I had no idea what this would do. Well, I knew what it was *supposed* to do, but my life had never gone as planned, so...

The smile disappeared from her surprisingly, wrinkle-free face. "And you understand that you could disappear, right? That this very well might not work just on your wings?"

I hadn't forgotten, but I was right in the middle of wanting to forget. I couldn't forget Anthony's face as he stormed out of my apartments. I didn't belong here. So I swallowed hard and nodded.

"No, I mean as in you may never come back. I don't know where this stuff could send you," Iris said, jabbing a bony finger at the bottle.

I swatted her hand away. "Yes, I get it. I get it."

She snapped off the gloves that looked suspiciously like they were used to handle radioactive substances and slapped them onto the glass shelf next to us. They clinked the tiny bottles together as they made room for themselves on the clean but cluttered shelf. Reaching into her back pocket, she pulled out a yellowed piece of paper. She shook it in the air to unfold it.

"What's that?" I asked as she handed it to me.

The paper had the blotched, scrawled hand-writing you'd expect from a quill pen. The effect rendered it almost unreadable. What I could read, I didn't like.

"What's this about not being liable?" I asked, crossing my arms across my chest.

While I was trying to decipher the rest, she slipped off the pewter pin holding her apron together. The ties dangled to the floor as she held out her other hand to me. I hadn't even read it yet, but maybe she had to make a change to it. I went to give her the paper back. She sighed, a pained sound in the back of her throat.

"Dagda be damned, you can't be serious," she muttered, grabbing my hand.

With a swiftness that didn't make sense for a lady of her age, she stuck the pin into me.

"Ouch!" I said, baring my teeth.

I went to pull it back, but she was already pressing it to the paper. The red of the blood seeped like spider veins through the back of the yellowed parchment.

Yanking my hand back, I stuck it in my mouth. Copper flavored my mouth and was gone as I sucked the pain away. The tiniest bit of interest flared in my gut at the taste. I froze with my hand still in my mouth.

Tor Mór, what was that?

A thought jumped into my head, but I pushed it away. I refused to accept it. There was no way the vampire connection in me was responding to the blood. Was there? Uncertainty and fear jumped around in my stomach. The first place I was going when I got out of here was to get answers. Too long, I didn't know what was happening to my body. No longer.

Iris pulled me back from my thoughts. "This is to cover my butt if you disappear, and the royal guards come looking for you. Because as much as I hate to admit you're a princess, that doesn't change the fact that you are. And I'll be damned if I go to jail for life just because I want you out of here."

"They could take you anyway," I said, warning clear in my voice.

Though true, it wasn't likely. Even though Mother could do whatever she wanted, she would be more likely to knight Iris if I was gone for good. I had to say something, though. I didn't like how she seemed too much like she was preparing for me to disappear completely.

I decided to call her on it. "How can I trust that this is even supposed to do what you say it is? What if this is an elaborate ruse to be rid of me once and for all? I know how much you hate me. Let's not kid ourselves."

She picked up her gloves and headed to the back of the shop. "Who's kidding themselves of anything? And, for the record, you don't know. If I were you, I certainly wouldn't trust me."

My mouth dropped open at her admission. She pushed the beads apart as she went into the kitchen.

Stopping, she called over her shoulder, "I have to get cleaned up. Take your potion and go. Oh, and lock up before you leave, would you?"

And just like that, she was gone, her wispy teal hair trailing after her as she rounded the corner.

She'd left a lot for me to think about. I turned my attention to the bottle in my hands.

Was I doing the right thing? The question looped on repeat in my head as stared, mesmerized by the iridescent shimmers swirling around in the glowing, red-orange liquid.

CHAPTER 30

*T*he crickets chirped in the clearing as the tall grasses slapped my legs. It was in the same clearing where I'd made my getaway with Kittie almost two months ago. Stray hairs snuck out of my ponytail, snatched by the wind. I wished she were here with me now. Her little sarcastic self would know what to do.

As it was, I was alone. Totally alone. For the first time since leaving Knockaine the first time, I had no one to turn to. I hugged my arms around myself. I couldn't even go to Anthony. He'd told me to go. After what had happened, he wouldn't want to see me right now. Maybe not ever. What if he'd been trying to find a way to let me go, and this had been the least painful way? From the hate on his face, I could believe that. I could tell he'd been preparing for me to leave once the wings were gone anyway. The edict from Mother had just made it easier for him.

I supposed I could thank her for that. My jaw ticked. At least I could thank her for one thing in my life.

I tried to tell myself it was for the best as I looked back at the potion. It sat on a log in the center of the clearing. A reddish glow bled to the surrounding grass, swaying in the wind. I'd set it down when I'd first gotten here and couldn't bring myself to go back to it.

What about those threats against Anthony and Avalynn's lives? Maybe I could ignore them if they were targeted at me, but they weren't. They'd been targeted at my friends. I'd never forgive myself if anything happened to them. Sure, it was probably Harmon. But what if I was wrong?

The hellish glow taunted me. What was stopping me? After everything that Anthony and I had gone through to get here...I wasn't going to back down now, was I? My feet started circling around the potion. My eyes never left the ominous glow. My legs even stepped over the log of their own accord. If my wings went away, there was no getting them back. I could always feign innocence with Mother. I figured since they'd come out of nowhere, I could say they disappeared the same way. She didn't need to know that there had been skin on the bed back at Sven's.

Sven.

He was another person I didn't want to think about. He'd hurt me with his disregard of my life. If it were only him, I would stay. I would. Wouldn't I? What if I stayed? I squashed the thought as quickly as it had come. I couldn't stay. I didn't belong here. Not only did I not belong, but none of the faeries wanted me here either. Their whispering behind their hands with scorn evident in their eyes still haunted me. Even if I could get past my own insecurities and find a real home here, how could I stay in a place where everyone hated me?

The answer was easy. I couldn't. I'd be damned if I would go through that heartache. Not again.

Making my decision, I closed in on the bottle. I swept it up, throwing off the cork in a single motion. It popped into the grass with a hiss. A haze of smoke plumed from the top with a couple winks of shimmer into the night, and then it was gone. The bottle was still warm as I stared at where the smoke had been. Had I imagined it?

Imagined or not, I was doing this. I made my own future. Cementing my resolve, I put the top to my lips. Iris' words floated back to me: It could make you disappear entirely.

The pressure of fear strained my temples. With a prayer, I threw the contents back. Bits of crunchy bone and hoof slid down my throat on a wave of copper. I struggled to take it all in one swallow. There was no way I could make myself drink it again if I stopped. And I didn't want to think about what was going to happen if I only ingested part of it.

The liquid changed to sludge, and I knew I was at the end of it. That was the exact moment where my stomach started to riot. It clenched against the contents spilling into it. Panicked, I felt it start to come out of my nose. I plugged my nose to keep all of it down. It slid, thick down my throat, but eventually, it went down.

My hands shook as I dropped the bottle on the ground. I wiped my sweaty hands on the heavy cotton of my dress. Dread overwhelmed me, sending my head spinning. Closing my eyes, I willed whatever was going to happen to happen.

It didn't take long before my stomach burbled and roiled. Bile rose in my throat. With a hard swallow, the burning dropped back into my stomach.

Then...

Nothing. Breathless, I waited. My heart pounded—any second. Seconds ticked by to minutes. After standing in the clearing for a handful of them, I felt more than a little absurd. Nothing had happened. It was a dud.

Cold, I kicked the log. "Damn it, Iris."

My toe throbbed. Now what? Was I supposed to go back to Anthony and tell him we had risked our lives for nothing? Ok, sure. I was happy I hadn't disappeared into thin air, but my wings were supposed to be gone. I had to have done something wrong. Iris would know what was going on.

Turning to leave, my foot caught the log that had been the object of so much of my consternation not minutes earlier. I went down. My instincts kicked in, and I beat my wings to keep myself up. It didn't matter. I landed on my ass anyway. The dead grass tickled my forearms. What in the name of Danu was going on? I reached my hands back to prove to myself what I already knew, that I had my wings. My mind reeled. I felt nothing but the cool, smooth skin of my back. No soft leather of wings. No rigid exoskeleton. Nothing.

No, they couldn't be gone. I could still feel the weight of their presence. I tried again to beat them, but nothing happened. No way. I reached back a second time. The same super-normal back I'd had my whole life greeted my touch. I laughed, the sound echoed in the clearing. I ducked, not able to keep the smile from my face. They were gone. She'd done it! I didn't know how or why I still felt their weight, but they were definitely gone.

I laughed into the night air. Realizing anyone could hear me, I clamped my hand over my mouth. Still smiling behind my hand, I looked around. No one came. I giggled to myself and got up. She'd done it. I was finally free. I could leave. Again.

That thought stole the smile from my face and filled my stomach with lead.

CHAPTER 31

*T*rees grabbed at my hair as I ran through the forest. I couldn't believe I was leaving. I'd walked right out the front door. All I'd done was wear a tank top, so the guards could see I wasn't hiding anything. Sure, they had slanted me looks, maybe even did a double-take when they saw I had no wings, but they couldn't stop me. Without the wings, they couldn't hold me. I wasn't a prisoner. Not technically.

But that didn't mean they weren't on the way to tell Mother and that she wouldn't be on my heels. Even on the night of her Midsummer Night's Eve Celebration, she'd want me under her thumb. Don't get me wrong, she'd do it under the guise of honoring me- anything to make her look less crazy- but I knew the real reason. She couldn't stand that I didn't bow to her wishes and demands.

I slowed down to squeeze through some dense trees. They'd serve decently for cover. It still unnerved me that I could slip between them without any problem. I'd never have been able to if my wings were still here. In the last month, I'd grown used to them, now it felt odd that they were gone, like a piece of me was missing.

It was for the best. I couldn't stay in that place. I couldn't ignore my own wishes and dreams and let them treat me like a pawn. And that's all anyone was to Mother. Her edict about Anthony and the baby had just been the beginning. I knew it. Not only because it was my mother, but there was something more. I could feel her sanity slipping away. What would have been next?

"Where are you going, loser?" asked a little voice in my ear.

I swung around and smacked right into a beech tree. A dull throb framed the world as I looked around. No one was there.

The voice must have thought that it was hilarious because it started laughing. It sounded familiar.

"Why are you always running?" asked a now-unmistakable voice. "That's got to be exhausting."

I put my hands on my hips, but I couldn't be anything other than happy that she was here.

"Ok, Kittie, show yourself," I said, a smile twitching my life.

My hair moved. Then I felt a weight lift from it. After a few seconds, Kittie was floating eight inches from my face.

This time I couldn't hold the smile back. "Look what the cat dragged in."

"Speak for yourself." She crossed her tiny ankles and cocked her head. Her hair fell over one black-fishnetted shoulder as she looked at me then pointed to her own wings. "Hey, aren't you missing something?"

"Something like that," I said, starting on my way again.

"So are you working on your creeper tactics? Or what? Why are you just waiting out here?" I asked as I picked my way through the trees at a faster clip.

She was quiet as she flexed her body in the air like a tiny dolphin.

Finally, she said, "It is forbidden for pixies to go into the faerie realm."

"Forbidden?" I echoed. "But how did Anthony get you to follow me then?"

"It was a secret. You know, under the radar." She put a finger to her lips in a mock gesture. "The King originally only agreed because he wanted to know if you were as crazy as your dear old mum."

"I thought you weren't allowed in the mound," I asked, my eyes narrowing in jest. "Besides, how do *you* know my mother is crazy?"

She gave a noncommittal shrug. "You can't expect us to not spy on our greatest threat."

That I understood. "So...what's the verdict? Am I as crazy as my mother?"

She tapped her lips like she was pondering, and then she said with an off-hand shrug, "Nah, it's just your personality that is shitty."

I rolled my eyes but couldn't help the laugh that came out anyway.

"Where are you going anyway?" She asked as if it had only occurred to her that I was heading away from Knockaine.

"I'm leaving. I don't belong in that place." I said, trying to keep the words nonchalant, like admitting it out loud to an outsider didn't hurt a million times more than hearing it in my head for my whole life.

She stopped and screwed up her face. "You can't honestly tell me you're just going to keep letting this crazy shit your mom is doing just keep happening. Anyone with eyes can see where this is going."

A shudder ran through my body. I didn't even want to think about what Kittie was saying. Mother had felt two breaths shy of a full melt-down for years. She'd just been getting crazier and crazier.

"Well, I'm never going back there. I hate Knockaine." Even as I said it, my heart twinged.

I leaped across the stream we'd come up on; my teeth clicked when I hit the other bank.

"I call bullshit," she said, flying across the river after me, pixie dust sparkling in the moonlight as she flew fast to keep up with me. "You look more alive than I've ever seen you. You don't get that from being miserable."

I had started running again but slowed it to a jog. I thought about what Kittie had said. Was she right? My mind whirred over the past week's events. It *had* been nice to be around people who understood what it meant to be fae. And not everyone had been mean to me. I know Avalynn had heard people talking about me, but then again, I hadn't exactly gone out of my way to sit down and chat with anyone. Maybe once they got to know me, they would accept me.

Not that I wanted to live in Knockaine. I cherished the freedoms of my life on the outside. But there was no denying the loneliness that had crept into my being over the years. Nothing felt like it could be eased. Until I'd been back at Knockaine. It hit me that only then did that loneliness vanish. I just hadn't wanted to feel caged. Maybe I could find a way to have my own life and be around my own kind. What if it didn't have to be all or nothing? I had loved being around my own people. How much I'd missed the Enchantette was proof of that. Thinking of the magical heart of Danu made my heart ache. The tattoo on my wrist pulsed.

That stopped me in my tracks. I needed them. As much as I didn't like to admit it, I needed them. Not in a desperate way. More like a quiet way that hummed in the background like the hum of cicadas.

And maybe, just maybe, they needed me too. Just look at those faeries I'd rescued. What if their being able to use their powers to fight could have gotten them out of that hell sooner? A decade, even a year, earlier would have meant more to them than caves filled with gold. Time was the most precious treasure in the world.

There was nothing in our schooling to show a young fae how to use their powers when they came into them. Who knows what other fae's lives were being impacted by the handicap? It didn't take a seer to know that without me championing it, the fae would likely never get the chance to learn how to use their abilities for fighting. I could do it. But it would mean going up against Mother.

My stomach rolled. I could do it. Everything in me screamed, I could. I didn't want to, though. Mother was crazy in every sense of the word. Who knew how she would react to the opposition from her daughter of all people. My throat went dry. Considering how unstable Mother was getting, it was a scary thought.

I had to do it, though. Not only did my people deserve better, but I was feeling no small amount of guilt about Sven situation. What if I'd exposed our existence to vampires? The very existence we'd gone to such incredible lengths to pull off. Sure, the vampires who'd known about us had died in the fire, but the possibility of them telling others was still there- no matter how small.

Kittie dipped in front of my vision, her little form shadowed by the moon behind her as golden pixie dust flittered down. "Earth to Cy. What's going through your boggle?"

"I'm going back," I said, excitement pumping through my veins.

Her little face broke into a huge grin. "So, you're saying I'm right."

I swallowed my smile. "Well, you had to be right sometime."

She stuck her tongue out at me.

Then a thought hit me. "You can't come with me, can you?"

Her little shoulders shrugged. "No, I don't suppose I can. When am I going to see your cringe-worthy face again? I'm kind of addicted to your crazy life."

I flicked at her. She dodged the attack with a smile.

"You're going to have to put up with me sooner than you think. I'm not staying here. I'll just be...taking more of an active role in things around here." She raised her eyebrow at that. "No, that doesn't mean Mother's removal. My people need me for change is all. And I'm going to help them get where they need to be. I'll be around. Just pop over to my place in New York City or The S.A.W. some time. I'm sure I can find new and exciting ways to make your life miserable." I said with a wink.

She pursed her lips. "Ok, but no more cages. You suck at making those."

"Oh, I *suppose*," I said with a dramatic sigh.

I wasn't great with goodbyes, so I turned around as I said, "See you."

"Bye, Largie!" She called after me.

I liked that little pixie. My feet started walking as my brain turned to the task in front of me. I still had to deal with the threats against Avalynn and Anthony. There was no denying the seriousness of it. They'd both been attacked already. Could I live with a friend's death on my shoulders? No, but if I could keep them safe until I found that person. Then I would make sure they never threatened anyone again.

If I hurried, I could still make it in time for the celebration. Anthony would be there. Maybe I could even start down the path of healing us. I had to make peace with my past before I could move forward. And I wasn't just moving forward, I was flying. Elation flew my feet across the uneven ground.

CHAPTER 32

*B*utterflies fluttered in my stomach as I strode through the entryway at a clip that was far from ladylike. When I reached the hall, my steps faltered. There wasn't anything from the exterior that would make me stop. I approved of the rose chiffon framing the doorways in a dramatic swoosh that dropped to the floor like it was paying homage to the entrants. It was what was going on inside me that stilled my steps.

Sure, people were going to question the absence of my wings. Probably more whispers than outright questions, but it would be on everyone's mind. That wasn't what looped through my mind, though. No, what went round and round through my head was that this was the Big Step. It was the first time I was coming to them as not just Cy but as their Princess. It was the first time I wasn't going to shirk my title but embrace it. My heart raced like it was gearing up to jump out of my chest.

Just because I was going to be involved in their lives didn't mean I wouldn't have my own. I would have to repeat that to myself at least a million times before I realized that it was actually doable.

Gathering up my courage, I stepped around the voluminous pile of fabric that had pooled below the doorways. If I didn't, my own organza skirt that was roughly the size of the Times Square Ball would grab it as I passed.

Petals dropped in a steady curtain, shielding any onlookers from the festivities. That surprised me. Elder Elspeth had to be doing that. It surprised me that she would leave Harold's side so soon after he'd come back. Then again, maybe he was here too. The thought gave me a measure of peace.

I took a calming breath. Focus. This was it. I stood so close to the petals that I could feel their little wisps of air as they fell. I took a deep breath. And as I exhaled, I stepped through the curtain.

The petals tickled my hair as I passed through. Some of them had to have been captured by my crown. It was a simple yet elegant affair with four filigree leaves reached for the ceiling. It signified birth: the birth of a new era. It had been in the history of fae since the beginning. I'd never worn it before today.

Not that I hadn't *wanted* to wear it. Breathtaking didn't even begin to describe it. It had a delicate V that came down over my forehead that had a diamond dripping from it. Tinier versions of which were snuggled into the crown's curves. Combs were concealed there to hold it in place. Not that it needed much holding. It couldn't have weighed more than a kitten.

No, I'd just never worn it because I had always thought it would be the equivalent of showing Mother she'd won. That I agreed to be under her thumb and rule. It was no secret that I didn't agree with dozens of edicts she passed down. But I'd realized tonight being a part of the system was the only way to help my people. Attack it from the inside.

So I wore the crown.

Mother could think what she wanted tonight. She would soon see what was coming.

When I stepped into the room, I stopped. The strands of diamonds draped across my exposed back pricked the delicate skin there at the jerky act.

They didn't hold my attention, though. Neither did the Sistine Chapel sized room I'd entered.

Don't get me wrong. The room was spectacular. The same roses from the entryway swept throughout the room from the chairs to the walls to the gossamer silk tablecloths laid out in squares on crystal tables. Mood lighting assured it looked like the dawn came to life. It didn't look dark, though. The crystals twinkling around the room made sure of that. Well, that and the faerie lights punctuating the threatening darkness, a quiet reminder of our heritage. The changing colored flames floated on an invisible current, flaring and blazing, their haunting light holding thousands of years of fae secrets. This room held all of the tantalizing things dreams were made of. Things that were just out of our reach. It was breathtaking. Intoxicating. Then again, I'd expect nothing less from one of Mother's Midsummer Night's Eve Celebrations.

What transfixed me was the man leaning against the far wall. Since a massive wooden dance floor separated the tables, and it was too early for dancing, he was directly in my line of sight.

The distance ensured I couldn't make his features out, but I could still tell it was Anthony. His lithe frame sported a black tux with a crisp white shirt framing his chest. The way it pulled across the expanse made me think it hadn't been fitted, but I knew better.

He was leaning against the enormous wall like he was solely responsible for holding it up. I knew the second he saw me too. He pushed off the wall. His body language said he didn't know whether to come to me or leave. I held my breath as I waited for his decision.

"Her royal highness, Princess Cybil," The royal barker called out next to me so loud it made me jump.

Everyone stopped to turn to me. Hushed exclamations pointed at me. I didn't know if they were commenting on the beautiful dress the royal tailor had put together, the fact that I was wearing the crown, or that my wings were gone.

If it was me, I would have been looking at the dress. Two lightning bolts winged up from the V of my bodice to frame my shoulders. The same design dropped down to the fitted bodice interwoven with a lightning and lace design was awe-inspiring.

When everyone rushed over, I had a sinking feeling it was because of the crown. There were so many people. They clustered around me, all talking at once. I smiled at the faces around me, trying to give everyone my attention at once. Pretending like I was succeeding at the goal.

"It suits you." said a girl with a heart-shaped face and a wreath of flowers on her head. She was from the third floor in the Royal Apartments, wasn't she?

"Always knew you had it in you," said an old faerie with a gnarly cane that looked like it was unapologetically fashioned out of a crooked, old tree. She also had a crown of brightly colored flowers. I smiled warmly at her positivity and her spirit.

A short man with a smile the size of the moon positively glowed at me. "We missed you, Princess."

Their words didn't surprise me. There was so much deception in the Fae Court you never knew who was your friend or who just wanted the next rung up on the social ladder. What did take me off guard with the sincerity in their faces, in the claps on my back? I rubbed my face trying to keep the crease off my brow. I thought nobody had wanted me here. Hadn't everyone been whispering behind their hands earlier?

"It's such a pleasure to see you again," said Wendy, her expression soft.

She looked incredible in lace, light blue kid gloves that were loosely clasped together over the skirts of a voluminous, peekaboo gown. But it was more than how she looked. A calm assuredness had replaced her timidness. I'd made a difference in her life. Goosebumps ran down my body. I'd done that. Me. And this sweet woman and her friends were the only the beginning.

I pulled her in for a hug. She gave a surprised little, "Oh," and then she wrapped strong arms around me. My heartbeat freed doves. This was the right thing to do. To be here for my people. I pulled away, dabbing moisture from my eyes.

"It's so good to see you, Wendy," I said, and it was.

It felt good to know she was doing well. Good to know I'd made a difference. She pulled away, a smile crinkling her eyes. Just then Harold dipped down, sprinkling orange glitter over the crowd. I smiled up at him. Maybe, it wasn't so bad being here, for a spell.

"Give the Princess space," said Avalynn pushing people to the side with her long arms.

She looked regal in a black, strapless number. The silk had a sheer overlay that started at an empire waistline and came up to knot in a delicate bow at her shoulder. With a deep bow, she reached a hand out to me. Wendy blinked in surprise but stepped back.

It was a little awkward, but I took her well-meaning hand. I'm sure she thought I was overwhelmed after having been out of the limelight for so long. And she was right in that I was a little overcome, but it had nothing to do with stage-fright and everything to do with knowing I was making the right decision. For the first time in my life, something felt good. Right. I wasn't sacrificing for them or for what I wanted. I was making choices for me. And it felt so damn good.

When we were safely out of earshot, she pulled me close and whispered, "Is everything ok?"

"Thank you. Yes, everything is fine."

She said, pinching at the skin on her throat. "Thank the gods. I wondered because I thought you'd said you were leaving, but you're here."

"I am, aren't I? I guess I figured it was time for me to actually help my people for a change. To stop running." I pulled a wry smile.

"Are you not...scared, though?" She asked as she plucked a rose from a nearby table and twisted the stem.

"Of course, I am. It's a whole world I'm going to have to try to navigate. Before, I didn't give a fig what anyone thought of me. I can't have that attitude if I want to actually help."

Her expression grew pinched. I winced. Oh, she wasn't talking about my new philanthropic adventure. How dense could I be? She was probably worried about her own skin.

I grasped her hand, holding it to my heart. "Don't worry about the attacks. Tonight, I'll speak to The Guard and make sure you have sunup to sundown protection until we put a stop to them. I'm not going to let anyone hurt you."

Her hands flitted like butterflies as they fidgeted over her dress. "It's not that I'm... I'm not-" then something caught her attention across the room.

I craned my head to see what she was looking at. Mother. She sat on a dais in all of her Midsummer Celebration splendor. My jaw ached as I spotted Dian Cect behind her throne. His mere presence rubbed me the wrong way. Though, I suppose anyone who killed their own children would make me feel that way. Even if he hadn't been the bane of my existence from a young age. He leaned down to whisper something into Mother's ear. What lie was he whispering into her ear now? She tilted her head, giving his words consideration, and then she nodded. My temples throbbed, the beginnings of a headache coming on.

"Of course, her Majesty has called for me. I must go," Avalynn rubbed her hand over her mouth, fixed her hair, straightened her dress, and was off before I could so much as get a word out.

Well, that was weird. She picked her way over to Mother, passing right in front of that same boxer's frame I'd seen from the other day. Harmon. Fire shot through my veins.

This was something we were going to take care of right now. No cat and mouse games.

My stride was the same as when I stalked towards him as when I approached a criminal. It screamed that I was taking him down. Very appropriate for how I was feeling right now. I'm sure it looked comical how my full skirts bounced around like they were unsure of what to do with such determination. I didn't care. This was one situation that didn't call for tact and diplomacy. Perfect. That was my forte.

Harmon's eyes landed on me as I walked up. At first, they widened in appreciation. Then they narrowed in hatred when he recognized me.

I didn't beat around the bush. "I'm staying, Harmon."

His bushy eyebrows rose as he took in my crown. "I can see that."

"Well, you better leave my friends alone," I said, making sure to give him a nice even glare.

"Why in the name of the Gods would I care about *your*

friends?" he asked, looking at me like I'd said the world was ending in 2 days.

At his reaction, I started to doubt myself. "Someone has been targeting my friends for the last two weeks. Are you trying to say that wasn't you?"

His face looked like I'd slapped his grandmother. "Of course, that is what I am saying."

"But what about the alley earlier today? You attacked Anthony." I said, holding my ground.

"The Messenger was attacked?" The way his eyes widened made me sure it wasn't him.

But then who was it? Could it be Mother? No, she wouldn't bother with warnings or the like. She'd simply take me out and have me executed, under the radar, of course. No need to cause a mutiny.

Harmon must have taken my silence as an accusation. He puffed up his chest and said, "If I wanted to kill my honor, I could think of far better ways to do it than attacking your friends."

"If you weren't attacking Anthony, what were you doing in that alley earlier?" I asked, not bothering to keep my accusations to myself.

"What are you doing? Following me?" He scoffed, disgust sliding down his face. When I didn't answer, he shook his head. "I was throwing away a plant for my brother-in-law. He killed it and didn't want my sister to find out. Not that it's any of *your* business."

He'd been helping his brother-in-law? Was that what normal families did? Families who weren't busy trying to prove their worth? Trying to prove that they still mattered?

I sighed. I didn't rise to Harmon's bait. This conversation had made it painfully evident that Harmon, though a jerk to me, was not only a good person but also not the assailant we were after. On the one hand, I was grateful I didn't have to go against him again. On the other hand, I was no closer to figuring out this mystery-from-hell than I had been.

Thankfully, I didn't have to worry about wracking my brain at this exact moment. A more pressing matter presented itself when the crowd parted to reveal Anthony, still resting against the back wall. I needed to make things better with him, like now. The need to ate at me. Even now, the time that had elapsed sliced my gut. His eyes seared into mine. Answers, he wanted them. Who could blame him? Things had snowballed so fast I didn't even know which way was up at this point. Talk about an unintentional mind-fuck.

The crowd closed again. I blinked then gulped down a shaky breath.

Harmon made a disgusted sound in his throat. "Do me a favor, would you? Leave me alone."

Before I had a chance to say anything else, he left. It was just as well. I needed to talk to Anthony, like yesterday.

As I started to walk away, a young faerie pulled on my skirts. "Are you ok, Princess?"

Blinking myself back to the moment, I looked down to take in her bright cheeks. Her purple curls bobbed as she belatedly remembered to curtsey. A smile curled my lips. She'd been so caught up in the world around her, she'd forgotten Court etiquette. She reminded me a lot of myself at that age. The fact that I stood here tonight spoke volumes about how much I'd grown as a person. I knew I had a real chance of making a positive change. I could tell everyone was open to it, from Sansonite to the people who welcomed me with open arms. And that made me feel pretty damn good.

"Yes, I think I will be. Thank you." My skirts billowed around me as I knelt down and wrapped her in a hug.

Her body was stiff for only a second before she melted into my embrace.

Giving her a quick pat, I released her and stood up. Her face beamed up at me.

I curtsied and said, "Will you excuse me?"

She blinked wide eyes at me and nodded. I gave her a little wink as I went to move through the crowd. The crowd parted at my coming. Ok, so being a princess had *some* benefits.

At the shift of bodies, Anthony appeared again. He stood there like he could wait all day. I could tell from the rigid lines of his body that he wasn't going anywhere. He wanted to talk. I could do that. It was the least I could do after the kaleidoscope of crazy he'd endured on my behalf the last month.

I left the heat of the crowd, my feet falling on the quiet of the carpet. Anthony's eyes never left mine. There was an intimacy. When I reached his side, he pushed himself off the wall. The erect posture made it clear he hadn't forgiven me. Yet. I decided to put it all out on the table.

"I'm an idiot," I said, not bothering to mince words.

He lifted an eyebrow. "True."

I smiled into a scowl, pretending he wasn't making me laugh.

"I have the worst judgment," I said, tapping a finger against my chin. I watched his eyes start to twinkle and added, "Probably of all time."

At that, he smiled a half-smile and tilted his head as if he were thinking about it.

Then he appeared thoughtful and said, "Quite possibly."

Seeing him smile made my heart fly. I stared at him. The low light caressed his honeyed hair. Carmel skin begged to be touched, but I resisted and looked into his eyes. Their teal depths caught me.

His straight eyebrows lowered as he regarded me. Then

his face crumpled, and his arms reached out to me. Grateful, I stepped into them. Relief sagged me into him.

"Cy, I know I can't have you-"

With an unsteady hand, I leaned back to clap my hand over his mouth. "Anthony, stop."

His breath came out, shaky against my hand.

Then he kissed my palm. Taking it in his hand, he separated my fingers and trailed his fingertips between the tender parts of my fingers.

He never took his eyes off my hand as he said in a whisper, "I've loved you for so long. But I know now that I'm not what you want. No matter how badly I want to be."

I cupped his nervous fingers in my hand and brought them to my chest. He smiled, his lips tight. Someone behind me caught his eye, and he brought my hand down to his side but didn't let go. I turned just in time to see Avalynn glide up.

She nodded to Anthony. Pushing an uncharacteristically wayward strand of bubble gum pink hair back into her coif, her gaze darted to Anthony and my intertwined fingers for a half a breath. A second later, they were back up to me like a moth's flight. "Your mother wants to see you."

My stomach turned. For all of my earlier bravado, I wasn't ready to face the plague that was Mother yet. I sighed. Would I ever be ready? Knowing the answer to that, I gave Anthony's hand a light squeeze. I had to go. After a moment's hesitation, he let my hand free.

He lifted his chin and raked me with sad eyes. "Thank you."

I knew what he was saying, thank you for giving us a chance. Giving him a chance. I couldn't quite get a full breath as his sadness weighed on me. Seeing him struggle against his hurt made me wish I hadn't, but I couldn't take back the past. Besides, our paths were how we grew. Changing it would change who we are, and I liked who I was.

Raising a hand, I gave his shoulder a warm pat. As far as reassurances were concerned, it sucked ass, but there wasn't much more I could do. I nodded to Avalynn and turned towards Mother.

She was a sight on her stage, raised above her subjects. Her rigid posture and her mouth's turn a fitting match for the formidable stone throne she occupied. Behind her Cecht, regarded the room as cold as a winter lake. It was a stark contrast to the towering birch tree to their left. The Maypole. It was completely bare except for the top of the tree where limbs fanned out like an umbrella. Moons and stars floated in and out of the lower branches. Haloing the treetop, sunshine trickled in without any seeming origin. Brenden's handiwork, no doubt. It made a heavenly backdrop to the bounty nestled there: grapes, sheaves of bundled wheat, and flowers. And oh, the flowers that were splayed out. Some had long stamens that showered bright lavender pollen on the leaves below them, while still others had dark purple berries nestled in their prickly homes. Their grape soda fragrance so potent I swear I could smell them from here. Woven into the branches hung wide ribbons, the same colors as the flowers above, draping to the ground. A little boy decked out in a wide-collared festival suit picked a rich purple one up and gave it a couple flicks. His buddies looked in horrified delight at the rebellious act. I smirked and continued on to Mother. Danu truly blessed us.

Mother lounged on her throne on the center dais. Roses of all colors and kinds, given to her as homage, were piled around her throne, two dozen deep. When I reached the edge of the platform, their perfume wrapped me in comfort. Snippets of happier moments flashed in my mind at the smell. A distant memory tickled my brain: roses covering the dining room table. Unable to resist their soft allure, I'd snatched one from the colorful pile. Laughter floated in from the next room. Had that been when Mother was the Goddess of Fertility, as Elder Elspeth had said?

Cecht turned to me. His eyes widened when he took me in. Dark hatred pulsed the vein in his head. My chin went up, refusing to be intimidated. No easy feat considering the way his fingers curled like deadly claws around the top of Mother's throne. He leaned down and whispered in Mother's ear. Her features softened, and she turned to me. Adrenaline shot traitorously through me at the sudden turn. Was she...happy to see me? Was she actually going to stand up for me? Whether she was or not was impossible to tell because her gaze turned to daggers when she saw me.

"What have you done to your wings?" She asked, with a sweeping gesture at me.

There was no mistaking the venom in her words. If I was dense enough to miss her tone, there was no mistaking the rage contorting her beautiful features.

Numbness slid over me. No matter her rage, no matter what it might foretell, I couldn't seem to care. Not paying any mind to the anger of one of the most powerful faeries in fae wasn't the smartest move I'd ever made. Still, I was too wrapped in my own thoughts to give more than a passing acknowledgment to that thought.

How stupid could I be? Did I really think she would feel anything but repulsiveness at the sight of me? I don't know if it was the memory of happier times, or the look that I had somehow convinced myself was love on her face. All I knew was I was hurt. My gut twinged as if to emphasize the point. I hated her. Or more to the point, I wanted to hate her because I was panicked to realize I still loved her. She could never know that, though. She would use it to hurt me, use it to make me a pawn in her game. There was no other way to explain the next words that came out of my mouth.

"So...how does one lose the status of Goddess?" I asked,

wiping the hurt from my face and replacing it with a look that could wither an evergreen.

Cecht jerked back as if slapped. When a deadly calm came over, Mother, I knew I'd finally done it: I'd crossed the line. For all that, her outward emotions stilled. That was the only part of her that did. Something else entirely started to happen to her. In an instant, her hair darkened four shades, bleeding from dark amber to a murky brown. Her face faded and flared, pulsing from a porcelain ivory to an ashen Sphynx as if stuck in a glitch. She seemed unaffected by the change and continued on.

"I did not *lose* anything. It was taken from me. Much like the only two people who ever meant anything to me." She said a verbal gut punch.

She'd said it to hurt me like I'd hurt her. I was never more sure of anything in my life. Still, the barb stuck like a fish hook.

"You have to care about me a little. Otherwise, you wouldn't have cared about my wings in the first place." I said, my mouth unwilling to accept what I already knew: she didn't care about me.

"And yet, you made them go away, anyway. Didn't you?" She whispered the last question like it pained her to utter the words.

They were almost quiet enough to where I didn't hear them. Almost. The knife in my gut twisted. On some level, I knew making my wings disappear would hurt Mother. That she'd seen them as a commonality between us. Something to bind mother and daughter. But what was I supposed to do? Leave them and live my life to make her happy? That wasn't living. I had to live life for myself.

"Didn't you?" She screamed them this time, the glitch on her face settled on the sickly crag.

What was happening to her? Why was she...changing?

This was bad. On some level, I knew it was. I knew I should be worried. Take cautions. But I couldn't make myself do anything. I was stuck in a mental bog, and it was sucking me under. I couldn't even answer her. My limbs shook so hard that my teeth rattled. I wrapped my arms around myself to try to quiet the shaking. My mind was blown. She had all but said I was right. That she cared. That she loved me. Never in my life had my mother said that to me. Not as long as I could remember. Had I killed that now? Had my getting rid of my wings pushed her away for good this time? She took my silence as much as admitting my guilt.

"I should have you flogged for your impetuousness. Do you know how many faelings would have killed to be given such gifts? You're a spoiled vampire whore, not fit for the title Princess." She said, rising out of her throne with every razor-edged word.

The volume of her voice had moved the ever-curious faeries closer. At this accusation, gasps rippled through their ranks. There was nothing like juicy Court intrigue, but this went beyond. Especially since Mother now looked less like the regal Queen, she had been mere minutes ago and now resembled a murderous Queen who had the life sucked from her. Her words cut deeper than they would have because of our people's presence, the same people I'd just vowed to help. They were a people wrapped in tradition, so I was under no disillusion that her points were hitting home with them.

"How could I want them?" I shot back. "They were your way of keeping me chained to this place. I will not be your pawn. But I am here, aren't I? I'm here to help our people."

"You care about no one other than yourself, you always have." She pointed a wrinkled, accusing hand at me.

Seeing the aged arm, what little color there was in her skin fled. Her hands flew to her face. Her head shook over and over again in disbelief of what her shaking fingers found: an old woman. The dark purple of her gown no longer protected luminescent flesh; it cradled crepey skin. The legendary amber glass hair had been piled high on her head, arranged to spill over the top of her gold crown in artful curls. Now, those same curls hung limp, seeming to be pulled down by the weight of the swamp-water brown she now was the unfortunate owner of.

"What have you done to me?" She whispered, horror cracking her voice.

Shock hit me at her words? I hadn't done this to her. Had I? It wasn't my magic. Was it? Wouldn't I know if it was? There wasn't any time to think about it because she swirled her arms around her in a dance like seaweed deep on the ocean floor. A ball of darkness enveloped her. This just excited her audience, which at this point was everyone in attendance. Shoulders bumped against each other as they crowded for a better look and the cavernous room erupted in a roar of murmurs. Then a light as bright as the sun flashed from the center of the globe in a pumpkin seed-shaped spear. Shit. Reflexively, I ducked, shielding my head. My heart drummed a double bass in my chest, all my senses attuned to the stage. The sound of hasty steps brought me back to my feet. A quick check to the left and right didn't show Mother, just dozens of faeries crouched down. Their faces buried into colorful skirts that no longer seemed joyous covered in the floor's dirt hundreds of feet had brought in.

I craned my head to see over the raised area. There she was. The black orb was almost to the discreet door next to a tall, spiraling juniper. I'd used it myself, the many times I'd wanted to duck out of a party early. It led to the kitchen building, but there was a small dirt path next to it that led away from everything. She was leaving. The swirling blackness moved among the crowd, many who were on their knees fervently murmuring devotions to the deep purple train that flew out from the blackness. The hysteria that fueled the words spoke of fear rather than adoration. But that's how the Queen of Fear and Illusion liked it. The door was thrown open. Cecht, obscured by the illusion before now, stepped to the side as the Queen sailed through. He slammed the door shut. I flinched. I half expected it to splinter under the force.

What in the hell was that about? What was going on? Why did my mom look like death? We'd fought before. Granted, nothing to this scale. It wasn't something I did, was it?

Black loomed into my peripheral. I drug in my kundalini energy so fast a little buzz of heat buzzed at my spine. Simultaneously, I twisted to the newcomer. A regal woman stood there, her brown hair neatly coiffed, and the clean lines of her dress screaming style the likes I'd never be able to replicate. The Wicked Italian Queen, Catherine de' Medici*[1] herself. It wasn't up to me to say if she'd earned the title. However, anyone who made their son state before all of his addresses, 'This being the good pleasure of the Queen, my lady-mother, and I also approving of every opinion that she holdeth, am content and command that...' wasn't precisely undeserving of the title either. I didn't ask why she was here. Her love of parties was well known and the Midsummer Night's Festival was one of the biggest parties in fae land. I left the magic crackle quietly in my palm. After what had just gone down with Mother, I'd be damned if I was caught unaware again.

"Such a shame," she said as she stared down the slope of her long nose, scrupulously assessing the closed door Mother had just flown out.

There was no humor in her rigid spine. No pep in her words. If the Wicked Italian Queen was this somber, real shit was going down.

"What is?" I asked, not sure I wanted to know the answer.

She waved a long, elegant hand to the stage. "It will be as Lapis foretold."

At this, I let go of the energy I'd been holding. Too disturbed by the thought to do anything but give my full attention to it. A cold chill swept through me. Lapis was the most powerful seer in all of Faerie. She was so in demand that she only saw Kings and Queens. She was never wrong.

"What did she see?" I asked in a hushed voice.

I don't know why I asked. It's not like I wanted to hear the answer. Quite the opposite, I most certainly did not want to listen to what the Wicked Italian Queen had to say. After the Croí had "blessed" me with the mark, I was afraid of what her answer might be. But it was like my body was possessed, and I couldn't stop myself from speaking the question aloud.

Her eyes stared, unseeing into the distance. "She saw pale skin and hollowed eyes. Of rotting teeth and hearts. The wailing death of a reign that would destroy all of Faerie as we know it."

Fear icicled down my back. Death of a reign. Mother's reign. Did that mean the start of mine? And if so, what? Was she saying I was going to destroy Faerie? The crown on my wrist burned. No way, that wasn't happening. I rubbed my wrist, wanting nothing more than the mark to just go away.

A clammy hand on my bicep pulled me out of my thoughts. I turned to see Avalynn, her face white.

My skirts poofed air into my face as I bobbed fast and low, "Excuse me, Queen Medici."

Deep in thought, she waved her fingers, never letting her eyes leave the closed door. I desperately wanted to ask her more questions, but from the look on Avalynn's face, this couldn't wait. I stepped to the side with her. It wasn't hard to do since people were still clustered in excited groups.

Avalynn handed me a rolled piece of paper. "I didn't

want to panic you, but a waiter gave me this. He said he was told to give it to you, but you were with the Queen, and he didn't know what to do." She worried her bottom lip.

I unraveled the curled paper, catching the edge as it threatened to unroll again. The words, simple and to the point, dropped the floor out from under my feet: WE HAVE ANTHONY. ROOFTOP. 15 MINUTES. ALONE.

Horror washed ice over me. Anthony was in danger?

"Who gave this to you?" I demanded.

Not waiting for an answer, I scanned the Great Hall. It was a rush of chaos, voices clamoring to be heard one above the other. A tide of fae rushing to the door in droves. A handful of teenage faeries pushing others back to give space to some of the Elders who'd gotten caught up in the maelstrom.

She stood up on her tiptoes to make sense out of the havoc. By the time she finally answered, I'd already figured out there were no waiters. "I don't see him."

So much for getting more information.

I strode to the door, my breath was far too shallow for the moderate pace. People tripped over themselves to get out of my way. Self-derision crawled into my throat. Danu only knew what they thought of me after what Mother had said. As if reading my mind, a regal woman in a paisley, lace dress stepped in front of me.

"Princess, is it because your Mother is borne of Bile that she...that she..." her hand clutched her throat like the words were being strangled off.

Such an abrupt introduction of something so out of touch with what all of my senses were screaming hit me like a slap to the face. I shook my head to make sense of what she'd said

The question out of my mouth was automatic. "What?"

She started to speak. The crease of her brow making her

distress evident. I didn't hear a word of it. My ears started to ring. I couldn't deal with this right now.

"I'm sorry. I can't right now." I said and pushed past her.

The offended intake of her breath I did hear, but Court niceties were so far outside of what I cared about right now it wasn't even funny. I had to get my best friend.

How could I be so stupid to think I could protect my friends? I'd promised Avalynn I'd keep them safe, and yet, I couldn't even keep them safe for a single night. Sure, I hadn't thought they would strike tonight. Not during a sacred festival. But these clearly weren't moral people. How could I have been so dumb?

I could feel every eye on me. Ignoring them all, I strode out of the room. No doubt, they thought I was leaving because of Mother. Better that they think that then jeopardize Anthony. The flower petals were still falling. I brushed them out of my hair as I strode down the hall.

Avalynn was right behind me, her kitten heels clacking on the polished floor.

"What are you doing?" I called over my shoulder as I broke off from the crowd heading out the door and rounded the corner that led to the stairs.

The diamonds slapped my back with little pricks of pain, and my skirts plastered themselves between my legs as I practically ran to the stairwell doors.

She huffed behind me. "Are you kidding? I'm not letting you go up there alone. Who knows what could happen to you?"

"They said *alone*." I reminded her as I threw open the metal door that led to the rooftop stairs.

"I know. I know…Here, how about this? I won't go out onto the roof if they are there. Otherwise, we go out and look for Anthony. I figure they weren't dragging him through the building while they delivered the note, so he probably is up there already. So by my estimates, we've got about ten minutes and two people looking are faster than one." She said.

I listened to her reasoning as we leapfrogged the stairs, two at a time. I had to admit it was pretty sound logic.

So I agreed. "Ok, but only if no one is out there."

"Right." She said, thinning her lips.

When we reached the rooftop door, I put my finger to my lips and ushered her to the side. When I was sure she was out of any possible line of sight, I threw some energy into my hands. It vibrated along my skin.

I opened the door with all of the subtlety of a creaky haunted house. A shiver ran down my spine.

With tension tight in my legs, I walked halfway out the door. "Hello? I'm here."

The rooftop consisted of an 8 X 10 cement pad that featured a massive crate and a small shed. Beyond that was the roof itself. Wood shingles wove together to create a picturesque peak. It made quite the picture when you were on the ground. Up here, it just looked like a death trap.

But death trap or not, there was no response. Thank Danu. With a nod to Avalynn to come on, I went the rest of the way out. Now just to find Anthony. I prayed Avalynn was right, and he was here.

The wind whipped around us as we split up. The small area meant there wasn't much to investigate, so this would be quick if Anthony were here.

I took the North half, first checking behind the crate. I even lifted the top to look inside. Nothing. Avalynn checked around the fenced part of the roof, leaning over the roof to make sure she didn't miss anything. She turned and shook her head. I checked my disappointment. The shed was next. When I was sure there was no one behind it, I let go of the energy that had started to stretch and burgeon like a balloon inside me. I didn't want to keep it too long. Unused Kundalini energy held for too long would be a disaster.

A padlock hung from the shed door. I looked up to see Avalynn's progress. Shock blanched my cheeks as I saw she was making her way across the peak of the roof. I tried to remind myself that she'd been an expert at the balance beam when we were growing up. Still, the way loose shingles skittered and fell as she passed them made me more than a little nervous.

"What are you doing?" I hissed across the expanse.

"Checking everywhere!" Avalynn hissed back, in an equally loud voice.

I flinched at the volume. We had to stay quiet, so I let her go and focused on the task at hand. We had to do this now before the heavy got here. I looked back at the lock that rested against the metal door. He was in this person-sized shed. He had to be. Light-headed, I rested my head against the wall as I worked through the problem and my gut knotted. Just how was I going to get in there? I couldn't break the lock with my magic because the whole building was made out of metal. Lightning and metal didn't mix. If Anthony was leaning against the side, it would kill him.

I rapped on the shed. "Anthony, are you in there?"

I put my ear to the cold metal. Nothing. Not that that proved anything. He could be gagged, or worse, knocked out. I gulped in deep breaths. I had to get it together. I wouldn't do Anthony any good if I didn't.

"He's here," Avalynn shouted over the picking up winds. "I can't reach him!"

Clasping my hands together, I pressed them to my lips. Thank the Gods, he was safe. Shooting to my feet, I dashed to the roof's peak, tossing a quick glance over to my shoulder to make sure we were still alone. So far, so good. Avalynn knelt over the edge of the roof; her skirts slapped the shingles in the wind. Precarious didn't begin to cover her position. We were so high up. You didn't get to fall from a height this high and live to tell about it.

"I'm coming!" My heart raced as I kicked off my heels. They hit the shed with a hollow thunk, thunk. "Be careful!"

I drew in a deep breath. Holding it, I placed a foot onto the thin line where the shingles met. An ominous rumble came from above. The sandpaper-like shingles buckled under my weight. How old was this roof anyway? It certainly was in no shape to be crossing. Still, I had to get Anthony. To my relief, it held.

Trying not to think about how we would get back across this slip and slide nightmare, I focused on shuffling one foot in front of the other. Letting out a deep breath, I kept my course. Thunder crashed above me. Still, I pressed on. Thunder clapped. Once. Then, again. Then, again and again, and again. What in the name of Ba'al was going on? The heavens opened up, and rain poured down in crystal curtains. My teeth started to click together. Whether it was from nerves or the cold, I didn't know.

"Slow and steady," I whispered to myself in between the click of teeth.

An even more thunderous crash came right after the other. It reverberated deep in my chest, knocking me off balance.

"Shit." I gritted out as I lost my footing on the slick tile and went down.

Avalynn must have seen me falling because she screamed, "Cy!"

She was too far away, though. Throwing my leg out, I managed to catch the other side of the peak. I slammed down onto the V. Pain spiked up the edge of my thigh, but gods be, I was alive. My pulse thudded in my throat. Ba'al wasn't making this easy. Focusing my thoughts to the heavens, I prayed.

"Please, Ba'al. Please make the rain go away. I need to get to my friend. He needs me." Thunder cracked closer, this time accompanied by a crackle of lightning that lit the sky. The Goddess of the Atmosphere was angry. I did not know why, but I closed my eyes and pleaded with her, "Goddess, I know not what I have done, but I beg your forgiveness. Please help me. Let me pass in safety, Ba'al. Please."

Lightning flared, and thunder crashed in a deafening crescendo. Then just as quickly as it started, it vanished. There was only the slightest trace of wind, as I fervently gave my thanks and got back on my feet. My bare foot slipped on the slate when I took my first step, but without the wind, I was able to regain my balance.

"Hurry, they could be here any minute!" Avalynn practically shouted.

My stomach churned at the smack of reality. Yeah, that helped. I took a deep breath. She was right. If they came through that door, we would be in the middle of a full-blown battle. On top of a slippery ass roof. The thought of such a gut-twisting act made me move a little quicker.

I really wished I still had my wings. It would be so much better if I could rely on those. Where were my wings anyway? I know they were supposed to disappear, but they weren't gone. I knew they weren't. Even now, I could feel the weight of them. The difference was I couldn't feel, see, or use them. What had the Nevermore spell done to them?

Thankfully, with the weather cooperating, I was at Avalynn's side before I knew it. Her feet pigeoned the sides of the peak as she rose to her feet.

She went to move around me. "He's tied up on the ledge. I can't reach him. Maybe you can."

I went to go around her, but as her words sunk in, I froze,

"Your arms are longer than mine. How can I reach him if you can't?"

"Help me. You have to get me out of here. My wings are tied." Called Anthony's voice, clear as a summer day from the other side of the roof where he was on the ledge.

"I don't know, but we can't just leave him there. Maybe you will see a way to get him up that I can't." She went to go around me again.

I didn't like it, but we were running out of time. I stopped her again.

She practically growled. "What?"

Her reaction shocked me. It was so uncharacteristically Avalynn. Maybe she was just as stressed as I was. Everyone reacted to stress differently.

I said the next slowly so as not to spook her. "That's fine, but let me straddle the roof, so we both don't die up here."

She didn't look happy with my suggestion. In fact, she didn't look ok at all. She looked like she was fraying at the edges.

Despite that, she said, "Fine, fine."

So I did as I'd said. I tried to grip the roof with my feet as I lowered down, but it was like trying to grab sand. More shingles fell away as I landed harder than I'd anticipated.

"Fuck." A dull ache between my legs punctuated the sentiment.

Avalynn hoisted her skirts. I ducked down to make it easy for her to get over me. She balanced herself on my shoulders. With the grace of a dancer, she stepped over me.

"Ok," She said when she was safely on the other side.

I looked up at her and gave her a nod. The wind had snatched pieces of hair out of her updo. They plastered themselves to her elegant features. Features that were currently taut with determination. I could see her lips tremble. She bit it and nodded back.

This had to be hard for her. She wasn't used to this kind of action.

Now that I was down here, I questioned the logic of getting back up. I decided against it. Instead, I crawled the last few feet on my hands and knees to the edge of the building and looked over.

The distance to the ground loomed at me. Just looking down that whole way made me dizzy.

But it wasn't the distance or vertigo that floored me.

It was the fact that the ledge below was empty.

Anthony was nowhere to be seen. What in the hell?

Then it came crashing down on me. It was Avalynn. She'd created his voice. Like she'd done when we'd played as kids.

I turned around, the world moving like it was in slow motion. "You-" was all I got out before hands shoved my back. I tried to turn in time, but I wasn't quick enough.

My hands gripped the roof as my legs tumbled over my head. Against all odds, I was able to keep my grip. Probably because what I'd managed to grab wasn't shingles, it was just wood planks that swooped the edges of the roof in decoration.

Desperation fueled my limbs as I held on for dear life. "Avalynn, what are you doing?"

"You're supposed to be gone. You weren't supposed to come back." She screamed, tears choking her voice off.

Floored by her words, I tilted my head back to see her. She leaned over the ledge. The whites of her eyes stood out in the dark of the night as she looked down at me. The wind picked up, whipping her hair and dress into a frenzy that matched the storm brewing above. I tried to pull myself up. Excruciating seconds passed before my arms gave up the battle and straightened again, unable to take the added strain.

"What are you talking about?" I practically shouted as my

triceps started to shake. "You know, it doesn't matter. Just help me up."

"What am I talking about? What am I talking about?" She laughed a high-pitched, hysterical laugh. "How about the fact that your mother was grooming me for the Crown. Me? It was everything I'd envied you for, but then you just left. Then when all of my dreams are coming true, you come back? No, no. That just isn't happening. You had your chance. This is *my* time. Mine, you hear me?"

She punctuated her words by bringing her dainty heel down onto my fingers. Pain exploded. I fought to keep my grip all the while my mind put the pieces together. Her. *She* was the Heir Anointed.

"Stop," I screamed through the pain. "I don't want to rule. I don't. There are things I want to change, but I don't want to rule. You can have it. I don't care."

That was the gods' honest truth too. I didn't want to be Queen. Along with being able to live freely among humans as a fae, I had resigned myself long ago that was never going to happen. This wasn't the time to go into that, though. My fingers weren't going to hold much longer. How could I get out of this? There was a ledge below me, wasn't there? If I could touch it, I could drop onto it. I pointed my toes. Trying not to move too much, less I dislodge my aching fingers, I felt around for the ledge. When my foot hit it, I realized it was just out of reach to simply fall on. It wasn't that wide. Years ago, it had been home to a statue. But it had fallen during a prank gone awry.

At my declaration, uncertainty clouded her face, then she pushed it away, hate blazing anew. "You're lying. You have to die. You have to. Since you won't leave, it's the only way."

She brought her foot up to smash down again. I flinched. There was no way I could take another one of those. As it was, my arms were visibly shaking.

Making a split-second decision, I took the last of my effort to lift the hand she was aiming at. When she brought it down, I wrapped my fingers around her ankle.

The intent was to pull her off her feet, but I didn't even have to pull because my other hand gave way with the added pressure. It brought her down. With a crash that mingled with thunder shuddering the night sky, her head smacked the back of the roof. I grabbed her ankle with both hands.

With a prayer, I swung myself towards the ledge. The momentum pulled Avalynn down the roof. I could hear her smashing the shingles above as she slid down the roof. It wasn't enough to get me there, though.

I swung again, harder this time. The force arced her off the roof. Her screams tore at me as she fell. But there was nothing I could do. For her or me.

My fingers gave out. Desperate, I flung myself at the ledge. Hope twisted inside me as my feet hit. Then my stomach dropped as they kept sliding. The backs of my legs hit the edge, and I fell.

Panic jerked my body. Sweet Danu, this wasn't happening. As I felt the cold night's air rip past me, there was no denying it.

Despair clenched my eyes shut. I berated myself for taking that damn potion. Avalynn's screams stopped. She was dead. I didn't have to look to know it. And I was going to be next. I could've just beat my wings, and I would be safe. But I couldn't now. All because of that damn potion. It was so unfair.

I could feel my wings. Why couldn't I use them? I beat my wings just like I would have before. Nothing happened. Nothing.

I knew I was getting close to the ground. It was so unfair.

I whispered my sorrow to the air hurling past. "I should never have taken it. Never, never, never."

Just as the last word passed my lips, I felt my wings jerk upwards. Shock wrenched my eyes open. My fall slowed to a slow drift like the first winter snow. Had I really felt my wings? Tears pricked my eyes. Even though it didn't make sense, I beat my lost appendages furiously. This time it worked. I wasn't falling anymore. Cold air pressed in waves against my bare back.

I was flying. And thank the Gods because I was a mere 3 feet from the ground. Pressing a hand to my mouth, I let out a strangled, thick laugh.

Faeries started pouring out of the building as my feet crunched on the pebbled roundabout.

"We heard screaming," said a teenager with purple, too-tight curls and skirts as big as a barbie house.

Her voice bounced as she ran towards me. When her gaze fixed behind me, the color left her face, and she pulled up short. I knew what had her transfixed, but I turned anyway. I think I looked because I wanted to make it more real.

And there was nothing more real than Avalynn's twisted body on the pavement. Her face looked almost peaceful as her eyes stared at the stars. They stared unseeing at the night's beauty. I tried to come to grips with it for a second longer before I turned away. Avalynn, my friend, my confidant. She'd been behind all of the threats all along.

Numbness settled over my body. This young girl shouldn't be here. I took her attention away from the nightmare in front of her with a hand on the shoulder. When she didn't look, I gave her a gentle shake. That brought her big eyes to me.

I tried to keep it together as I said, "We need to let someone know. I can't go. Will you?"

She nodded absently. Her face was still blank. I pushed her back in the direction of the building. As she walked away, I caught Stacia out of the corner of my eye. The strangest expression was on her face: pity. I felt like such a fool for accusing her, for not knowing it was really Avalynn. Avalynn. Another thought hit me like a freight truck. What had she done to Anthony?

Panic climbed my throat. I picked up my skirts and started to run to the building. At that exact moment, Anthony ran out. Seeing him alive and well stopped me in my tracks. I pressed a fist to my mouth as tears of gratitude welled up in my eyes.

I ran the last few steps to him, flinging myself into his arms. His arms came around me.

The intensity of his grip didn't lessen as he said into my hair. "I thought it was you."

It took me a second to realize he was talking about the dead body.

I pulled away from him, realizing he still didn't know about Avalynn. "It very well could have been. Avalynn was the one making all those threats."

"What? Are you kidding me? But you guys have been friends forever." He stepped around me to gape at where her form lay on the ground again like he had to see it for himself.

His head cocked as if seeing her for the first time. More than anything, I wanted her to get up and explain everything. Her words would make sense. I could help her through it, tell her she could be Heir Apparent. That everything would be ok. Her future was going to be all she'd ever dreamed. My chest squeezed. That conversation would never happen now. Outside of a small memorial service, she had no future. And I'd never be able to know the grief my friend was going through. Never be able to tell her it was ok, she had nothing to worry about. Life could be so unfair.

It took me a couple of times, but I finally was able to speak. "I know. Trust me, no one is more shocked by this than me. I don't know what I'm more grateful for right now, that you are ok or that I am."

He looked to the side and looked back at me. "What are you talking about? Of course, I'm ok."

"Avalynn told me that you'd been kidnapped. I thought maybe she did something to you. She was pretty far gone."

Even saying it had me reliving it. I shivered in the chill of the night.

Anthony rubbed my hands together and said, "I was fine. She told me I was needed at Bardais for an emergency. When I got there, nobody knew what I was talking about. I knew something was off, and when I went in, nobody knew where you two were, just that you had gone off together. I was just going to go look for you when I heard the screams."

Just mentioning the screams pulled at my gut. Avalynn was dead. And for what? Senseless jealousy.

Anthony's fingertips grazed the tips of my wings. "So they're not gone after all, huh?"

My wings. I reached back. Velvety softness met my seeking fingers. I didn't know whether to laugh or cry. All of what we had been through had been for nothing.

"I guess not." The knowledge sat like lead in my stomach.

"But where had they gone? And why are they back now?" Anthony asked.

"I don't know. They came back after Avalynn pushed me off the roof." It was hard for me to talk about.

Anthony must have sensed it because he folded me in a crushing hug. I squeezed him back just as hard, grateful to have him in my arms.

As much as I didn't want to think about it, he was right to question the wings, though. In fact, I'd had some of the same questions myself. And there was only one person who could solve this mystery.

CHAPTER 33

"Well, damn," Iris said by way of greeting when we walked into Spells of the Poppet.

Frankly, I was surprised she was still here. We'd come straight from the party, so it was quite late. Granted, her shop was attached to her house, but you'd think she had boundaries. Maybe she and I had something in common.

I hoped she was referring to the wings and not the fact that I was standing here, alive, so I said, "You're telling me."

She came around from behind the counter, smacking her hands against her dirty apron.

"You took the potion?" The way her mouth tensed and her eyes narrowed, it didn't look like she believed me.

"Every last drop," I affirmed, trying not to let the stress of the day show on my face. I shuddered as I remembered the thick liquid crawling down my throat. I could almost taste it.

My dress knocked against the close displays as I made my way to her. Anthony caught a bottle that wobbled and then fell.

When I reached her, she put her hands on her hips. This time the tired look on her face couldn't be misread: it was the look of defeat. Even though I had no reason to want to help the old, kitchen witch feel better, I couldn't help the need to do just that.

I gave her a wry smile, "Well, they did disappear for a bit...but they came back."

I finished lamely. As if standing here in my current state didn't tell her all she needed to know. Of course, I left out that I was in the middle of being pushed off the building when it happened. No need to be overdramatic.

Processing the new information, I could see her tongue push against the inside of her cheek. Finally, she asked as if not totally clear she'd heard right, "They disappeared and then came back?"

I nodded. Anthony bobbed his head up and down too, as if she might need confirmation of the fact. Considering the witch's and my tenuous relationship, there was nothing wrong with the added support, I suppose.

"Huh..." Her eyebrows drew together. She tapped her lip, pointed her long finger at me, and said, "Let me get the book."

We made our way through the maze of shelves while she retrieved the book from the back. She dropped it onto the counter in front of us again, much like last time. Funny how things could be so changed yet feel the same.

"What were you doing when the wings came back?" she asked as she flipped to the page with the potion on it.

My cheeks grew hot. We were going there. Great, how did I explain what had happened without admitting that even my friend had wanted to kill me?

After throwing a handful of options away, I settled on, "I...ah- was falling off a building-"

"She was pushed off a building," Anthony said, cutting me off.

That tidbit brought Iris's head up.

She gave a humorless chuckle and said to me, "Someone wants you gone worse than I do, huh?"

"Wanted." I clarified. "You're still at the top of the list as of about an hour ago."

I said the last with some jazz hands to add levity to the situation. I'm sure it wasn't lost on Iris either that she could have killed me with the potion when she had the chance. If I could make this a little easier on her by keeping it light, maybe she would see I appreciated it. An hour ago, I wouldn't have been grateful for something like that, but an hour can do a hell of a lot to change your outlook on things.

She acknowledged my unspoken communication with a sparkle of respect in her eye. It was either that or the light hitting her eyes just right as she turned back to the book.

Her fingers skipped the part with all of the ingredients on it and went straight to the section below. She mumbled to herself as she skimmed over the passage. Her hand covered her mouth as she read through the verse a couple times.

The third time she read it aloud, the words muffled behind her fingers, "Never will your troubles bother you again unless you speak from the never. Only then will never be at your door."

No one said anything. The silence hung heavy in the air like a muggy, summer afternoon.

When I couldn't take the silence anymore, I asked, "Ok, so what in the hell does that mean?"

Iris tapped the book and then looked at my wings again. Her gaze went distant, and she started to pace behind the counter.

"Never will your troubles bother you." She tapped her finger against her lips. "...unless you speak from the never."

She pointed her finger towards the ceiling as she walked, "...unless you speak from the never. Only then will never be at your door."

When she said it like that, one word stuck out in my mind: door. My stomach twisted with foreboding. She stopped in front of me so suddenly the dried bats behind her swayed.

"Did you say anything before your wings came back?" she asked, jabbing her finger in my face.

I thought hard. Something tickled my memory. "Now that you mention it, yeah, I think I did."

"What? What did you say?" Her eyes bore into me.

Their intensity made my heart race. I struggled to remember what I'd said that could have been so critical. Nothing came to me. Dagda be damned, how could I be expected to remember what I had said when I was falling to what I thought was my death?

Finally, I threw my hands into the air. "I- I don't know."

She slammed her fist down onto the book. The violence of it made me jump.

"That's not acceptable. Think!" Her teeth bared as she said the last.

I don't know how she expected me to remember something like that, but I tried again since it clearly meant something.

"I was thinking about how I wish I hadn't taken the potion." The words were hard to say. How could you admit something like that to the two people who'd helped you? Especially when one of them had risked their life? There was no way to make that ok. There was no way around the embarrassing revelation, though.

"Did you say you wished you *never* took the potion?" Iris prodded, her face pinched.

When she said it like that, a flash of memory hit me. "Yeah, yeah, I did. I think I said, 'I wished I never took the potion' then if I remember correctly, I think I was crying and said 'never, never, never.'"

I didn't like to admit to her that I had felt so weak, but I'd like to think it was understandable considering I had been falling to my death.

Urgency shook her voice as she urged me to, "Do it again."

"Pardon me?" I blinked, not sure what she was asking.

"Do it again. Say never three times...like you did." She said, her hands starting to tremble.

"Ok...sure..." I tried to sound confident, but I swallowed against a suddenly dry throat.

I didn't want to say the words. Saying three little words seemed so easy. In fact, to not say them would have been more crazy. But every fiber in my being screamed not to. I licked my dry lips. Iris had more experience in this arena, and if she needed me to say them, I would do it.

My pulse was in my throat as I spoke the words. They came out slowly like they were being pulled from me, in a whisper into a room that now felt as dead as night. "Never...never...never."

I didn't feel anything, but the color drained from Anthony's face. Iris's head dropped.

"They're gone, aren't they?" I asked Anthony.

I knew the answer, but I had to ask. He nodded in confirmation.

Iris's teal, kinked hair swayed back and forth as she shook her head. Her eyes were round like she'd seen a baby snatched up by a hawk, "This can't be..."

Excruciating seconds ticked by, stretching me thinner and thinner. When she didn't elaborate, I said. "What can't be?"

She shook her head. The somber act on such a lively woman was as loud as a scream. Dread pooled in my belly. This must be really, really bad.

"Iris, you're scaring me," I said with a laugh, but it had no mirth in it.

"Do you realize what we've done?" She asked, her husky whisper so low I almost missed it.

"Clearly, not. Tell us for the sake of the gods." This was from Anthony.

His hands were balled at his sides like he wanted to strike something.

She lifted her head to give him a dead stare. "Let me tell you what we did, *Messenger*." She said the title like it was an insult. "We've opened the door to the Never."

"The Never?" I asked, not knowing why it sounded familiar.

She didn't let go of Anthony's angry stare as she answered me. "Yes, the Never. The place where nothing real exists. Where everything is nothing but magic. Magic in its rawest form."

"Is that...bad?" I asked.

She laughed a low, dangerous laugh that made my skin crawl like I'd seen a cockroach. "Bad for us? Quite possibly. Something could come through the door with your wings. Pure magic isn't meant to exist in our world. It's only safe through the conduit of our bodies. There's no telling the ramifications of it getting into our world in its purest form." Then she swung her gaze to me. It pierced me. "But bad for you? Definitely. Because if you can draw those wings out of the Never, that means you can be drawn in. A doorway goes both ways, you know. And not only would there be no way back for you, but you could change the course of magic for the world, forever."

Fear tickled my throat, and I said in a hushed voice, "Forever is a long time."

She ignored my attempt to be lighthearted.

"I've never heard of a doorway being opened before. I'm going to call on some covens. There has to be a way to fix this." Then she pointed to where my wings had been. "In the meantime, don't you call those wings again- as in ever. That door needs to stay closed. We can't take any chances."

I nodded my agreement. Awful didn't begin to cover how all those possibilities sounded. If Iris wanted to scare me into submission, she'd succeeded.

"What do I do until you find answers?" I asked.

"Just live. There's no telling how long any of this will take. So the only thing you can really do in the meantime is live. And just forget that your wings ever existed. As of today, you don't have them."

All I had to do was live my life. Talk about an impossible task. Knowing the fate of the world's magic rested on my ability to keep in line when following rules was a skill I failed spectacularly at daily wasn't a comforting thought. And I couldn't exactly get an A for effort here, not this time.

CHAPTER 34

*T*he cab zipped away, pulling the door I'd just stepped out of shut behind me. New York City cab drivers had places to go. Far be it for them to worry about little things like their customer's lives. I looked up at Gaige's townhouse. With its peaked windows and the scrolled doorway, it was a slice of goth wedged into the cityscape of Manhattan.

Part of me said I should go home first and get freshened up. But I was way too frazzled about Mother's change and the unintentional death-to-magic portal that I couldn't bear to go there and be alone. I needed to talk through everything with someone I could trust. And there was no one better to do that with than my best friend. Considering the frantic voicemails and messages I'd gotten from her, it sounded like she needed to see me just as badly. It made sense. The last time she'd seen me, I was being tossed into the back of a Thomas' car. She probably thought I was dead.

A guttural scream pierced my thoughts. Gaige. I knew it immediately. Panic froze my veins. I couldn't move. Then the stained glass windows on the second floor burst outwards, raining colored glass down on me. It was all I needed. Panic melted to fuel my legs, and I flew into action. I threw a shoulder into the solid doors. Shards of glass bit through my coat on the impact. I'd never reach her in time this way.

Screw it. In desperation, I held my hands close to the handle. Then I threw as much energy as I could into the lock. Lightning shot in a small arc, followed by a loud pop. That was the only invitation I needed. My heart slammed in my chest as I pushed open the door and rushed in.

Fire gleamed off the red-veined marble floor. Where was Gaige? My gaze sped up the double-winding wrought iron staircases to the balcony overlooking the first floor. Flames shot out from over the railing. Gaige stumbled onto the landing, her lithe body engulfed in flames.

THE END

Thank you for reading *Death Charmed*!
If you can't get enough of the world of the Fae join our
newsletter:
YOU'LL GET YOUR VERY OWN FREE BOOK *TODAY*!
Click here to join!

MESSAGE FROM THE QUEEN

Thank you so much for reading *Death Charmed*! I hope you loved reading it as much as I did writing it! Reviews are the life-blood of an Indie author. If you could pop over and leave a review, it would mean the world to me!

Drop a Review for the Book Here!

ABOUT THE QUEEN

Erica Reeder is a *USA Today* and International bestselling author of Urban Fantasy who uses glitter as a territorial marker. Kids, boyfriend, you name it. If it's got glitter on it, it's hers. Besides an infatuation with glitter and all things fantasy, she is a Queen with an unreasonable passion for writing. Whether throwing her characters a demon or hiding pixies in pants, there's always fun to be had. Come be a part of it in so many places either at www.ericareeder.com, where there's merchandise that will spellbind you, and of course, books that will steal your breath and enchant your heart. Or you could join our Facebook Group: Erica Reeders Fae Court to have daily fun. OR for less interaction but no fewer goodies, you could JOIN THE NEWSLETTER, WHERE YOU'LL GET YOUR VERY OWN FREE BOOK *TODAY*!

BADASS WOMAN FROM HISTORY

Catherine de' Medici, Queen of France, is a guilty pleasure of mine. Part of me thinks I shouldn't select her as the Badass Woman From history because she was referred to as an Evil Queen. (Kari Bovee 2017) However, if we look closer at her story, it seems closer to what we've all become to understand regarding history: the victor tells the story of history. Her husband, Henry, took her cousin, Diane de Poitiers, on as his official mistress and spent most of his time with her over their 26 year love affair. The length of their affair was torturous for Catherine because he clearly loved his mistress and not her. (Barbara McNally 2017)

She was a rare breed though and loved her husband still. They produced 10 children, only 7 which made it to adulthood. They were constantly in her thoughts. As a firm believer in "soothsaying" she consulted with psychics on a regular basis about them and her own life. When she was given the bombshell that her husband was going to be killed in an upcoming competition, she begged him not to participate. He ignored her warnings though and died of jousting injuries 12 days later. (Barbara McNally 2017)

Furious and hurt, she wanted to take back her life. Her first order was to force Diane to give back the crown jewels and the Château de Chenonceau that her husband had gifted her cousin with when she was his mistress. Then Catherine banished her. (Reign Wiki 2017) Next, she oversaw her son's coronation. The 9-year-old King Charles IX was in no position to rule, however. So she "presided over his council, decided policy and controlled state business, and patronage". (Reign Wiki 2017) In essence, she was the queen, if not in name, for sure in act. Times were violet and the country was on the brink of religious civil war. In fact, the entire time her sons ruled, which she would oversee the ruling of three of them, the country was on the verge of civil war. (Reign Wiki 2017) She was tenacious though and smart. In fact, "some historians believe her sons would never have remained in power without her cunning and sharp wits." (Barbara McNally 2017) This can be evidenced by when Prince Francis became king at 15 years old. Before all statements he would give the disclaimer "This being the good pleasure of the Queen, my lady-mother, and I also approving of every opinion that she holdeth, am content and command that …" (Reign Wiki 2017) It should be known that I have instructed my own boyfriend that I'd like him to repeat said disclaimer before everything we do. He laughed. I mean...I don't see what's so funny.

Anyway, back to Catherine de' Medici.

Her cunning tactics in political intrigue, policy, and during wartime are fascinating in and of itself. However, when you add into it the fact that she was every inch a lady the entire time, it becomes fascinating to me. Strong women throughout the ages are typically depicted as Asexual, as being mannish. This simply is not the case with Catherine. She was every inch a woman and reveled in it. Even when she was married at the tender age of 14, she stood out as such. She was seen wearing the world's first pair of high-heeled shoes. (Barbara McNally 2017) And she was fierce too. When her husband's interest in her had waned, she threw "lavish cross-dressing parties where men dressed as women and women went topless as men." The intention was to garner his interest again, but even though it didn't work, the parties were said to be "legendary." (Barbara McNally 2017) Her love of parties didn't stop there either. "Throughout her time as Queen, and Queen Mother she" threw so many "banquettes" and "extravagant parties" that the entire kingdom actually held yearly Catherine de' Medici's Court Festivals. Reign Wiki 2017) Can you imagine having such epic parties that people held them every year in your honor? Now, that is someone who knows how to find the magic in life! It's quite commendable when you consider the constant pressure she was under and the immeasurable loss of so many of her children sons and her husband. When she was married to the King at such a young age, never could she have imagined she would not only be forced to endure such heart-ache but also have to lead an entire kingdom. She did it, though. Successfully and with style and grace. And for that the Evil Queen, Catherine de' Medici, is our Badass Woman From History.

COURT INSIDER SNEAK PEEK...

USA TODAY BESTSELLING AUTHOR

ERICA REEDER

GOBLIN
CURSED

A CY VANGUARD, FAERIE PRINCESS, NOVEL

Get *the next book in the Cy Vanguard Series!*

"Take off your shirt." Bab commanded as soon as I opened the door for Sven and all of his 6' dreamy glory.

I resisted the urge to bang my head against the wall. Talk about the first thing I didn't want to think as soon as I laid eyes on the man who'd betrayed me and broke my heart. His dream-come-to-life status had been revoked. And I needed to keep that in mind when he was around.

"Can I have my own thoughts?" I complained out loud.

Sven's guarded look melted and I could feel his palpable need to gather me in for a hug as he asked, "Is it so bad?"

"Sure, you can," Bab responded. "You want him to take off his shirt too. This is a win for both of us, honey."

With a sigh, I motioned for Sven to come in. I refused to regret having him over just because the voice in my head couldn't seem to behave. I refused to acknowledge Bab just might be right and pushed down the tingles shooting through me as Sven's jacket brushed over me when he passed.

I ignored my vagina and Bab as I stayed behind to duck my head outside and look both ways for those pesky goblins before I shut the door. Just one more thing to add to the list of things that were slowly driving me crazy.

When I came back in, Sven was surveying me with hooded eyes as he leaned a hip against the cabinet. Was he thinking of the time he'd put me on that very same counter and kissed me silly? My heart thudded in my throat. I sure was.

"Gods, just kiss him already, will you? You're killing me here," groaned Bab.

"Do you have to do that?" I complained. This time I was careful not to brush against him in the tight space as I moved into the living room. Space was definitely what I needed when Sven was in the equation.

"Do what?" asked Sven, opening his arms wide.

"Prop yourself against a random object like some sort of GQ model." I said, narrowing my eyes at him, as I sat onto the couch. I grabbed a fluffy pillow and sat it on my lap, punching it for good measure.

A grin lit his face at my words, but to his credit he did move away from the counter.

"GQ model, huh?" He prompted with a twinkle in his eye as he came into the living room.

"You're missing the point. What I mean is do you HAVE to pose?" My face got hot. I was pretty sure this was my problem, not his.

He looked to the empty space on the small couch next to me then searched the room and spotted the one other chair in the room. He only paused for a second before moving to the soft pink chair. I ignored the disappointment in my gut and the "Boo's" from Bab as he sank his lithe frame into it.

"I'm not doing it intentionally, I assure you." He said, the smile on his face still watted to a 1,000. His next words took the smile from his face though. "So why don't you tell me what's been going on?"

I blinked against the tears that suddenly found their way into my eyes. I put my socked feet on the couch and pulled the pillow to my chest.

"Gods, where do I begin?" I said into the pillow. "Well, let's start off with the fact that I was kidnapped by the Boogeyman."

Sven leaned forward in his chair. "I'd heard tales of The Boogeyman. He is real then?"

"Oh, yeah. He sure is." On one level I was proud my fellow fae was so notorious that everyone knew him, but on a more practical save-your-ass level, I wanted to steer everyone clear of him.

"I've heard mostly bedtime horrors, but there was one story that was attributed to him in Transylvania that has always stuck with me." He said with a cocked head.

I found myself nodding at our unintentionally shared memory. "Oh, yeah. How he killed invaders to his land in a fit of rage and put their bodies on posts to keep out others. Vlad the Impaler historically gets the credit for that, but it's not the truth. Vlad just took credit for it because it increased his power. The Boogeyman let him because he didn't want to attract headhunters. He hunts. He is not the hunted."

"So how is it that he came to be hunting you?" Sven asked, intrigued by the revelation.

I threw my arms up in frustration and let them drop back down to the sofa. "By some miracle, my mother apparently had a favor the Boogeyman owed her, so she sent him to bring me back to the mound."

He rolled his eyes in amazement and said incredulously, "I can only imagine what agreement led them to that end.

Yet, here you are. What has happened after that, my little faerie?"

I was like a locomotive engine, after I got going, I couldn't seem to stop. I told him about everything. Leaving the part about Anthony out (there was no need to pour salt on wounds,) I told him everything about the deadly scavenger hunt I'd had to go on to get out of Knockaine: escaping Goblins, a deadly horde of werewolves on a full moon, traveling to another world, the death battle in Hell, all of it. The fact that one of my old childhood friends tried to kill me and I couldn't save my best friend from a tragic fire seemed like an appropriate segue to my new split personality friend, after all that was the straw that had broken the camel's back, so to speak.

I talked well past the sun sinking into the horizon, through the incredible colors of the sunset painting the cityscape in pastel rainbows, and through the hundreds of lights that popped on, one at a time, into the inky darkness.

"And now I'm in some messed up game of hide-and-seek with these so-ugly-they-are-adorable goblins who want to kill me. Dagda knows why, though." My gaze, which had flickered back and forth between the vampire to my left to the scene out my window that changed like a digital picture frame, rested on the darkness.

He was quiet for a long time. Right that second, I would have given anything for him to come over, wrap his arms around me, and tell me everything was going to be ok. To not think about anything more complex than his hands stroking my worries out of my hair.

To Sven's credit, he absorbed it all, adding thoughts, feelings, and exclamations in the right places. He even gave me psychologically sound advice when I told him about Bab. It made me feel cared for, like someone gave a shit. I don't know what I'd expected when I'd agreed to let him over, but it wasn't this. Honestly, given the emotional place I was in, I probably would have had sex with him if he'd tried. I needed to feel loved, and at the base of it, that was one way to achieve that. In fact, I'd half expected him to make a move on me after listening to me prattle on for a bit. But he just let me sit in silence. Let me process it. Maybe I didn't know him as well as I thought I did.

"Oh, yeah. We'd let him ravage every inch of your body." Bab said on a half-sniffle.

The ridiculous comment was enough to take a little of the weight from my maudlin thoughts. I laughed and had to agree. "You're right about that."

Sven, who'd been listening intently, blinked in confusion and asked, "I like being right as much as the next man, but may I ask, what am I right about?"

I covered my mouth with a hand, horrified. "I didn't just say that out loud, did I?"

Sven raised an eyebrow and thinned his lips before cracking their compression with a pop and saying, "Yep, you sure did. So what am I right about?"

I couldn't exactly tell him that I wanted him to come over here and mold my body like newly wet clay. Looking down to pretend sadness, I racked my brain for the last thing he'd said and grabbed onto it.

"That I need friends." I said, hoping he would buy it.

This time he did move over to the couch. I could feel the couch dip under his weight. The fluffy cushions sank in. My abs were not up for the unexpected challenge, and I struggled not to slide into him.

"It's a dumb thing to struggle against." Bab noted sagely.

I rolled my eyes. I couldn't respond, though. I'd forgotten how to breathe because Sven had taken my hands in his. My eyes flew up to meet his. His gaze held what could have been construed as need for a fraction of a second before they shifted back to the care that I'd seen for countless hours.

"You have a friend, Cy. I'm your friend." he said, a passionate need to be heard stitched into his face.

Pretty words, but I knew when it came down to it, they didn't mean anything. When it came down to it, he was just going to do what he wanted. The memory of the all-consuming anger I'd felt when I realized what he'd done to mark me came back over me. Sure, it was an echo of it now, but I clung to it. He'd marked me. For life. Do you know how long that was for a faerie? It might as well have been eternity. The buddings of anger was enough to pull my hands from his. I knew he could sense the shift in me because he grabbed my hands and pulled them to his side fervently.

"Look, I've been doing a lot of thinking. What I did was wrong. If I could undo it, I swear by the Mother, I would. I justified it in my head that it was for you too, to keep you safe from other vampires because without a mark you were fair game for any vampire to take you and make you theirs. But while that was part of it, it wasn't the real reason. The real reason is I wanted you all to myself. I didn't want to give you up. Wanted you all for myself. And now, I don't have you at all."

He took a breath. The protest that it wasn't his decision to make sprang to my lips. It was mine. My mind. My body.

Then he continued, "It was wrong of me to not give you the choice, not let you make your own decisions. You are your own person and deserve to do so. I know you didn't list me and what I'd done as part of what you've been through, but trust me when I say I am fully aware of how all of that must be affecting you too. To fear a species and then have the one you opened your heart up to betray you like that. It must have hurt like nothing else."

On one hand, he was right. On the other, he could never

know how much he had hurt me. My breath hitched in my chest.

"I've never loved anyone like I loved you." I found myself whispering before the logical part of my brain could keep the words in.

Sven inched closer, the heat of his knee searing mine. His hands came up like he wanted to take my chin in his hands. I could feel my lips part. The little traitors.